POISONOUS PSYCHE

ANGRY GREEK GODS SERIES BOOK 2

<u>TRIGGER WARNINGS</u>

Please be advised that this book (and the entire series) will be **<u>gory</u>**.

Other triggers worth mentioning are:

- Attempted murder
- Animal cruelty (mild) (no harm of pets)
- Blood
- Cannibalism (heavy)
- Emotional abuse
- Gore (heavy)
- Hallucinations
- Incest (Greek mythology)
- Kidnapping
- Murder
- Occult
- Poisoning
- Profanity
- PTSD
- Religion
- Suicide (very mild & brief)
- Torture
- Violence

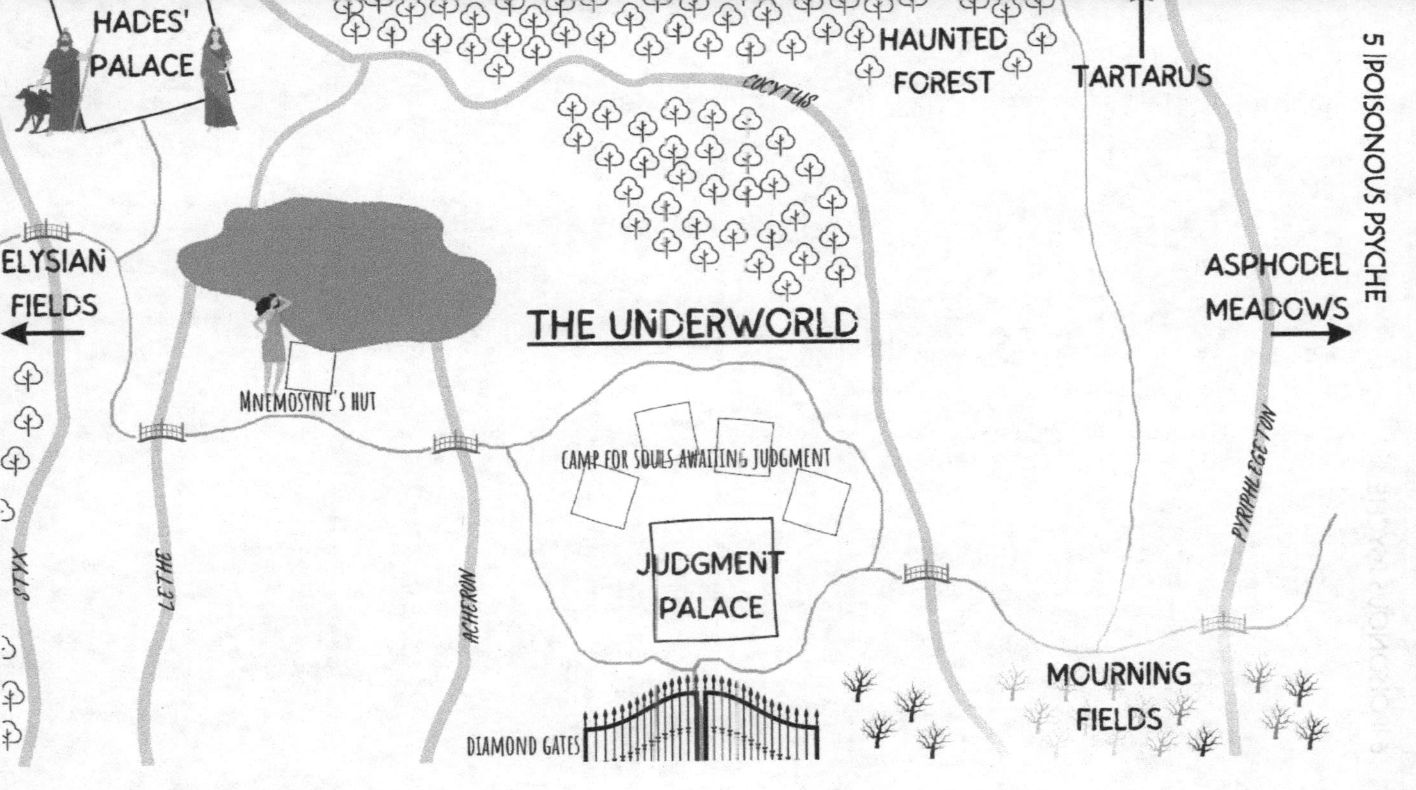
HADES' PALACE
HAUNTED FOREST
TARTARUS
COCYTUS
ELYSIAN FIELDS
THE UNDERWORLD
ASPHODEL MEADOWS
MNEMOSYNE'S HUT
CAMP FOR SOULS AWAITING JUDGMENT
PYRIPHLEGETON
STYX
LETHE
ACHERON
JUDGMENT PALACE
DIAMOND GATES
MOURNING FIELDS

‖1. YOU'LL KNOW‖

???

Leaves crunched under her feet; a sound she'd become familiar with, that resonated deep within. *Crunch, crunch, crunch.* Like crumbling paper, a crispy bite of chicken. Knuckles cracking, bones snapping.

The more she heard it, the more she remembered what she'd done. What she had yet to do. The more leaves detached from thin branches and swished to the ground, the more aware she was of time running low.

She gazed across the bushy field of slumbering crops, focusing on a small countryside home. It was quaint—weathered stone walls, faded olive shutters, a flimsy roof that looked ready to cave in. It didn't fit in with the modern cities she'd overviewed, which explained why it was so tucked away from civilization.

Still as a statue, quiet as a mouse, she waited. For a sign of life, for proof there were inhabitants in the house. For the green light revealing they were *targets.*

She needed that green light, needed the certainty it brought. Then, she'd make her move.

Stumbling backwards, she braced herself against a tree-trunk. A dizzy spell crashed over her, muting her senses as a distant but pleasant picture came to mind.

The Olympus palace, encircled by its massive, glistening gates. The foundations floated atop a steep mountain, with chunky clouds concealing it from human view. Sunlight poured from the heavens, basking the grounds in a golden glow. She could have smiled at the image, at the memory of the faint hymns playing from the gardens, the scent of ambrosia-filled pastries wafting up from the kitchens.

But something within her rumbled, growled, yanked her away from the merry sights to remind her of her task. Her dreadful, gloomy task.

The cottage came into view once more. She'd gotten closer while she'd been in her dream-world. Much closer. She no longer needed to squint.

Someone skipped by the window. Chatter and footsteps, followed by silverware clinking and scraping on plates.

They were eating.

Perfect.

A few more steps allowed her to peek through the stained pane, to witness them digging into a meal of pheasant, potatoes, and greens.

Blood gushed through her veins, fast, fast, *faster,* prompting her to muffle a squeal. With each bite of food they scooped up, the surge inside her amplified. Her extremities tingled, her belly bubbled, her vision blurred.

And there it was, at last—the dim green glimmer that indicated her next victims. Invisible to the human eye, it was like a blanket that only she could see; a filter flickering over her eyesight to signal her of her next targets.

Them.

Her heartbeat sped up, echoing in her eardrums.

Convince them. Drag them into the cause.

She winced, a tiny twinge inside urging her to fight the thirst ravaging her; but it was useless. She'd tried before, and failed. Nothing stopped this craving.

Convince them. Save them.

The yearning took over. It dug into her scalp, burning through her brain, slithering down her spine as it enhanced her muscles. Her skin prickled, her stomach expanded, and her saliva thickened with the familiar yet unwelcome taste of poison.

It's time.

Her hand left a luminescent print on the doorknob as she twisted it and tugged the door open. She never knocked—the green light meant she didn't need to.

A cozy, fire-lit ambiance within welcomed her. A woman, a man, and a young boy sat at the narrow table, pausing their spoons near their mouths as they sighted her.

The man stood up, frowning. "Who are you?" he asked, in a foreign tongue she identified as French.

She pounced before he could take a single stride in her direction. Her nails were like talons as she drove into him. But instead of slicing at his flesh, she crushed his arms, pinning him to the ground, under her weight.

Her touch immobilized him. Her acerbic aura made him submissive, relaxing his jaw, numbing his muscles. Once certain he wouldn't resist her, she pried her lips apart, and a smoky substance squeezed up her throat and out of her mouth. Clover-colored fumes laced with vibrant violet puffed over him, soaring, soaring—until they shot into his nostrils, his mouth, his eye-sockets, his ears.

Once the mist had seeped into every cavity of his body, he

became stiff. He blinked once, twice, three times before nodding.

She removed herself from him, and he stood with ease. As if she hadn't just plowed into him, as if he'd never lost control of his motor functions.

She veered to the woman and child, both in awe at the scene, shocked into silence. She pointed the man towards them.

"Robert?" The woman slid before the youngster, shielding him. "What is happening?" She also spoke French.

The man snatched his wife's wrist. His other hand took hold of her jaw and squeezed it to force her mouth open. He blew the green and purple haze into her, watching as it shimmied down her throat, luminescent through her light skin.

She shuddered, swallowed—then turned to the juvenile. A frightening violence flashed in her eyes as she repeated the intoxication ritual on her son, who had no means to stop her.

All three of them then spun to *her*. Alert, obedient. Ready. *Success*.

Her pale pink tunic flowed in the breeze whisking in through the open door, and wisps of her straw blonde hair rubbed over her forehead. She pointed towards the outdoors, a slow smile spreading over her lips. "Feast. Gain strength. A war comes."

They didn't wait for her to say it twice; in a flash, her three newest victims exited, trudged through the field, and disappeared into the neighboring woods.

She followed them. The man crouched near a tree, still as stone—then jumped at an unsuspecting deer grazing near the forest entrance. He sunk his teeth into its furry flesh and tore it apart, splattering its crimson blood onto tree-trunks and rocks. His saliva sizzled onto flowers and bushes that wilted at once, dying from the toxins his body now contained.

She smirked, excited with how fast he'd shredded the animal.

Nearby, the woman was slumped by the beginning of a meadow, attacking a defenseless rabbit. She ripped off its fluffy ears, morsels dribbling from her mouth as she chewed. A messy pile of insides gathered at her feet, but it didn't disturb her in the slightest.

In the meantime, the husband had located another deer, and was busy draining its juices onto his tongue. The boy had climbed a tree, his fingernails like sharpened claws as he heaved himself onto a thick branch. He seized a few baby birds from a nest and slurped them up one by one like noodles. He burped, swallowed a few more, and cackled in delight.

The unknown one, satisfied with her duty completion, meandered the other way, leaving her deadly creations to roam the woods and continue to devour its inhabitants. She'd send them new commands soon enough; they knew to wait until that time came. The poison inside them controlled their thoughts, their motions; and *she* controlled the poison.

She had to wait, too. Wait for the next batch of innocents to twist and warp to her orders. She never knew where she'd go, not right away. But somewhere, another family would bend to her will, drink her venom, and grow strong by chowing down on wild beasts, big and small, fearless or frightening.

An army of poisoned humans for the upcoming battle.

Dazed, her footsteps airy, she braced for the new instructions that would soon pop into her head. The whispered words that would enter her soul and swim into her mind, repeating over and over until they tattooed onto her brain.

She wandered, barefoot, barely conscious. Insane, lost, lonely.

But never disobedient. Confused and conflicted, but always at the ready.

Wander. Gaze. Poison. Watch.

She almost stumbled on a rock, her mind battling its madness.

Wander.

She blinked, and the marble palace reappeared in her thoughts, begging her to remember who she was. Who she *really* was.

Gaze.

A flash—a lively courtyard filled with dancing nymphs and half-dressed men playing lyres, harps, singing out melodies that enchanted her.

Poison.

Flowers blossomed, draping over hedges, sprinkling their pretty petals onto the red brick passageways.

Watch. Repeat. Over and over.

She pictured the smile of a blond-haired man, sitting beside her, his hand caressing hers. Handsome, chiseled, enticing enough that she licked her lips. His amber eyes creased in joy, and his lips parted to speak to her—

His image dissipated as a gong echoed in her skull, heavy and harrowing, tugging her far from the images—memories or imagination, she'd never know.

"Focus. You'll know when it's time."

Her eyes closed, and she sensed her body lift and drift away.

She had no clue how many minutes passed, but when she next came to, she lay in a field of lavender and tulips, a refreshing aroma tickling her nostrils.

The softness beneath her sore spine soothed her—but the agony that raced to her temples pushed her to sit up and rub her forehead.

She'd been transported elsewhere, which meant it was time for more orders.

She took a deep breath, inhaling the flowery smells.

"More. Wander. Gaze. Poison. Watch. Repeat, over and over."

Despite her wobbly legs, and the incessant ache of her scalp, she got up. A house—much larger than the previous one—loitered at the edge of the meadow, calling her to convert its owners.

"Psyche...you'll know when it's time. Don't forget."

One step, another, another. Her bare toes dipped into the fresh soil. Her fingertips became empowered with atmospheric energy. The nearer she got, the more she felt tormented but tipsy. Unsure, but eager.

"Help them. Set them all upon each other. We will save the world."

Reminded of the last place, the carnage she'd caused, she hoped they'd spare the animals. The darling things she'd usually protect, but instead now set her new disciples to feast on. The innocent friends, sacred to her family.

They weren't her family anymore. Her only family was the poisonous liquid splashing in her abdomen, brewing, preparing to unleash and infect. And the voice guiding her every move.

These vulnerable,6 furry creatures were important; their essence was strong, their blood essential to her minions. To hell with what her so-called family would think.

"You'll know, Psyche."

||2. THE FAVORITE DAUGHTER||
ATHENA

Athena stared at the blinking letters suspended in the air before her. She traced a few more with her finger—*LUKUS*—and glared at the name as it trembled, as if laughing at her.

She had so little to go off of. How she wished Agent Arvantis was around to help her, but Aphrodite had wiped his memory. The human detective would be of no use to her now.

Backing away from the floating names and half-sentences, Athena fell onto her bed. Its plush, pale covers were almost comforting—but to her, in a time like this, there was no such thing as comfort.

Ruffling her messy mop of brown curls, she groaned at the matted strands sticking to her forehead. One glimpse at the mirror across from her—noticing her gray eyes streaked with red—she sneered. "What a sight I am."

Getting to her feet, she pressed down on her wrinkled tunic, desperate to make it somewhat presentable, and re-adjusted her breastplate.

"Athena, goddess of strategy? *What* strategy? I can't even strategically comb my hair."

She sighted the magic words still sparkling nearby.

"Oh, yes, remind me how I'm failing, would you?" She marched over to the floating list of potential evil-doers, to review the little knowledge she had so far, for the thousandth time.

Cup-bearers—nothing to report.

"Of course not, they're bribed." She swiped a finger to cross it out but made a mental note to interrogate some of the servants she often caught sneaking about at night.

Apollo—working on remedies for Eros.

Artemis—noticed diminished game/animals on earth. Strange?

She didn't always trust the twins, but she doubted they had a major role in this situation. Apollo wouldn't try to cure someone if he had caused the carnivorous rage.

"But…that doesn't clear him yet." She split them up, sending Apollo to the left, Artemis to the right.

Hermes—too busy traveling between here and Tartarus.

"He might have leads," she wrinkled her nose, "but he's our connection to the deceased who aren't speaking. He had no part in transporting the souls of Eros' victims."

Hermes—sly thief and flirtatious boy, he was. She'd never accuse him outright, but he was never easy to read. Always hiding beneath his crude jokes or changing the subject to sports. Wincing, she shoved him to the left, joining Apollo in the *"uncertain"* list.

She had too many on that side already.

Hera—???

"Ugh," she moaned, sliding the peacock lover's name farther left than anyone else's.

Adoptive mother or not, Athena would never trust the queen of the skies. Not when she'd spent years plotting against her own husband and seeking retaliation out of jealousy.

Demeter—all she does is cry, she's not faking that.

Hestia—sworn to neutrality.

Zeus—!!! Never blame the king!

Shrugging, she whisked all three of them to the right, the *"non-suspect"* area.

Then came the two she often struggled to read. She had interrogated them separately, but their stories were so similar she had to wonder if they'd consulted one another first. Or if they were innocent as they claimed.

Ares—would he use violence on his son and daughter-in-law?

Aphrodite—proved her innocence, but never cared for Psyche...

She tapped her cheek. "I have no clue where to put them."

For an instant she thought of separating them—Aphrodite to the left, Ares to the right—but she abandoned them where they were, too conflicted to choose.

Aphrodite hadn't kidnapped Psyche, but she might have known more than she claimed. And Ares would do anything to protect his lover.

She moved *Hades—awaiting interrogation* and *Persephone—pending* upwards, as she had yet to obtain their stories. A pinch in her belly prompted her to want to stick Persephone in the suspects column, but she was a victim, too.

Grimacing, she threw *Poseidon—nope* to the right. Though she definitely didn't care for him, he wouldn't dare harm Psyche or poison Eros. He had little time to try, and still harbored feelings for Aphrodite, anyway. Zeus and Hades always monitored him because of his earthquake-inducing tantrums, so he'd never escape their scrutiny if he were off kidnapping goddesses and provoking gods into carnivorous rages.

Suppressing a chill, she tossed *Hephaestus—likely uninvolved* to the non-suspects, no matter how it irked her. Their history made her wary of him, but he wouldn't have time to organize someone's disappearance.

And I'd rather not chat with him more than necessary.

Dionysus—who in Tartarus knows?

The dazed and drunken deity was a mystery to her, so she tugged him towards the suspects. His frenzies, albeit controlled nowadays, bothered her. When she first approached him to ask questions, his lips were violet-hued, and his breath smelled of wine. He couldn't enunciate a single sentence that made sense.

All other names she flicked upwards or to the right; all but one.

Athena—?

Did she trust herself? For all she knew she might have been under a spell or intoxicated. But she had no memory loss or blackouts and could account for all her actions in recent weeks.

She snapped her fingers, and her name vanished with a *poof* of yellow smoke.

On the other side of her room were the other facts—dates, cities, outlines of locations, victim's names. Every detail of Eros' carnage. She wasn't too familiar with American geography, preferring to survey her chief city of Athens and its Greek surroundings. But Eros had concentrated on the United States, striking major areas, leaving terror in his wake—so America was where she had to focus.

Zeus had sent down a team to wipe out memories and calm the citizens. The gods would have had quite a crisis on their hands if their king hadn't reacted so fast. They had sufficient issues to handle, with Psyche's location still a question mark.

Her disappearance signified something big; that someone targeted Olympian deities, messing with their minds, enraging them, confusing them. The sooner Athena discovered the culprit, the better. Who knew where Psyche was and what *she* was up to? Eros had caused soulmates to rip each other's hearts out; Athena panicked at the idea of what more could happen if a psychotic goddess was on the loose.

She whirled to her suspect list. "Is it one of you? Or…someone, *something* else?" She scratched along her jawline, her shoulders sore, her spine electrifying with pain. "What am I not seeing?"

The suspended words evaporated in a sky-blue smoke as she walked through them, headed to her closet. She wrenched the giant metal doors open and dug through the piles of coppery armor and rusted weapons, to salvage her aegis—the special shield fabricated from Medusa's head. She pulled out her favorite sword, a gleaming immortal material she couldn't pronounce the name of, and extricated her old bronze helmet from a pile of headgear.

Throwing the shield and sword onto her bed, she set the helm atop her frazzled curls. It weighed on her skull, causing recollections she didn't wish to see, but preparing her for what might come.

Blood. Screams. Lightning cracking over navy skies. The clinking and clanking of swords, the chopping of limbs, slicing of extremities, the sangria colored stains on muddy earth.

Shivers spiraled up and down her spine. "Goodbye, goddess of wisdom." She spun to her reflection, watching her eyes shift from gray to yellow dotted with blue. Her dress magically shortened, and her breastplate widened to cover her upper arms and below her breasts. "Hello, goddess of war." She summoned the sword and it launched from the mattress, its hilt nestling into her palm as if having always belonged there.

I've missed this.

She'd ditched her other persona because of Ares, unwilling to argue with him about proper war tactics. But now…her father counted on her. He wanted *her* to retrieve Psyche, then confront whatever beast had marked her. Zeus wanted the old Athena back.

A knock caused her to drop the blade.

"Yes?" She removed her helmet and smoothed out her hair, tugging at the hem of her gown as the door opened.

Hebe, her sister and chief cup-bearer, appeared at the threshold. "Father wishes to see you in the throne-room," she said, her eyes duller than usual.

"Did he by chance say what he needed?" She puffed out her torso. "I am working on the suspect list." She followed the girl out and secured her door with a few enchantments.

Hebe shrugged. "He told me nothing. But he seemed…anxious. I'd hurry, if I were you." Inclining her head, she scurried to the left, down a darkened corridor leading to one of the service staircases.

Athena meandered in the opposite direction, gliding onward to her father's favorite meeting place. She wandered by portraits of heroes she'd guided, all smiling at her, encouraging her. The sconces brightened as she approached, illuminating her passage to the larger, marble-lined hallway that led into the throne-room.

Heavenly sunlight swarmed her as she stepped into the rounded chamber, sighting the circle of empty thrones atop the dais, and the biggest seat of all towering in the middle. Zeus sat atop the latter, straightening up when he saw her arrive.

"Ah," he said, standing as she approached, her soft soles barely making a sound on the polished, mirror-like floors.

"Father." She kneeled, but he waved her up and tugged her into his arms.

"No need for formalities, dear daughter, we are alone." His chin nuzzled her, and a sweet scent of honey and ambrosia filtered into her nostrils.

Despite his affection, she had no trouble detecting the quiver in his tone, and the twitching of his limbs as he pulled away and returned to his seat.

"Father," she shifted her weight, "if you've summoned me for answers, I must remind you a few weeks is little time to solve such a mystery. Even for a goddess like myself."

His sky eyes narrowed on her. "I'm aware. But that's not why I asked you here." He twirled the end of his beard around his finger. "I have news that might help you. Reports from local lesser gods in Europe. They've noticed abnormal human behavior and instantly associated it with the behaviors Dionysus shows during his *festivities*." She opened her mouth to complain about the wine-drinking god, but Zeus raised a hand to stop her. "It's not him; he's been partying up here since before Eros ran off to the United States."

Humans and frenzies? This is about to get gross.

"They claim something is slaughtering animals. Game, mostly."

"Right, Artemis mentioned that," she said, crossing her arms, tipping forward to peer at her feet.

"Yes, but these are additional sightings. Whatever is killing these creatures...is also devouring them *raw*. Skin, organs, flesh, parts of bones. Carcasses were found in forests, wiped clean."

Her forehead creased as pain flared to life in her scalp. "Oh, dear."

"Indeed." Zeus expelled a heavy breath. "I've heard of no being that likes to do such a thing, not in eons. And humans…they wouldn't, not the ones I created. They cook animals first. The individuals I oversee do not have such gruesome violence in them, do they?"

"Well…" She sealed her mouth—asking him where he'd been for the past few centuries while his bloodthirsty warring son oversaw his precious planet wouldn't aid their situation in the slightest.

Luckily, he'd given her the power to shield her thoughts—including from him—meaning he wouldn't have access to her demeaning beliefs about Ares.

"Pan found gnawed bones in puddles of blood. Decaying flesh. Horror scenes. To be truthful, these weren't unlike the crime scenes Eros left behind." Concern etched over the king's face; a worry Athena hadn't seen in him in centuries.

"So you're asking me to investigate those areas, then?" She pinched her lips. "Do you plan to strip me of my powers, as you did Aphrodite, and pair me up with some smart-ass, dimwitted skeptic of a human to look into this brutality?"

Zeus' gaze darkened and he squared his shoulders.

Oh, no. That was too much.

Her eyebrows shot up as she clapped a hand over her mouth. "Father, please, forgive me, I'm under a lot of pressure—"

"—No!" He jammed a sandaled foot to the ground, making the throne-room's foundations quake and the marble pillars wobble, threatening to crash. It wouldn't be the first time everything shattered in the wake of Zeus' rage.

Athena dropped to her knees and bowed her head, zipping her lips shut.

"You'll interrogate Eros, in his mother's presence," said the king, his voice low in his throat. "She's a true witness of this mess."

She lifted her chin enough to spot him angling against the back of his stone chair.

Aphrodite—not a goddess she enjoyed spending time with. But she couldn't show her honest feelings at his request; he'd send her flying out of the castle with a zap of his thunder.

"You need to uncover a way to link his behavior to these animalistic, ritualistic events going on in Europe. And figure out if Psyche has anything to do with it, if Eros believes she might be pushed to commit such acts." He cracked his knuckles, and on instinct she shuddered. "Then you'll descend to earth and question these local deities, demigods, and your immortal heroes. We must decide if any of them could be suspects."

Rising, her knees weak, Athena bowed. "As you command, Father."

"Based on all this, you may be able to pinpoint Psyche's general vicinity. And stop her, if she's the one creating this carnage." He ran his fingers through his curly locks and sighed. "Most of these beings are sacred to us, and if Artemis finds out the extent of the damage—"

"—she won't. I mean," she cleared her throat and averted her gaze, regretting having interrupted him, "you made my thoughts impenetrable for a reason. To avoid interference with the investigation. So she won't get wind of this, not more than what she found out on her own. If you keep her confined to the palace, like everyone else...I can pursue this without disturbance."

Zeus set his elbow on his armrest and his jaw on his fist. "Well said."

She flinched. "Where is Aphrodite? So that I might go and get that part over with."

"Play nice," said Zeus, torn between a chuckle and a grunt of displeasure. He knew better than anyone how the goddess of love and Athena weren't friends. "She doesn't deserve such heavy judgment on your part. Don't forget she brought Eros home and prevented his chaos from getting worse."

"Fine, but—"

"—but nothing." His sternness returned as he stiffened and pointed at the exit. "She's in her room, waiting. And aware of what I've asked you. You'll go to Eros together, and then you will come to me before you leave for Europe. Understood?"

Athena bobbed her head again. "Yes, Father."

She spun on her heels, frowning once Zeus could no longer view her expression.

Great. This is…great.

"Find the truth, favorite daughter of mine," he added, his tone booming across the room as she reached the door-frame. She craned her neck to watch him stretch in his chair. "Find Psyche."

Dread uncoiled in her gut, its snaky scales scratching her stomach linings as she ambled to Aphrodite's room.

‖ 3. RILE ME UP ‖
EROS

Eros stared out at the gloom surrounding his enclosure. Plunging, never-ending silence stared back.

Shifting about on the hard, twin-sized mattress, sheets dangling to graze the concrete floor, he groaned at the sensation of the sweat-coated pillow under his neck.

The dungeons weren't cold and terrifying as one would expect. Instead, they were dank and swampy, with a foul sewer smell that swirled in his stomach, making sleep feel near impossible.

His only way of preserving his sanity was to picture Psyche standing at the entrance, a torch illuminating her fair complexion, flames dancing in her azure eyes. Her golden mane swishing as she tiptoed closer, her calming aroma of fruit and flowers falling over him like a soft blanket of bliss.

He snorted, and the image dissipated. "That'll never happen, not here."

He'd never leave the dungeons, nor would his wife return. He deserved such mistreatment anyway, didn't he?

He had to take responsibility for his actions while under the effects of the toxins that still flowed in his godly blood. "Godly?" He peered at his palms, still viewing the blood that had long since been washed off. "Yeah, super godly."

The word *poison* played on repeat in his mind. Fast, fast, *faster,* making him dizzy, drowning him in shame and despair. Prompting questions; who would hurt a love god? Who would harm his delightful wife, the deity of souls?

Souls. *Soulmates.* Soulmates eating human hearts.

"Stop—"

A blurry, woman's outline grew in the dungeon entryway. Wearing a silky nightgown, she held up a thumping heart to her mouth, pointing at him. "You," she said, digging her fangs in, splattering scarlet liquid everywhere. Chomping, chewing, her teeth were stained red, and droplets drizzled down her clothes.

"Stop!"

His horrific murderous tendencies haunted him—whether he was awake or fighting for slumber.

"Leave me alone," he said, flicking his wrist to banish the ghosts forcing themselves into his recollections.

Instead of fading, the picture shifted, and a foggy-silhouetted man joined the woman, taking the oozing organ from her. He smiled, his striking blue eyes holding Eros' gaze as he, too, sank his fangs into the still beating heart, blood blasting all over his messy mane of ebony hair, dribbling down his well-defined jaw.

"Lukus?"

That was new—the FBI agent had never popped up in his visions before now.

Eros lurched up from the mattress and ran to the metallic bars. "Lukus...no, I'm so sorry."

He squeezed his eyelids shut, willing the detective's figure to fade, but when he reopened his eyes, Lukus' face had crept closer, his nose mere inches away. He munched, and munched, and *munched*, morsels of the heart spewing from his mouth and lodging onto Eros' cheeks.

"Stop, *stop!*"

Eros raked his fingers through his curls, scratching against his scalp, rocking back and forth. Unable to differentiate between reality and imagination. Stuck between torture and truth, his legs bent, and he crumbled, smacking his forehead against the enclosure.

The visualizations vanished as footsteps fluttered down the hallway leading to the prison doors.

Eros perked up. He tipped his ears close to the bars and waited, listening, praying.

Is someone coming to rescue me?

He flinched—no, not rescue. Persecute. Interrogate. Punish.

He'd had enough of their questions; so unless this person came with news of Psyche, he had no interest.

With a huff, he heaved to his feet and marched to the bed as the door creaked open…to reveal Aphrodite.

Aphrodite. The one who had stopped him. The one who'd brought him to his senses. Her power, her fury, her ability to destroy him for the deeds he'd committed—

But she wasn't snarling at him, wasn't charging her energy to hurl it at his chest.

She flashed a weak smile as she set her torch near the door. "Son."

"Mother?" He took two steps forward, then froze, catching more movement from the hallway.

She's not alone.

"Who…who is there?" On instinct, he hugged himself, wary of

who else would brave the gross dungeons for the likes of him.

Aphrodite padded over, and he remembered how she'd kneeled before the cage, not that long ago. She'd been wracked with worry, with guilt—not eager to tear him to shreds as he'd anticipated. No…she had rescued him. She'd stopped Zeus from killing him.

"It's okay, son." Her melodious voice, her heavenly nymph's song, settled into his lungs and allowed them to expand. Allowed him to breathe. "Come here…let me look at you."

Though hesitant, he crept over. "Mother…" His leather pants chafed as he walked, making him cringe.

She reached between the bars and brushed his cheek, wiping the tears he'd unwillingly unleashed. "My boy," she said, sliding her fingertips through his oily, unwashed hair. "I promise, we're working on a cure. Something to get you clean, so we can release you. I hate seeing you stuck in here, but…it's for *your* safety, too." Her strawberry blonde locks lowered over her bare shoulders as she leaned in. "I wish I could swear all will be well, but…I can't."

The second person made its appearance, prompting Eros to gasp and jerk away. "Who is that?" Shivers scattered down his spine as he was unable to perceive their aura.

Aphrodite moved out of the way and left room for a woman in gleaming armor, a short-hemmed dress stopping at her bulky knees.

"Eros, hello," said Athena, her voice cautious, but her body language far from afraid.

"Zeus sent her," said Aphrodite. "She's here to interrogate you properly, this time. Have you calmed down since she was last here? Are you…conscious enough to answer her questions?"

He recalled the visit from the goddess of wisdom, and his insides bubbled. Not that he had anything against her—of all the deities, she was the most level-headed, most days. But he was in no mood for questioning. Her probing would worsen his unease.

It will rile me up… they should take my reluctance as a warning.

Athena's tanned, youthful face inched up to the magical bars. "I'm sorry to push, but your responses are crucial in helping me locate your wife." She was taller than most goddesses, her knees bruised, her posture stiff. Yet there was a certain beauty to her ruggedness, to her muscular arms and ungraceful hands.

He got lost in the intricate designs of olive trees and owls on her breastplate. "How can you find her?"

"I think you were poisoned by the same concoction, though it had different effects on each of you," she said, eyeing his disheveled appearance, a pinch of pity in her features. "Understanding your trauma might tell me which direction to look for her."

His mother, a stark contrast from Athena, wore a loose-fitting tunic, exposing her creamy skin and enhancing her warm, sexual aura. "It would help, son."

Help… but can I trust Athena?

They both scanned him, trying to pry into his thoughts. He winced, a tart and tangy taste in his mouth. "I…can't. I'll lose it. Again."

Athena's owlish eyes connected with his, digging into his soul. "I understand it's difficult, but…this is important. Remember; you can't harm us. These bars are enchanted, and Aphrodite and I are empowered Olympian goddesses. We won't let you do anything."

Her reassurances were flat, meaningless. His sanity would suffer if he spoke, if he brought his experiences to life.

"Son." Aphrodite's musical tone lost its charm. "Do it for her. For Psyche."

He gulped.

Psyche.

Her ghost gallivanted about his head, reminding him why he went crazy in the first place. "Fine," he shoved up the sleeves of his shirt, "what do you want to know?"

He'd do anything for Psyche, but kept his distance from his mother and aunt, in case his thirst for revenge returned.

Athena cleared her throat. "Well…when you were provoking your murders…how did you feel? Like you craved the killing? Or something within made you?"

Eyebrows scrunching, he rubbed his neck. Had he been orchestrating it all? Or did someone command him, whisper orders into his ear, manipulating him from afar?

"I think I was in control. I don't recall hearing voices…but maybe there were some in the beginning." His words triggered a vague recollection. "One voice led me to the Underworld. To…steal Cerberus' blood. But after that, I murdered on my own instincts." He joined his hands behind his back, desperate to hide how they shook.

Aphrodite reached out to him again. "You weren't in your right mind, son, we're aware of that."

"She's correct." Athena never removed her gaze from him. "But…were you always in control? Or were there times when you didn't wish to coerce your soulmates into eating each other's hearts?"

The onrush of ugly flashbacks made him queasy. He wobbled side to side and stumbled forward, almost slamming his forehead into the metal again. Aphrodite grabbed his wrist and squeezed, but her touch brought him no reassurance.

"I…don't know. I'm sorry, I can't remember all the details." An uncomfortable warmth crawled up his forearm, cruising to his shoulder and up his neck. "All I see are visions of my crimes… Specters of those I killed. Gore and blood." He gagged as the images splayed out before him again and again. "I'm not sure I wanted to slaughter them all…it was an obligation. Like I was doing it to free them, save them. Like such a gruesome death was the only way."

Aphrodite's grip tightened, and his eyesight blurred.

"So…you didn't see yourself as evil." Athena's tone became gentle, distant. "You assumed you were doing it for good." She squatted beside Aphrodite. "My next question will seem strange."

He nodded; if he opened his mouth he might be sick. The spectral woman from earlier hovered nearby, slurping up the juices from the muscle she clasped in her bloody hands.

"Did you ever think of murdering animals, too? Or strictly humans?"

Through his hazy view, he saw Aphrodite look at her in confusion. "What does that have to do with any of this?"

Chomp, chomp, chomp.

Eros' rib-cage constricted, his heart thrumming quick, *too* quick, shooting electricity up his limbs. He jolted backwards, out of his mother's grasp.

"Eros?" The goddess of love gasped. "What is it?"

"There have been horrible animal deaths throughout Europe the past few weeks," said Athena, ignoring Eros' sudden shift in demeanor. "The carcasses are similar to the messes you left behind, according to Zeus."

"Animal deaths?" Eros' voice strained, slicing up his throat. "Animals are eating each other's hearts?"

"No…*something* is eating them raw. Skin, organs, nibbling on bones. Leaving little remains." Athena stretched up to a standing position. "Some of our local gods found them, and they informed Zeus."

Eros' sickness still swelled in his gut, but he straightened up, too. "I didn't care for animals. My carnivorous desires concentrated on humans."

A sudden pang in his lower abdomen had him gritting his teeth, locking his heels to the floor to not hunch over.

The toxins...brewing...

"What are Psyche's thoughts on animals? Does she eat meat?"

He snarled, glaring at Athena with an urge to jam his nails through her breastplate and into her chiseled chest. "You would dare accuse Psyche of such a heinous thing?"

"Son, calm down," said Aphrodite, distancing herself from the cell. "No one accused anyone."

Athena's biceps bulged as she folded her arms. "I can't deny the link. Someone poisoned her, same as you, Eros. And she's missing...and animals are turning up horrendously butchered. Do you not see it?"

His heart banged so hard it tugged at the vessels connecting it to the rest of his body. It hurt. It screamed, screeched, blinded him with fury and hunger.

No...not again. Not now, not here...

Athena was oblivious to his suffering. "Eros, I need you to answer. Did Psyche have any grudges against animals? It might mean the poison finds deeper, well-hidden emotions and brings them to life."

Her words were muffled as the obnoxious pounding of his heart resonated in his ears. He didn't recognize the rhythm; rapid, but out of anxiety, not poison. It wasn't his heart he heard; it was

Aphrodite's. And in the background...Athena's, slower, more prepared, less frightened.

He wasn't supposed to hear them. The magical enclosure was supposed to block his skills.

"So does that mean," Aphrodite slipped backwards, "he wanted to kill humans, deep down? Wanted to destroy the gods?"

Athena set a fist under her jaw and grimaced. "No clue. We're still analyzing the traces of the potion from his blood."

Blood.

His calf muscles tightened.

Blood, blood, blood.

The venom was reactivating, traveling to his extremities, prying into his veins.

Athena rattled the cage. "Tell me, now! What do you remember?"

Eros saw red. Vibrant, vivacious, violent.

He dashed up to her, startling her into hopping several feet back. He couldn't touch her, but he *felt* her; her doubts, her concerns, her heart speeding up.

"She...loves...animals," he croaked, a perilous pain jabbing into his temples. "Your insinuations are triggering me, Athena. Riling me up."

Aphrodite whimpered. "Eros—"

One growl in her direction and she flew to the door. "*No.*"

"Son..." Her timbre trembled, coming from far, far away. "We're not saying she did it, only—"

"—*I don't care.*" His voice was no longer his own. It was dark, barking, bitter. As the two goddesses glanced at one another, whispering, he growled again, prompting Athena to guard Aphrodite, shield her.

"Eros, relax—"

"—no."

Ferocious hormones awoke in every cavity of his body. An angry intonation repeated in his ears, over and over—his inner turmoil begged to belch fire at her.

Aphrodite. The one I wanted dead.

He chortled, and the deities shriveled, slinking farther away.

I want them all *dead.*

"There may be a connection between your behavior," Athena swallowed, "and these recent murders. And Psyche's vanishing. It's inhuman…ungodly. Whoever, or whatever, took her might be executing the poor creatures in some sacrifice. Or fueling on their flesh. But I'm on your side, Eros. *I'm on your side.*"

She was a soft summer breeze; and he yearned to unleash a deadly storm to knock her over.

"Shut up," his fists bunched, "now."

The more she talks, the worse I'll get.

His consciousness veered between his normal, loving nature, and the ravenous rage that clogged his arteries, lodged in his mouth.

"I answered you." His nails pierced his skin. "I can't help. Not with…*this*…inside."

"Eros, let me—"

"—*you provoke me!*" His speech whipped out like a tornado, billowing over to blow the two goddesses against the prison wall. *"Get out!"*

Neither of the women put up a fight; they retrieved their lantern and withdrew, their hastened footsteps climbing back to where they came from.

He deflated, darkness seeping into his cage once more. The twinkling energy wrapped around the bars seemed to wink at him, daring him to try to break through.

I don't think this thing can hold me much longer.

||4. AN UNLIKELY DUO||
ATHENA

The poison still flows in Eros, and it's volatile.

Athena and Aphrodite's steps resonated as they climbed the stone stairs leading up to the main mansion. Athena's pace was quick, eager to get to work; but Aphrodite lagged. The dungeons were far under the principal lodgings, and the goddess of love wasn't used to such exertion.

But exhaustion wasn't the only thing bothering Aphrodite, Athena knew. She slouched, shoulders inward, wringing her hands.

"It'll be okay," said Athena, half-hearted and uncertain.

Aphrodite let out one of her signature exaggerated sighs. "But will Apollo find an antidote? Because I doubt anything will be okay."

They'd always disliked each other, but today, Athena had to be the bigger person.

Clutching the torch as she gritted her teeth, she slowed down, allowing Aphrodite to catch up. "I don't believe he is necessarily the best god for the job, no." She hadn't suggested it in front of Zeus, but in her gut, the deity of medicine and music lacked the skills to analyze such dark poisons. "He's good with healing, but this is more of a curse. We don't have anyone in Olympus who handles those."

Humming in agreement, Aphrodite's expression darkened—in

concentration or in rage, Athena wasn't sure. "We need someone from the Underworld. Someone who has dabbled in obscure spells." Her melodic voice lowered, and her emerald eyes darted back and forth, as if fearing being overheard.

"Aphrodite?" Athena paused, one foot hovering over a step.

The strawberry blonde goddess stiffened, her voluptuous curves crashing into Athena's lithe muscles as she leaned sideways. "I told no one of this, least of all Zeus, but…" Her perfumed and oiled skin sent discomforting shivers up Athena's arms. "I had a visitor before the big meeting the other day."

Athena almost lost her balance as she lowered her foot. "A what? Who?" Her free hand grazed the rocky walls to regain her stability. She thought of her suspect list and bit her tongue, waiting.

With a semi-indifferent toss of her curls, Aphrodite resumed her ascent. "An unusual guest. A surprise one—"

"—enough with the theatrics." Athena puffed out a breath as she continued after Aphrodite, refusing to play into her guessing games. "Who was it?"

Swift as a bolt from Zeus' fingertips, Aphrodite's words hit Athena square in the face. "Hades."

"Who?" Athena's knees buckled and she nearly missed a step.

"Hades!" Aphrodite adjusted the décolleté of her strapless tunic. "He visited me."

The King of the Underworld, swinging by her room in secret?

The constant drip-drop from the spiraling ceiling and the flicker of the lanterns made Athena dizzy.

Hades. The one man in the family who never gave into Aphrodite's temptation, into her foolish seduction tactics. The one who only had eyes for his bride and though he'd cheated once, he'd never do so again. Had he finally succumbed?

Athena scoffed. "Does Persephone know that you've been having an affair with him? I thought Poseidon was your favorite of my uncles—"

Aphrodite grabbed Athena's upper arms and whirled her around, flames flaring in her gaze. "How dare you insinuate such a thing? With Hades?" She snorted. "No. Persephone and I have had enough drama, thank you. That's not what he came to me for."

"What then?" Athena ripped from her grip and dusted herself off, as if the love goddess' touch had soiled her clothes. "A love potion? Has his wife fallen out of love with him?" She jutted her chin to the steps, urging them to pursue their path.

More sconces waited ahead, meaning they were closer to the main palace floor—closer to the walls she didn't trust and the family she doubted.

We need to finish this conversation.

"No," Aphrodite grunted, "he warned me. He claimed whoever did *this* could still be lurking, listening to everything we say, watching all we do. He spoke in code."

Athena tightened her grip on her torch as sweat coated her fingers. Hades had always been a bit off, but this was more cryptic than she was used to. "In code? Disturbing, coming from the king of the dead." She struggled to hide her concern behind her fierce facade. She trained herself to be neutral, to never show emotions; but lately, her skills had been tested. Too tested.

"I agree." Aphrodite cocked her head. "He kept looking out the window, viewing the courtyard, seeing things I couldn't. Was he poisoned too? He was stranger than usual."

With a cringe, Athena threw her arm out to halt Aphrodite's

strides. "Wait. Was there anything he suggested that would have made him suspicious?"

Aphrodite puffed her chest out, her breasts pressing against Athena's forearm. "What do you mean?"

"I mean," Athena gulped and yanked her arm away, "he's been neutral for centuries. But did he give the impression he might be drawn to the darkness that surrounds him?" She glanced ahead—her thoughts were veiled, but anyone would hear Aphrodite's. This stairwell was the safest place for them to exchange such information, no matter the dingy odors and gloomy atmosphere.

Aphrodite shifted her weight, her ocean eyes stormy as she bit her lip. "I don't suspect him. I can't. He didn't appear malicious. But…tormented. This creature intoxicated his spouse, too."

"True." Athena angled against the wet stone wall.

"So…maybe his anger has deranged him? He's imagining things?" Aphrodite twirled a strand of hair around her finger. "He seemed persuaded that something much bigger than all of us was at play. He frightened me." As she pivoted to Athena, her tunic clung to her body, wrapping over her silky silhouette as she crammed a hand to her heart.

Athena's throat constricted. Aphrodite *was* a beautiful being, but they weren't friends. They were sisters—though neither made any effort to act as such. "Hades can be difficult."

Shoulders raising, Aphrodite glanced askance. "Right."

"What?" Despite her reluctance to be in Aphrodite's personal space, Athena slid forward. "What is it?"

"Well…" Aphrodite massaged the back of her neck. "Before he dashed out, he mouthed something to me. A name, I think. But no matter how many times I review the scene in my mind, I can't figure out what he tried to say." She proceeded up a few steps.

Stunned into silence, Athena followed. Before either of them realized it, they had reached the top. Too soon; they weren't done exchanging essential information.

Athena set the torch in its holder by the metallic door leading inside the Olympian homestead.

Winded, Aphrodite panted as she stopped to fan herself; but Athena barely sensed a flutter in her torso.

"Look, I—" Aphrodite took hold of Athena's shoulders and pressed their noses together. "You must go to Hades. Before you go above ground, before you speak with anyone else. He knows something. He has answers, it's undeniable. Maybe not who the culprit is, but...I bet he has a hunch. Or knows someone who has more knowledge. Or...he's bound to secrecy, and that's what he mouthed to me."

Though she agreed, Athena yearned to break free from the woman's grasp.

"And...he has potions. Cures. A live-in witch," added the goddess of beauty, a sly smile appearing on her pouty lips.

"Are you mad?" Athena swiped Aphrodite's hands away. "Did you drink poison too?"

Aphrodite's sugary breath breezed over Athena's face as she slanted closer. "Go to the Underworld," she whispered. "Not to earth. You won't find answers there, not without Hades' help. He wants to help, I'm certain of it. He assisted me, why not you?"

"Aphrodite—"

"*Go to him.*" She seized Athena's cheeks and forced her to look at her. "He'll be safe in his realm, more able to speak. You can detect what dared to hurt my son. I beg you."

Immobile, lost in thoughts that caused her to forget where she was, Athena closed her eyes.

The Underworld. Dead souls ferried by Charon. Cerberus and his three heads of sharp teeth.

She swallowed and cringed at the acidic taste sliding down her esophagus.

Aphrodite's parted lips and tantalizing aroma weakened her senses. "The Underworld. Hades' palace. I've never been, but…you're the wise and brave one, no? The smartest of all deities. You shouldn't hesitate, Athena."

Subtle sounds of a harp and hushed laughter came from nearby—they were too close to the door.

Athena tugged Aphrodite away from any potential eavesdroppers. "Zeus will never allow it," she mumbled, scratching under her breastplate.

A soft moan escaped from Aphrodite. "You might have to use a ruse to fix that, dear." She smirked, entering her comfort zone. Seductive subterfuges and plots were one of her specialties. "You're unfamiliar with lies and tricks…but you may not have a choice if we want answers." Sensuality slithered from her pores as a smoky scent swirled around Athena, trying to entice her.

Such behaviors never swayed Athena; not now, not ever. She wrinkled her nostrils as Aphrodite's sticky, sweet stench attacked her nose.

Aphrodite circled her, oblivious to her disgust. "This is important, friend. Hades has connections to realms we don't. He's associated with creatures who might be aware of what's going on. And best of all—he has access to ingredients that might form potions to save my son. Everyone seems to have dismissed him, but…I won't." A violent violet shade shimmered to life in her eyes as she stalled before Athena. "You might have to step out of your area of expertise, for once. For the good of us all."

Clearing her throat, Athena slipped sideways. "I suppose you're correct." A shiver spiraled down her spine. "But…what about Father? I've never betrayed him. I'm his most trustworthy advisor. His favorite daughter. What happens if he learns the truth?" She scowled, racking her brain for strategies, past battles to draw inspiration from. "I don't know how to lie, like the rest of you."

Aphrodite's sickeningly tart presence was overwhelming. "Oh, precious Athena. Sweet, innocent offspring of Zeus." Her fingertips trailed along Athena's arms, provoking horrid images to flash in her mind, burn her scalp. "Do you need help?"

Against her will, against the churning of her stomach and the screaming in her eardrums, Athena nodded. "I do. I can't do this on my own."

Aphrodite giggled and skipped out of the way, allowing Athena to breathe again. "Leave it to me. I'll come up with something. This is for my son, after all."

Pinching the bridge of her nose and regaining her bearings, Athena blew out her cheeks. "It is."

"So…a fib good enough to fool Zeus." Aphrodite paced and paced, her dress draping over her perfectly sculpted limbs. After a few minutes, she halted and squeaked. "Yes." She twirled to Athena, an air of triumph in her features. "Tell him Hades summoned you. You can't refuse an invitation from a king! He'll have no alternative but to let you go." She batted her lashes, proud of her excuses—proud of her ability to stir up schemes. Gone was the flirtatious goddess of beauty—this was a skilled liar, a conniving creature of pleasure.

And yet…her idea was flawless. "Yes," Athena huffed, "and now I must find a way to execute this without Father reading right through me." Groaning, she gestured at the door. "Go on, then, you did your duty. You leave first…as if we were separated coming upstairs. Pass the throne room, but don't stop. Please, be your usual dramatic self to not rouse suspicion."

The beginnings of a plan germinated in Athena's head as Aphrodite disappeared into the palace.

Can I be like my siblings and fool my father?

Zeus knew her well, probably better than any of his children. Would he see through her uneasiness, even without access to her thoughts? Would he remove the magic to gauge her deepest intentions?

With a sigh, she slipped into the decorated hallway, fixing her face into one of concern; which wasn't hard, since worry ate at her insides that very moment. A single wrong move, a wrong word, and everyone would doubt her.

She, like Aphrodite, had to be her usual self. Rigid as ever, her heart about to plop out her mouth, she marched to the throne-room.

Zeus was there, atop his seat, in a meditative state.

Can I convince him?

|| 5. FEAST YOUR EYES ||
PSYCHE

Heavy smoke released from Psyche's mouth, spewing out of her chest in waves, cascading into the unwilling woman's throat. The latter shivered under the poisonous goddesses' firm grasp, her lips gliding apart to accept the toxic gift. The infusion took effect, and her organs swelled, drinking in the purplish haze, making her spellbound, submissive. Her eyes turned to a sickening green as her stomach gurgled.

"Yes," whispered Psyche, "now eat, child." She pointed at the nearby farm animal enclosures, smelling them, salivating. "Eat. *Eat.*"

The woman's features lit up as her legs twitched in anticipation. She stumbled to the first gate, hopped over it, and leaped up to a white-maned horse that she sank her teeth into without hesitation.

Such things would usually derange Psyche. She'd curse anyone who devoured such a precious animal, and vomit at such a heinous sight. Now, she was envious of the delicious scent of meat, and oh so hungry at the vision of the animal's shimmery ivory coat being splattered with red.

She grinned.

Gain your strength, my sweet.

The chewing was deafening, and chunks of horseflesh flew over to Psyche, almost hitting her in the face as she approached. Rubbing her hands together in delight, she slithered past the gate.

Become stronger so I may rescue you.

The recently converted lady's eyes glowed an ethereal emerald as she deserted the near-empty horse's carcass and unleashed a heart-wrenching squeak before pouncing to the next enclosure. The lambs.

Psyche's smile widened. Such delicate creatures. Meant to be devoured, to fill her soldier's bellies and empower them.

Feast, my pet. Enjoy yourself before the fight.

The words whirling in her mind were always so cryptic. Often, they sounded like *someone else,* though she heard them in her own voice. Despite the confusion, she obeyed without dispute. It was second nature, as if she gave herself the commands.

Yet somewhere beneath the haze, beneath the toxicity…she knew it wasn't her. But she'd never dare protest. That liquid flowing in her, cruising through her blood, would consume her if she denied its requests. No matter how odd and gruesome, she was aware of the internal struggle that would take place in her if she didn't comply.

In any case, she became used to the tasks. She liked them, as they woke emotions in her she'd never experienced. They energized her, made her powerful, useful, a veritable goddess.

Psyche returned to the bloody scene ahead and her heart fluttered with pride at the sight of a lamb wriggling about, thinking to escape its death.

Those poor, sacrificial animals.

How she wished she had an altar to pray; a place to thank the gods for offering such pleasant morsels to them, to beseech their wisdom—

"No!"

Something growled inside, shaking her skull, pinching her eardrums.

"There's no time. We must gain force and defeat the gods, not thank them."

She tried not to wince at the pain searing in her temples. At the agony the voice within produced, at the threat it conveyed.

"Humans must win. I must save them."

The savage woman made quick use of the lamb, then threw its remains to the side. She glanced at Psyche, lower lip puffing out, craving more. Asking for permission.

Psyche gestured at the barn a few feet away; there were pigs inside, she could smell them. "Go. *Feast,* child."

Flashing a smirk of crimson-stained teeth, the woman scampered off and burst through the wooden doors, attacking the first pig she located.

Psyche tiptoed over to witness the hogs screech as their entrails splashed against the door with a disturbing *squelch.* Their grunts grew so loud she had to cup her hands over her ears. A sudden nausea navigated up her throat.

No...no...can I infuse them and leave? Must I watch? I'm wasting time!

The growl occurred again. Louder, fiercer, piercing into every cavity in her brain. She squeezed her palms closer to her ears, but it wouldn't stop, wouldn't relent.

"Stupid...question," she rocked back and forth, "*stupid* question."

The crippling pain in her scalp wouldn't cease.

Stay...I am their mother. Teach...then leave them be.

She shut her eyes and willed her muscles to relax, praying for her rebellious mood to pipe down before she got in trouble.

We'll be reunited in the ultimate moments... to take down the gods.

"Yes..." she hummed, her heart thrumming as her objectives made sense all over again. Though the tones dishing out orders in her head felt unfamiliar, she knew they were *her* orders. *Her* decisions. Where else would they come from? Who else would have access to her innermost thoughts?

Maybe she'd always desired something more than what her love-struck husband could provide. Maybe, after all this time, she hated being a secondary deity, the wife of the son of an Olympian. The poison inside revealed her true nature, her true needs. Blood, flesh, and a human army to put an end to those who oppressed her.

Warriors to rescue us lesser deities from those who abuse their power.

A pig leg soared past her, and she swerved out of the way as it launched out of the shed. A trance-like, uncontrollable cackle croaked from her as she stared at the woman plowing through the carnage, ripping flesh from bones, crunching away.

She'll be thankful... dedicate herself to the cause...

"Keep eating, child." She took a step back. "Wait for my signal."

A hefty wind whipped up her skirts, yanking her from the barn. She recognized it; a signal, a warning.

Time to go?

She had little chance to isolate herself, as her eyelids slammed shut against her will. Chomping noises dissipated, smells of pork guts faded. All sense of time evaporated. She floated, solemn and soothed as a light breeze brushed against her cheeks. Though she couldn't see anything, she was sure she'd left the farm, her body on its way elsewhere. She never had control over the direction.

Seconds, minutes, hours passed before the forces controlling her permitted her to take in the new location. Waves crashed in the distance ahead. A slowly setting sun turned the sparkling sea to hues of grapefruit and canary. Seagulls screeched overhead and startled her.

She flipped around to familiarize herself with her surroundings.

A *Centre Touristique* loomed before her; a brick building with lofty windows plastered with postcards and flashy signs offering discounts for transportation and lodging.

Intrigued, her feet melting into what felt like sand, she pushed past tourists who peered at her in stupor. They wore sweatshirts and pants, hats and boots; she was barefoot and in a revealing pale pink tunic. She heard them scolding her as she meandered by, ogling her luminous skin, confused about her zombie-like demeanor.

Their comments were in French. A handful in English, one or two in Italian. They had no effect on her as she paid careful attention to the name of the town mentioned above the tourist center's sign.

Nice, France

She recalled the city from a few visits with Eros. A lovely area—but not overcrowded with animals to feed her fledgling army with.

Why am I here?

She padded a few paces down the boardwalk lining the beach, viewing gift shops, ice cream stands, quaint restaurants serving *crepes* and chilled wine. And though she craved to continue onward, a whim—the voice—encouraged her to return to the sands behind her.

With no reason not to heed its request, she spun on her heels and ambled past the tourists still calling out to her, telling her she was crazy. Telling her to cover up, to put some shoes on, to not go for a swim in this weather.

Their insults muffled as she slid into the water. An icy sensation skidded up her legs, her core, her shoulders, refreshing and cleansing her.

A detour? For a...bath?

The internal growls dispelled her questions.

"Do not challenge your commands, Psyche."

She waded farther until the waves lapped at her knees. Then her middle. Her breasts. As she prepared to let the water submerge her, a soft, distant wail halted her.

She squinted, swimming around to face the shore. It wasn't her voice, nor was it the roar that usually resonated inside her. It was something, *someone* else. It sounded familiar.

Though the toxins polluting her insides prevented her from exiting the water completely, she tried to push through. Tried to break free from the hold her intoxicated blood had on her.

The wail, so clear yet so far, so impossible to ignore, tugged at her heartstrings, beckoned her close, closer. With the water now lapping at her ankles, she sniffed the air, desperate to figure out who or what that voice was. What it wanted.

She finally had her feet out of the water, but the inner poison burned in her gut, moaning, forcing her to crouch and grab at her belly.

"Stop...I must go..."

She attempted to lift one leg, but barely got it a few inches off the wet sand before it slammed back down.

"No...you cannot."

She clicked her tongue, heaved in a massive breath of the salty air, and once more hoped to pry her foot from the ground. But it was no use; the thrashing in her scalp overpowered her as it hauled her backwards. Far from the beach, far from that beckoning cry she yearned to identify.

"Your mission, Psyche... complete it. Carry on. Continue."

She flung her arms up and down, well aware she'd appear as an insane psycho drowning in the glacial October Mediterranean sea. But those who mocked her earlier were nowhere around now.

"Dive. Eat. Then resume your purpose."

Dejected, she slouched, as more waves whipped against her torso.

"Save the world."

Shivering—from the frigid liquid or the voices haunting her, she wasn't sure—she bent her knees until the ocean swallowed her whole.

||6. LIES AND RUSES||
ATHENA

Zeus' gray marble throne glittered as the afternoon sunlight peeked in from between the massive pillars.

Hands fidgeting near the ruffles in her short tunic, Athena strode up to him. His eyes remained closed, his expression neutral, his limbs immobile. He was meditating, but had he sensed her arrival, nonetheless? Could he sense her panic, her distress, the fears fluttering to life in her chest?

"Athena," he said so suddenly she came to a halt. He pried one eyelid apart, then the other, and she fixed her face at once. "What troubles you? Your footsteps are uneven. Was the visit with Eros more disturbing than the last?"

My footsteps. My damn footsteps gave me away?

The tips of Zeus' sandals grazed the tiled floor. "Tell me, child."

"Yes," she said, her chin drawn down by gravity and guilt. "That is part of my issue, Father." She refused to get any closer, wary he'd spot the concern in her posture and her unstable breaths.

But the distance made no difference, as he groaned, stood, and marched up to her. His sky blue gaze poured into her as if analyzing every fiber of her soul. She winced, bracing for his anger. For the first time in her lengthy existence, she wished she could run from him.

"Share those issues, Athena. If you don't, I'll lift that spell I put on you…and I really don't want to read your thoughts." He appeared calm, but his voice boomed, bouncing from wall to wall.

She straightened up.

Lie. Everyone else does it. Lie, lie, lie. I can lie.

"As I was returning from the dungeons, I received a message." Her palms slicked with sweat, and she sent them behind her back, wiping them off on her dress. "An emissary from the Underworld, some…harpy-Erinye hybrid creature…"

Zeus wrinkled his nostrils. "Ah, yes, my favorite means of receiving mail from Hades."

Athena thanked her lucky stars Hades had once told her how he relayed information to his brother. "Yes…and it brought a report from Hades, but for me. A summons."

"A summons?" Zeus' brows joined. "For you? From Hades?"

"He wants me to go to him. In the Underworld." She gulped, worried if she opened her mouth too wide Zeus would see into her rib-cage and notice her heart's incessant beating. "He claims he has potential leads on the case to recover Psyche. A few suspects for me to interrogate down there."

Lie, lie, lie!

Flinching, Zeus crossed his arms. "But he sent a messenger to summon you? Why not come here himself?" He huffed. "I long ago removed the restrictions on his travels. The gates won't deny him if he asks for permission from me."

She hadn't thought that far, hadn't mustered up the full story behind Hades' fake invitation to his realm. She regretted not enlisting Aphrodite to produce the lie for her. But one ounce of hesitation…one slither of doubt, and Zeus would remove the protective veil over her thoughts.

"I have no clue, Father. It was cryptic. No sooner had I read his words that they burst into flames. It sent Aphrodite squirming off to her quarters."

Tangling his fingers in his graying beard, he bunched his lips. "That explains why she whooshed past here, not long before you arrived. I assume this messenger wasn't much to her liking, either."

Athena had difficulty containing her snort as she imagined Aphrodite facing an eerie and ugly Underworld creature the likes of which haunted most deities' dreams. "Indeed. And the note was clear. He requested my presence, as soon as possible, to discuss matters he preferred to keep…under-ground. Does that mean anything to you?"

She prayed to every other god in existence that the almighty Zeus would accept her mediocre acting. That he'd believe her lie. She'd cross her fingers if she could—a gesture she'd heard humans did for luck—but he'd see it. Tall as he was, overlooking her shoulder, he'd know.

His normally plump cheeks sagged and the thunderous power in his aura faded. "Well," he pivoted and returned to his throne, but didn't sit, "he must fear the culprit is *here*. In the palace. So he wouldn't want to confer his ideas with you in a place he feels unsafe."

"Ah." Her tension eased up. "I understand that." A sour taste lingered on her tongue; she'd succeeded in lying, yet no satisfaction came to her.

Zeus mumbled. "Under-ground." He paced before his throne. "I suppose I understand that, too. But why would he be so nervous here? *I* protect this place! I'm the King of the skies! Does he not trust me to keep my family safe?" He growled, his calves bulging and stiffening as he stomped to and fro. "We need his knowledge…but he won't come to us. Something isn't right."

Panic hammered into her skull, its vicious vibrations traveling down her spine and creating tingles in her extremities. "He's only being cautious, I presume."

Zeus paced from one end of the room to the next.

Athena worried he was circling her, trapping her, cutting off her exit routes should she need to clear out. Her lungs constricted and perspiration cloaked her forehead. "Father," she coughed, "whatever his reasons, I must go. I can't ignore a summons from a king."

He ceased walking and pirouetted to her, his expression clouded by concern. "But…there's something wrong with it. The timing, the location, the manner of delivering it to you… No, this won't do. I'll summon him here first, for some explanations—"

"—but if he's afraid, what makes you think he'll come?" She stilled, then clapped a hand over her mouth as she collapsed to her knees, realizing she'd yelled at Zeus. "Oh, heavens, Father…my king…forgive my outburst, I—"

"—no." He was quieter than she'd anticipated. "He'd come, even if apprehensive. You don't know him like I do."

Battling with her quivering lower lip and the weakness in her knees, she heaved to her feet. "It's not an excellent idea to meet him. And you may find his methods strange, but I get it. Something in these walls worries him, and I have to say I get eerie chills when walking down our hallways, too. These grounds aren't what they used to be, Father. To force him to travel here would worsen the issue, no?" She strung the words together so eloquently that she wondered how she hadn't stuttered.

Zeus scanned her, half-turned in her direction, his other half basked in the sunlight peeping in between marble pillars. His shadow loomed behind him, reaching so far across the room that Athena nearly crumbled at the sight of it.

Rubbing his forehead, Zeus muttered under his breath as he sat on his throne, lacking his usual grace. He leaned over, forearms pressed against his thighs, head in his hands. "It's odd, even for him. I've known him my entire immortal life, but maybe not as well as I thought. No…he never reveals his cards until the end."

Athena tiptoed nearer. "What do you mean?"

He whipped his head up so fast she immobilized. "I'm uncertain if I…if *we*…can count on him."

Once she regained control of her motions, she ambled to the seat beside him—Hera's, its surface sending a scent of sugar and roses into her nose.

She couldn't deny Hades was a peculiar deity. He kidnapped his bride, tricked her into living with him, and spoke in enigmatic ways. But he was fair to all souls that soared past his gates, never insulted his siblings, nieces, or nephews, and accepted his brother's bastard children.

Unlike Poseidon, my other beloved uncle—a selfish jerk.

The trident-sporting god caused her to cringe, and though his throne was far off to the side, she could smell its seaweed and salty odor.

"Has he ever given you reason to doubt him? Hasn't he always followed through on promises, obeyed all rules, and treated everyone with kindness?" She pulled at a loose thread in the hem of her tunic. "Would he not welcome me with open arms and take care of me while I'm in his home?"

She suppressed a shiver; she didn't want to voyage to the

Underworld, no one ever did. Aphrodite suggested it, which meant it wasn't a brilliant plan. It would backfire.

But…she had to do it. Something about the land of the dead intrigued her, and a hunch hummed inside, prodding her…telling her she'd uncover answers there.

"*He* is not what disturbs me most," said Zeus, his eyes shifting to a midnight blue as he fixated the white floor-tiles. "I trust him, if not one hundred percent…but he's not alone in that realm."

Kneeling at his side, Athena grasped the extent of his fear as she touched his arms. He trembled; and Zeus, the mighty, marvelous Zeus…never trembled.

How is he so frightened of a place he's never been?

"Father? What aren't you telling me?"

He wouldn't spare her a glance, keeping his focus on his feet. "That territory is full of monsters. What if our manipulative captor is with Hades, hm? What if, as we speak, it's laying out a deliberate trap for you? Summoning you down there with Hades' methods, intending to poison your mind as well? Or what if Hades has finally gone dark? What if he wants to ambush you?"

She'd never witnessed her all-powerful father so hesitant, his posture so shriveled and shrunken. So reluctant to risk his darling daughter.

Crawling before him, she dared to touch his chin, to make him look at her. "No. Those are wild hypotheses, and you mustn't assume they're reality. You must trust your own brother would keep me safe. He'd allow no one to hurt your favorite child. He owes you and would never turn against you."

Though she'd lied before, these words were truths. Hades *did* creep everyone out, but he wasn't evil. Persephone wasn't evil. And if either of them fell into that bucket of sin, Demeter would blow up the planet in indignation.

Hades was smarter than that, anyway. He had to know more, as Aphrodite said. And Athena, the goddess of wisdom, was the only one with the logic to figure out his cryptic messages. Even if he hadn't officially requested her presence in the Underworld.

"He has answers. And Persephone…she was attacked, too. She'll have her own recollections to give. The judges, or those monsters you mentioned…they'll all have something to add. As the lead investigator in this case," she inhaled a breath, "it's my duty to communicate with them. It's my job to visit the Underworld."

Zeus lidded his eyes. Silent, debating with his inner self, his mind shielded from her, he pondered her speech.

Hades has overseen it for centuries. Nothing to be wary of.

Tartarus and its fiery depths were the danger, but she had no intention to venture there. And no reason to.

Rising up so swiftly he knocked Athena back, Zeus trudged to the middle of the room, fists on his hips. "Your counter-arguments are quite valid," he said, so softly Athena had a hard time hearing him, at first. When he whirled around to her, at his full, majestic height as if he hadn't been cowering mere moments before, he glared. "A summons is a summons, but you're not going there alone."

"My king?" Athena scrambled to a standing position and adjusted her skirts before they exposed too much of her. "With you? No, you can't leave Olympus unattended! Your wife—"

"—is lovely," he shot, his gaze hardening at his daughter's near-slight of Hera. "But *I'm* not accompanying you. You must speak with the only god who can travel with ease between realms. If he agrees to take you…then you may journey to the Underworld."

Athena's resolve shattered.

No...please, anyone but him.

"Hermes? You want him to go with me?"

"Don't act surprised." Zeus' lips spread into a lopsided grin—this amused him? "Hermes is the only one with such access. That's my condition."

She bit down an urge to tear her hair out. Or to laugh at her father's joke—except it wasn't a joke. He might have been grinning, but Zeus meant what he demanded. He knew of her and Hermes and their disagreements...but didn't care.

"He's away on business at the moment—" Zeus glowered at her as she snorted in disbelief, "—but someone will notify you once he returns."

Turning a blind eye to Athena's pouts of protest, he tipped an imaginary hat and strolled out of the throne-room.

Athena chewed on the insides of her cheeks to not howl in rage. Hermes would never agree, and if she tried to bargain, to ask for a favor...

Of all the deities to owe something to...Hermes is at the bottom of my list.

She'd never reach the Underworld.

||7. BETRAYAL||
PSYCHE

Feed, my pet.

Psyche ogled a teenage boy sinking his teeth into a deer. His eyes rolled back with pleasure as the flesh melted in his mouth and oozing red juice drizzled down his chin.

Gain your strength. Let the tender meat fill you up. Prepare you.

She'd posted herself nearer than she usually would while witnessing a new cultists' first meal, but she couldn't help it. She had to pay attention to the amount of food he took in and be at the ready to encourage him to ingest more.

Reports of unfinished carcasses had reached her—via the mystery voices in her head—and the news had horrified her. Wasteful…and unwise.

They'll be on to us. We must finish every last slice.

Crimson liquid splattered all over the adolescent boy's hands. The shiny substance produced a delectable scent Psyche licked her lips at. How she wished to swipe her tongue over his fingers and slurp up the remnants of his feast…but she had to wait until he was done.

None of those in her army had been caught yet, thankfully. But if anyone noticed them wandering around with deer skin dangling from their mouths, bloodstains on their ripped shirts…the gods would thwart her plans.

I can't have that.

The boy proceeded to chow down on the deer, keen to devour it in its entirety. Psyche was jealous of his squishy chewing, the juices splurging out, spilling all over the pasture. The raw purity of the beast made her grin. Her belly rumbled, gurgled—but she hunched forward when the pleasure suddenly became pain.

Her intestines twisted, her lungs constricted. A tiny timbre in the back of her head yelled at her to stop, *stop.*

No.

It was too much. She'd had her fill and needed to distance herself. The voice within rang to remind her she shouldn't be greedy; the morsels were for her creatures, not for her.

The youth looked up, licking his bloody lips. A few sizeable chunks were already beginning to rot on the ground before him.

"Finish it," she said as he blinked at her, his tongue frozen, his ethereal purple eyes focused on her. She squinted at him and wondered for a moment if he understood English.

We are still in France...

She repeated her words in French, pointing at the carcass, urging him to keep tearing off pieces of flesh.

The boy gaped at her, unmoving and silent. How she yearned to read his mind, to see what her intoxication had done to his brain. Did *he* hear voices, too? Were those voices confusing him? Did he need a fresh dose of poison? Had she not breathed enough of it into him?

Though her inner self was urging her to leave, she reached forward to take hold of the boy, to find a way to sense his level of toxicity. To send another cloud of it into his bloodstream if needed.

But when her fingertips brushed his shoulder, he jolted up so quickly that she stumbled.

Her heart thumped as she watched him straighten up, cock his head, and take a step towards her. She flinched and skidded away, but he dared another stride. Another.

She swallowed, some of the poisonous mist getting caught in her throat as he lessened the distance between them.

"Stop." She thrust her palm out, hoping to halt him. But he paid her hand no heed, and snarled, hunger in his expression as he bared his teeth.

Had he spotted another animal behind her? She veered around to discover that…no, they were alone. No other beasts loitered in the surroundings. So why was this ravenous teenager roaming closer and closer to her?

"Go to your food!" She waved at him, but he continued forward as she took small steps back. Her French was rusty, her panic worsening her accent. "Stop this, right now!"

She hopped aside, hoping he'd hurry past her, but he didn't. He followed her moves, zombie-like, thirsty for *her*.

Two feet separated them, and every time she steered herself backward, he took a bigger stride of his own. His nostrils flared as he sniffed the air. Sniffed *her*.

This isn't supposed to happen. Why is he charging at me?

"Stop this, this instant!" What other language could she try to get into the boy's head? Ancient Greek? She didn't know the long-lost language, but perhaps a few words of modern-day Greek…

His eyes, rimmed with violet and green, narrowed on her. His mouth foamed with saliva as he flashed his fangs. He growled—and lunged to grab her.

With a whimper she dodged him, leaping sideways; but he swiped at her as she regained her balance. To avoid his bloody nails, she leaned backwards, which caused her to lose her stability again and collapse with a hard *thud*.

Somewhat stunned by her fall, she gasped, searching for the energy to haul herself up to her feet. But before she had a chance to try, he pinned her into the dewy grass, slamming her head against the ground.

What is happening?

"Stop! *Stop!*"

The voice inside was screeching, screaming, begging her to spit out her venom to immobilize him. But it was too late; he shoved his salivating mouth against her neck and dug in. His dirty teeth broke through her skin, and droplets trickled out.

She closed her eyes, dejected, accepting her fate—

A whoosh of air and another *thud* later, and she was no longer in the field. No longer weighed down by the rabid monster she had created.

Opening her eyes, her vision blurry, she panted. She had teleported without meaning to.

How did I do that?

She smacked a hand to her neck but felt nothing—no bite marks, no bruise, no blood. As if her disciple hadn't jammed his teeth into her, attempting to drink from her.

Woozy, she sat up, and her surroundings became clearer. She lay on a twin-sized bed, under sticky sheets drenched in sweat. There was a scrunched straw pillow beside her, and a stuffy scent slithered into her nose.

"Where…am I?"

The room was compact, lined with wood, devoid of decorations. A bedside table to her left, and ahead of her she noticed a decrepit sink, a bucket—she gagged when she realized what it was for—and a curtained window.

Soft breathing from the floor prompted her to peek down and see *him*. The youngster who'd violated her, nibbled on her neck. He slept. His appearance was identical to how she'd seen him only instants ago…but without the snarling, the sneering.

Was I dreaming?

She stood up, dizzy. Her legs were weak and her abdomen tight as she dabbed at her neck again, still in disbelief. It had felt so *real*. In the mirror above the sink, she took a peek at herself—no wound. Only her pallid face, her ghastly blue eyes and tangled, faded golden hair. But no scars, no trace of anyone ever having tried to eat her.

Why would I dream such a thing?

She spun on her heels and viewed the boy. So innocent, with his chest moving up and down as he slumbered. Peaceful, as if he'd never assaulted her.

"He finished that deer…" Visions popped into her brain; like lightning, striking her fast, prickling her scalp. "He obeyed…then we went to sleep inside the cabin…in here." She tousled her curls. "What was in that fish I ate?"

Desperate for clearer air, she tiptoed to the door and pried it open. The bleak atmosphere outside knocked her backwards. Blood, rotting flesh, decay. She smiled. It was a stench that meant she'd fulfilled another piece of her purpose.

Yet her worries were there, besmirching her happiness. What if one day she *did* lose control? If she failed and her beasts feasted on her? On humans? What if that nightmare…was a premonition?

She crept over to where she'd watched the boy eat earlier. The once vibrant green grasses were tinted red. Abandoned bits of meat and gnawed bones nestled there, harassed by flies. With a quick flick of her wrist, she erased the damage to ensure the area remained neat. Untainted, as if nothing had ever happened. *No proof.*

Had she done the same at all other hot-spots? She needed to travel to them, check on her army, discover if they were eating woodland creatures, as ordered…or if they were disobeying her. She needed to wipe the scenes clean.

"Hide the carnage. Avoid unwanted attention from authorities."

Convinced, she began to retrace her steps—but her interior being moaned with such vigor it stilled her. Her legs wouldn't cooperate.

"No…more madness to spread. More to infect. To feed."

She cringed as the voice echoed in her cranium, crackling and corrupting. Deafening and powerful.

"Time runs out. Must move on. Cannot risk discovery. Pets…will fend for themselves."

Her mouth twitched as she pleaded to speak her mind, to oppose her internal self's commands. "And if…they turn…on each other?" Her fingers bent as she tried to form fists, and her spine arched, ached. "What if they…hurt others…I'm meant…to save? If they…ruin…my progress?" She sank to her knees, temples throbbing, belly boiling.

"A dream filled with your fear. Fight harder, Psyche. Stop the nightmares."

Nearby noises in the woods startled her. She wasn't sure who controlled her movement, but she gazed in that direction. Someone yelled; a mix of whistling screams that sent Psyche toppling over, writing around on the ground and hissing.

"Ignore it...more poison...strength. Smarter...creatures need...more..." She convulsed, and on the inside her neurons fired up and tried to shake her normal self out. The part of her that wanted to investigate the noise, to return to previous places, to fix her errors.

"One dose suffices. They'll receive more later. No more than necessary...or it was all for naught."

The poison bubbled, brewed, steamed. It fueled her, halted her convulsions, gave her the desire to move on. To infiltrate someone else's mind, bring them to their true purpose. To save humanity from the gods.

Her tunic was soaked from having rolled around in the bloody grass, but at last, she had some control over her limbs. She peered at the house, praying her insanity hadn't woken the boy. Praying he'd know what to do...and what *not* to do...once she left him.

"Farewell, my pet." She hoisted herself to her feet, seething, scowling. The scorching ache was fading. "Time to make more. Rest, wander, eat. I shall see you for the ultimate battle."

||8. PLEADING WITH THE PEACOCK||
ATHENA

One inhale. One exhale.

Athena's breath fogged up the mirror as she placed her bronze helmet atop her tangled tresses. She prayed for confidence, intelligence, and strength. She prayed to succeed.

Lying to her father was step one in her deception. Next…she had to confront Hermes. Beg for his help, plead with him to venture off on a dangerous mission with her. Knowing him, he'd accept…but with terms she'd dislike.

Once the headgear settled, its cool interior soothed her throbbing skull. She batted her eyelashes at her reflection—and gagged, reminded of Aphrodite's earlier seductiveness.

"Ugh, no." She spun away, half-laughing, half-crying. "That's not me."

She *was* beautiful. Many had said so. Many had tried to seduce her. But she wasn't the deity of beauty. Her wits and wise words were her weapons, along with swords and spears. She hoped a few well-placed phrases and compliments would entice the ever-flirtatious Hermes; because she'd do nothing rash, nothing like Aphrodite would.

She hated Aphrodite's intuition. How her counsel had been the alert that prompted Athena to lie to Zeus. To obtain his permission to pursue her agenda. To save Psyche. But she never would have guessed she'd also involve her boastful, hotshot little brother to assist her. Because if she had, she would have never omitted the truth from her father.

I would have never taken it this far.

With one last glance, and keeping the helmet on for luck, she strode down the corridors of Olympus. Head held high, shoulders pulled back, nostrils flaring—

Flaring. Her nostrils only flared like that when one particular scent reached them. A swish of sweet vanilla and majestic magnolia and disdain—and it came from the mighty Queen of Olympus.

"What do *you* want?" said Athena, swiveling to see Hera parading up to her, as if to attack her from behind.

Sneering, her large, light brown eyes glowing with their usual cruelty, the goddess of marriage grinned. "Why the rush, dear daughter? And why the attitude?"

Tightening her fists before she smacked the woman's cheeks with all her strength, Athena inclined her head in a quick gesture of reverence. "I am to meet with Hermes, majesty. So if you'll please forgive me…I will continue on my way."

Athena twirled to resume her trek, but Hera shimmied over to block her, her peacock-patterned robes roving in front of her like tentacles. "Are you? That's interesting." Hera giggled; a stomach-curdling sound Athena always despised.

"No time for your mind games, Hera." She huffed, wishing she was clutching her spear, to thrust it forward and ward Hera off.

Hera's grin widened, and her chestnut curls glittered in the semi-darkness. Even without her matrimony veil to cover her features, she basked in refinement. The glimmering crown of sapphires atop her head was meant to intimidate and demean. "You can spare a few moments for your queen, no?"

As the woman glided around her, wicked and snake-like in her movements, Athena's pulse quickened. "But Hermes—"

"—can wait." Hera angled against a wall, and her nose wrinkled in disapproval as she sized Athena up; she never appreciated her outfits.

"Fine." Athena rolled her eyes. "What is so important?"

Most Olympians sucked up to Hera. They cowered in her presence, reveled in her glorious aura, praised her accomplishments. But Athena disregarded such pleasantries. With their history, she owed Hera nothing. But she usually hid her hatred, remained polite.

Not today.

Her impatience boiled on the inside. Did Hera not know she was on business for Zeus?

Hera moseyed towards the opposing wall, taking her time, trailing her tremendous tunic's tail along the floor. "For someone who fought beside me in the Trojan War, you're so hostile, Athena." Though her voice was poised and pleasant, poison hid in it.

Athena scoffed. "You're one to talk—"

Hera raised her hand. *"Ah ah ah,* no need to reply." She snorted at Athena's scowl. "I'd expect more caution from a divinity such as you. More discretion. But I should not place my expectations so high."

"How dare you—"

"—*me?* Queen of Olympus? How dare I what?" Her airy chuckle caused chills to crawl up Athena's arms. "Oh, I'm so disappointed. Really, I wanted to think the best of you, but…"

"Think the best?" Athena's heart skipped a beat. "What are you about to imply?" Hera loved to get her in trouble, so what scheme had she concocted this time? "How did I offend you, step-mother dearest?"

By being alive? Unwed? Uninterested in sex?

Hera hated that Athena was the favorite child. The favorite goddess.

"You didn't offend me." Hera cleared her throat. "I said, disappointed. I'm upset by your hostility towards someone who is privy to your secrets."

Athena hiccuped. "What?" Her muscles tensed and her jaw hurt from clenching so hard. Had Hera seen her excess of exchanges with Zeus today? Was she expressing her usual jealousy out of boredom? Had the situation with Psyche put her in a mood? "Is there a point you're about to make, instead of spewing out cryptic nonsense?" Athena tapped her sandaled foot to the floor and groaned. Hermes traveled often, and if Hera made her miss him…

Hera's smile turned sour, and her eyes darkened like two puddles of deep, dingy mud, threatening to swallow Athena whole. "Sweet girl, for a goddess of wisdom you can be so daft at times." She rubbed her knuckles against her brilliant blue bodice. "I overheard you and Aphrodite in the dungeon entrance. And your conversation with Zeus after." Snickering, she slanted forward, getting into Athena's space. "You're a treacherous little liar."

Athena's semi-strong facade melted. "Oh." Her cheeks flared with heat, and she whipped her head away to not reveal her frustration.

Great balls of Cerberus—I hadn't anticipated that.

On a stupid whim, as panic pirouetted in her, Athena jammed her arm out and pinned Hera to the wall, covering her mouth with her other hand. "How?" The queen whimpered, but Athena compressed her forearm deeper into the woman's breastbone. "We were discreet and quiet. So how in Tartarus did you hear? You were lurking, weren't you?"

Hera's eyes shifted to a soaring sky-blue and her skin glowed gold. She sucked in a breath, then shoved Athena off her with all her godly energy, sending her spiraling and slamming into the opposite wall. "Never lay your filthy hands on me again, you bitch." She sneered as she dusted herself off.

Crap.

Athena shouldn't have allowed her temper to turn her into a turbulent idiot. Despicable as she was, Hera *was* the queen. No matter her taunts, assaulting her would lead to a severe punishment if anyone found out.

Fixing her crown, Hera stuck her chest out and pursed her lips. "You know damn well I have access to every square inch of the palace." Her glare was so intense it burned through Athena's skirts.

Her intestines knotted under the woman's scrutiny, her extremities tingled, and her flesh was on fire. Reluctant, she gulped down her pride and bowed. She had to apologize.

If I don't grovel at her feet...she'll tell Father.

"Yes, majesty." Athena straightened up and clasped her hands behind her back. "My sincerest apologies. I have no clue what came over me." If she didn't choose her words carefully, Hera would destroy her. She'd have her thrown off the case...meaning they'd never locate Psyche. And if she told Zeus, he'd not only forbid the trip to the Underworld, but he'd lock her up beside Eros. And never trust her again. "I beseech you…don't worry Father with my actions." She winced, struggling to hide her annoyance, her wariness, her discomfort.

Hera had never intimidated her before, because Athena excelled in word-wars. She always beat her to Zeus when they had complaints about one another. But today, Hera had come prepared. Her mischievous aura troubled Athena, and her gloating proved she had real leverage.

The queen let out a satisfied moan. "Ah, the power I have over you. The delicious, unyielding knowledge I hold. Zeus won't doubt it because, let's be real, he doesn't want you to visit our beloved Hades. So any excuse to stop you he'll accept as valid." She fingered the silver pendant dangling from her neck, twirling and twirling until Athena was hypnotized.

For an instant she imagined herself strangling the queen with the necklace. Twisting it around her delicate neck until her face turned tomato red and her heart stopped.

Gritting her teeth to erase the perfect picture, Athena lowered her chin. "I'm aware, majesty. So what is your price?"

Hera cackled. "Your mind is concealed, but how I crave to read your thoughts right now."

"Majesty," Athena dropped to her knees, realizing she had to use drastic measures, "please. Reveal nothing to the king. It would shatter him, leave him weak. We need him strong. An unidentified evil being is on the loose, targeting us, preparing a gruesome end for us. Psyche holds clues to this, I'm certain. So I must find her. Fast. Hades…has my answers. Please."

Don't be a selfish, rotten witch, for once.

Hera pressed a finger to her chin, her royal blue nails digging into her skin. "Hm…let you off the hook? For a price, you said? But…I finally have the upper hand. This is difficult." The subtle smirk on her lips showed she was enjoying every second of the torture.

Another surge of rage rippled through Athena. She grimaced; Hera was never rational. She'd put all immortal lives in jeopardy to win an argument, especially against Athena.

But to Athena's surprise, Hera huffed and flicked her wrist, allowing Athena to rise. "Fine. I'll say nothing. The memory of your begging and bowing will have to quench my thirst…for now."

"For now?" Athena got to her feet and adjusted her dress hem. "You can't be serious."

A cloud of resentment hung over Hera's gorgeous face. "Someone else will out you, I have no doubt. If I heard you, who knows who else did! And besides, I'll have more delight when Zeus discovers the truth later. Because he will. His darling daughter lied to him? I see it now. *Oh, Hera, my love, you've been right all these centuries to mistrust her, to disagree with her foresight.*" She cringed as she nudged Athena out of her way and waltzed down the corridor. Her fluffy train dusted the floors as she scurried off to, Athena assumed, her chambers. "Good luck! Looking forward to the grand finale—your showdown!"

Once she was out of sight, Athena shivered.

I should have seen this coming.

She was born an adult; but now, more than ever, she wished to be a child. To hide behind her father's throne, sit on his lap and cry in his arms, use her innocence to convince him to forgive her.

But it was too late. She told the lie, and she had to maintain it. Believe it. Hermes was next, and she wouldn't let her latest tirade with Hera destabilize her.

For Olympus.

||9. HUNGRY AGAIN ||
EROS

"No!"

Covered in sticky sweat, Eros sat up and gasped. He struggled to figure out his surroundings—the bars, the concrete, the sink, the mirror. As his vision adjusted, he spotted his leather jacket on the floor, and stared at its creases as he waited for his pulse to normalize.

His temples throbbed, squeezing every ounce of semi-sanity from him. Immortal or not, poison-induced nightmares were terrifying.

Removing his black t-shirt, he gagged at its foul perspiration stench. More sweat drizzled down his torso as he tossed the thing across the cell. His muscles ached and as he stretched, they didn't lose tension. If anything, they pained him more.

How he longed for a glass of ambrosia nectar and a bowl of grapes and a nymph to play a timid tune to lull him into relaxation.

"Ah, but I don't get ambrosia, do I?" He snorted, bringing himself back to reality. "Apollo says it activates the virus. Food fuels it. Happiness rouses it." He reached for the cup of lightly rose-flavored water on the nightstand and recoiled as he sniffed it. "*Rose water.* Who in Tartarus do they think I am? Some kind of prissy?"

He flung the glass against the cage and smiled as it exploded.

Sparks of magic fizzled as shards collided with metal, and the transparent, flowery liquid poured all over the floor. It didn't flow out into the dungeon entrance, since the enchantment kept everything in the cage.

"Great, now this place reeks of sweat *and* flowers."

His eyes wanted to release tears, but he refused to let them out, too angry for sadness. Too enraged to cry.

I've had enough of this damn prison!

Ignoring the buckling of his knees, he barged up to the barricade and winced at the energy it shot into his being as he touched it. Electricity surged, seared into his skin, but he didn't let go. He rattled, shook, gritted his teeth as he roared, punched, then kicked—but nothing changed. The power holding him in didn't lessen, and his complaints were to no avail.

"Let me out of this fucking hole!" No one was near to pity his whines. The dungeons were miles below the Olympian Palace, and no one would hear him. He didn't care; he had to unleash his frustration somehow. They'd given him nothing to blow off steam, nothing to distract him. "I'm a *god*, dammit! Let me out so I can find my wife! Only I can locate her and none of you can deny it!"

He yelled at no one in particular a few more times before falling backwards and landing on his behind. More pain flared up his spine as he looked at his hands, noticing the burns breaching his skin, charring it. Without his full powers, he wouldn't heal fast, like he used to.

She's in danger…I could tell from that dream.

Visions plagued him every time he tried to sleep, but *this* one had been different. Since he and Psyche had been married for centuries, he had no doubt he'd be aware if something went wrong with her.

He'd envisioned her wandering in a field of lavender. Her hair undulated behind her in a brisk breeze, and her eyes were lackluster, glazed, watery. Her tunic was ripped in ways that would usually arouse him, but there was a shift to her demeanor that horrified him. Skin paler than it had ever been, and fingers spasming with an uncontrollable power, she spoke to him…but he had no idea what she said.

The sight sickened him to the core, so he shot up and shook his head, willing the despair out of his mind.

"Psyche…my Psyche." He tipped back to glower at the ceiling, praying to see through it, to see his family. "I couldn't sense you before, but…in here I sense you less. So much less." Something pinched in the rear of his neck. It spread more ache up to his jaw and behind his ears, and he lowered his chin. "I couldn't feel your heart…and I fear what that means, my love. Where is your heart?"

The pinching happened again, but more of a stabbing jolt. It voyaged down to his groin, spreading down his legs, up to his rib-cage. He heaved forward and bent over, gagging.

"What…what is…"

No…

He worried he was about to puke his guts out, but instead of expelling liquid, he drank in the air. It coursed down his throat and freed his lungs from their constriction; it swirled into his belly and undid the tight knots. A foreign yet oddly familiar sensation slurred from his shoulders to his fingertips, from his hips to his toes, from his cervical spine to the tips of his dark blond hair.

The poison is waking up.

As if answering him, his insides grumbled, growled, groaned.

Words he didn't understand repeated in his mind, and the flashing picture of scarlet splotches on dirty floors made his mouth water.

He was…hungry. Not for ambrosia, not for grapes. He slid a hand over his bare stomach and his abdominal muscles clenched as he dug his nails into his own flesh.

Then came the nausea. Nerve-racking, numbing, never-ending. "No…no getting sick…deities don't throw up…"

As he wobbled back and forth, the dizziness subsided, and the sickness became…anger. Vicious, visceral. Like a bright sky shifting to clouds of bitterness, zipping open to drop heavy rain all over his face. The frustration seeped under his pores, traveling through his veins to awaken every irritated fiber in his being. Like an overflowing river, a deluge, the rage drenched him, wiping away anything in its passage. Love, sadness, confusion—all drowned in the sea of his wrath.

"Yes…" The poison. There it was. Sweet, sensual bliss. Delectable aromas of flesh and blood and death. "Ah…I missed this."

He shuddered in pleasure at the recollection of men and women licking their lips, reaching out, plunging hands into chests. He grinned at the image of them chewing on beating hearts, slurping up arteries, savoring the juicy organ of life and love. Squelching morsels, drops dripping into puddles of blood.

Though he never ate the hearts himself, he loved to watch. That nasty naughtiness in his lower half when he peeped, spied on his charges…he fed on that. The invasion of privacy, the anticipation and adrenaline arousing him as he sentenced his soul-mates to death. Blood, ash, decay; mortal creatures killing each other to provoke the gods.

Step one.

"Oh, yes…I have missed it."

All this time, stuck in his enclosure, it was as if he teetered at the edge of Mount Olympus, bracing to jump. But now, free at last, the wind whipped through his locks as he fell. He happily dove into the red pool that once stained his nails and his gold-tipped arrows.

No, he wasn't poisoned; he was alive. Intoxicated with the desire to hunt and kill, to purge the world of those the immortals loved most. Those who worshiped them. Those they extended special protection to without even knowing it.

Their playthings…

"Oh, what will my family do now that they're gone? What will they do once I return to work? How will they entertain their lazy selves?" He rubbed his hands and salivated at the suggestion of massacring all those of his kind.

He *had* listened to the goddesses' hearts earlier. His strawberry blonde mother, worried, frantic, far from her usual obnoxious self. And his brown-haired adoptive aunt, maintaining a steady facade that he knew was about to crack open.

The bars were sturdy, yes; but not as much as they thought. The magic in him might soon beat the magic used to contain him.

I might…break free.

His mission was unfinished. He had to pick up his rampage where he had left off. So many American cities to corrupt, lovers to lure together and assassinate.

Strolling up to the enclosure, he sniffed at the radiant energy barring him from escaping. His fingers caressed the metallic surface and though the shocks hurt him earlier, they now made him smirk. If he focused, sucked in enough of the delightfully negative aura, he'd be able to blast the bars away. He needed to channel his madness.

"They'll pay for keeping Psyche from me." He rolled his wrists, cracked his knuckles. "She's out there. Alone, lost, and famished. She needs strength; she needs venom. I'll give her some." He snorted. "I'll bring her a godly heart to munch on. And together, we can take them all down."

All his cramps vanished. The throbbing, the brewing, the heaviness—all faded from him as he clasped his hands in prayer and closed his eyes.

He needed a weapon. Something to kill his way out of Olympus.

My arrows.

Where were they? Had they been left behind in the warehouse? Or had someone taken them? He had to summon them, or trick someone into bringing them to him.

He smacked his lips as he visualized himself jabbing at Aphrodite, spearing her from navel to neck. Or at Athena, slitting a gash under her pretty jawline. His leather pants became tight as his erection grew, blurring his concentration. Their deaths turned him on more than anything ever had.

Oh, how delicious would his revenge be? How rewarding and refreshing? But how to get it?

A rugged figure came to mind; a youthful, half-clothed god whose voice was a melody and whose chiseled chest inspired mythical songs. Whose skin was the sun itself and whose healing abilities were unparalleled.

Apollo.

He chewed on his lips as his member hardened, threatening to burst through his breeches.

"He has access to the cells, to test cures on me...so *he's* who I'll trick. He'll be my first godly kill." He threw his head back and guffawed. "An honor!"

Apollo's semi-naked silhouette had woken desire, yes; but Eros' bulge erected more as he thought of the deity sprawled across the dungeon floor, submerged by his own inky blue ichor.

"Psyche can have his heart," he squeaked, clapping as he hopped up and down. "She'll be secure, then we'll wage war."

He danced about, an exquisite tune filling his ears, muffling the footsteps approaching the dungeon door. With his eyes closed and his chants so consuming, he had no clue that someone entered, walked up to his cage, lifted their arms—

A blaze of lightning zapped him, and he stilled. Every limb locked in place as he tumbled backwards, plunging into a dream-world of nymphs and satyrs and golden goblets of burgundy blood that he mistook for wine.

||10. ENLISTING THE MESSENGER||
ATHENA

"Shit! You dimwitted, toothless fucktard of a goalkeeper!"

Cringing at her half-brother's foul language, Athena knocked on Hermes' door.

"I will curse your entire family of morons—"

She knocked again, louder, and recoiled. He'd picked up on so many awful habits from humans—nasty insults included. She recalled his bursts of lashing-out when play-fighting with his brothers. His desperate thirst to prove himself, his desire to trick and trap—

"You're supposed to keep the ball out *of there, not throw it in, you ass!"*

"Hermes!" She banged on the door, far from eager to have any sort of conversation with him. But the sooner it was over, the sooner she'd never have to grovel again. "Let me in, I need to talk to you!"

The sports program Hermes had been watching went silent, and his footsteps pounded up to the door that he wrenched open.

"What?" There he stood, his white travel tunic barely clinging to the private parts it was meant to cover. At least he wasn't in his ceremonial outfit—the one that let almost everything hang loose. His blond locks were pulled into a messy bun and a few strands framed his youthful face as his eyes widened. "Athena?" He crossed his arms and smirked. "And what brings *you* to my side of the palace? And to interrupt such a fantastic football match?"

She glimpsed into his quarters and spotted the television that he had muted, still displaying images of men kicking a black and white ball. Every few seconds they tripped dramatically. "Fantastic?" She scrunched her nose. "Were you not screaming at the screen a minute ago?"

Hermes frowned. "I was yelling at the stupid American goalkeeper who dares to call this sport soccer but is unclear on the rules." He waved at the television, and it shut off. "What can I do for you?"

Athena cleared her throat, stiffening at his too-relaxed demeanor. "I won't waste your time. As part of my investigation into Psyche's disappearance, Hades has summoned me to the Underworld. He claims to have important information to give me. Something he didn't want to reveal here, in Olympus." She'd rehearsed it in her mind, and though encountering Hera had delayed her and worsened her dread, her speech pleased her.

Hermes' cocky grin and the shininess of his broad chest destabilized her more than she wished to admit. "Ah, and let me guess—Father demanded that I accompany you?" He clapped in exaggerated excitement, his hair flopping out of his bun and his tunic traipsing a little too far upward. "Did I win a prize?" He flexed his dark, bare arms; a trick that worked on every other goddess but Athena.

She rolled her eyes, doing her best to remain unimpressed. "No prize, no. But yes…Father requested that you guide me down there, since I don't know where the entrances are. I'm unfamiliar with the realm itself. So you…" she nearly gagged, "are my only hope." Her gaze shifted from his glowing face to his chiseled torso and sculpted abdomen, and then to the flimsy sheet covering his bottom—

With a shrug, she focused on her sandals as her cheeks overheated. She prayed to Zeus that Hermes hadn't caught her staring, because he'd use any weakness as a means to torture her. And one of his favorite weaknesses was virgins.

My virginity is sacred…he can't take it from me.

His flirtatious demeanor disappeared. "Well, come in, then." He motioned for her to follow him into the room. "Did Hades actually summon you?"

When he locked the door, she shuddered. She'd never been this far into his quarters before, and discomfort settled in her belly, heavy and nauseating. How many goddesses and servants and nymphs had spent hours here? How many had exited *without* their virtue?

She swallowed and set her gaze on a closet a few feet behind him. "He did."

"Are you sure?" He stretched as he meandered to the other side of his room. "Because I visit the Underworld on a weekly basis, and I don't think he's ever summoned anyone from Olympus. Not even Father."

Athena perked up, wary of all the lies, of the acting; she was getting in over her head.

Hera will love *this.*

"Yes, as I said, he did. Why would I lie? Why would it seem so preposterous?" Her voice trembled, and Hermes' eyebrows arched. "It isn't. He believed the culprit might wander about our palace hallways, or so Aphrodite told me."

He flinched. "Aphrodite."

They had a history—illegitimate children and secret sheet tumbling while hiding from Aphrodite's husband and official lover. But everyone knew Hermes had feelings for her.

Because of those feelings, an idea bloomed in Athena's mind; if she used Aphrodite against him…he might be more inclined to obey Zeus' orders.

"Yes, Aphrodite." She accentuated every syllable and tried not to relish in his unease. "You trust her judgment, do you not?"

"I do." He flinched. "But *did* she tell you that?" He pressed down on his tunic and looked askance. "I didn't realize she and good old uncle Hades were buddies."

"Come now, would it surprise you?" Athena squirmed on the inside; Hermes had annoyed her so many times, making him jealous was a sort of personal revenge. "Even he can't resist her forever. But I don't care who she's friends with. Hades summoned me, and I can't ignore it."

With a groan, Hermes fell onto his bed. "Because it's a king's summons." His feet dangled from the large mattress of his four-poster bed, and he twirled a portion of his silky covers around his finger.

Sports-themed posters were plastered on every wall, each player glaring at Athena. As she inched farther inside the suite, she noticed the trophies and the sports equipment cluttering corners and shelves and nightstands. With a shiver, she realized everything in the lodgings was stolen. *Borrowed,* he'd say, but everyone knew the truth. Hermes was the god of thieves, and he never hid it.

He shot up and ambled over to the ornate mirror above one of his dressers. "Oh, Athena." He grasped a navy perfume bottle and spritzed under his jaw and between his pectoral muscles. An overpowered but crisp cologne reached Athena and she waved her hand near her nose.

"What?"

Is he considering it? Or about to refuse?

"It's…so nice of you to visit," he said, admiring his reflection, tracing his fingers down his middle and lingering at the border of his tunic.

Fury twisted her intestines into tight knots. "Hermes." She snapped at him, but he didn't budge from his own image. "Do I have to tell Father I must decline a summons from the Underworld because my brother is too busy ogling himself and watching football? Or," she took one stride forward, unwilling to get too close, "will you take me? I don't have all day. Psyche is missing, and every moment counts. Her husband is in the dungeon, driving himself crazy and awaiting a treatment that may only be available in the realm of the dead."

He glanced at his fingernails, keeping his back to her. "Hmm…I understand the urgency, yes…" He made a pouty face then fidgeted to and fro. "Poor Eros."

Was he serious? She had trouble reading Hermes. Of all her siblings she was least friendly to him, and with reason; on multiple occasions she'd ruined his love life. Every time she passed him in the hallways, she wondered if he'd ever seek revenge on her. If he'd shove her into a closet and try to take what was most precious to her in retaliation. Funny and charming as he was to mask his anger, he'd never forgiven her.

"Hermes." She closed her eyes and inhaled, recalling Aphrodite's words. *Lie.* "We tolerate each other, you and me. I'm certain you're fabricating a list of excuses to avoid this, but…Father demanded it. So if not for me or for Psyche, would you do it for him?"

Without so much as a peep, he brushed past her and crept into his walk-in closet.

She blew out her cheeks. "Your games won't work with me!" She waltzed over to the wardrobe, intent on raising her voice and shaking him—

But she froze at the sight of him naked; tunic discarded, everything exposed, *everything* on display.

"I wonder which one to wear," he said, holding up two pieces of thin cloth, comparing them.

His imposing privates prompted her to gasp. "Oh gods," she murmured, pulling away before the image tattooed on her brain forever. "That was…inappropriate."

His singsong voice mocked her. "My sweet Athena." She grimaced as he slid beside her, preparing to spin from him if he was still in the nude. But he wasn't—he'd chosen the peach-colored tunic that was longer than the first. He tousled his curls, releasing a fresh, fruity scent that she hated to admit she didn't dislike. "So prude, so innocent. Isn't it high time you see what all the fuss is about? Me, my exploits, my accomplishments—"

"—no!" She growled, furious that she'd been correct; of course he'd use his *goods* against her, as leverage.

Did he know she was bluffing? That Hades hadn't called her to the Underworld? Did he want her to confess?

"Come on." He slithered before her, his eyes illuminated with pride, his chest slick with oil. "You were impressed, yeah?" He winked as he gestured to his manhood, luckily covered by his clothes.

She shook her head and skipped out of his field of vision. Her family members always looked in the other direction with deities and their often incestuous acts, but she didn't condone it. If ever she were to donate her virtue to anyone, it wouldn't be to someone as disgusting as he.

"You're so immature." On the verge of giving up, she bolted to the door. How could she have thought she'd convince Hermes to support her? He was an over-sexualized, over-dramatic, orgy-loving ogre.

"Wait!"

Against her will, she gritted her teeth and swiveled to see his features hardening as he squinted at her. "What?"

"You and I…we're siblings, but not friends, yes?" He stepped towards her, and her heart raced. "Meaning I could accept this proposal, but tell me, *sis*…what's in it for me? Why would I help you?"

She wrapped her hand around the doorknob, but still faced him; no way would she turn her back on him now. She had to prepare for a quick escape. "Because…we're family?"

"Family." He snorted. "You didn't think of that in our past, did you? I've tried to get over it, to overlook your cruelty towards me, to consider you an ally…but I can never forget what you did. You, the favorite, the spoiled. It's hard to live in your shadow, were you aware?" Another stride, and a whiff of his intoxicating scent invaded Athena's nostrils again. "Hard to not hold all you've done to me against you." Despite his words, lust lingered in every motion of his arms, every sway of his legs as he walked to her.

He wanted…payment.

The kind I can't give.

He'd come so near her now she envisioned his dark,

unblemished complexion and the tiniest trace of whiskers developing below his nose. "Hermes." She thrust her hand out to halt his progress, but he didn't seem to care. "Please, don't be rash—"

He rammed his torso into her palm and licked his lips. "It's not rash, it's normal. *You're* not normal, Athena." He chewed on his lower lip to suggest hunger, ravenous passion.

Athena wouldn't fall for it. She unleashed a far-from-feminine roar and used a slither of her energy to drive him backwards before it was too late. "Enough!" His famished glare strengthened her resolve. "Help me! It would help you, too, don't you understand? This being, this creature that's targeting us…we're all at risk, including you. The sooner I locate Psyche and extract the poison in her and analyze it…the sooner we'll figure out who or *what* is doing this."

Regaining his balance, Hermes tucked a strand of hair behind his ears. "But…why can't I get what I want in the process?"

Her insides churned. "Please…use your logic, not your manhood. Use the wit I know is in you somewhere."

He grunted and the fire in his attitude faded. "Why?"

"Because Father favors you, too. Why else would he have asked *you* to be my guide?" She wasn't sure how true it was. Zeus did love all his children, but Hermes often got on his last nerve.

"Ha!" He scoffed and twirled on his heels. "That was funny. The goddess of wisdom has a sense of humor!"

She panicked. "He'll reward you." Intrigued, he craned his neck and narrowed his gaze at her. "For aiding me in solving the case, he'll give you gifts. More items to display. Show off to your conquests. Or…more conquests."

Hermes tapped his fingertips to his chin. "Rewards.

Hmm…yes." He marched over to another armoire and opened it, stepping inside to rummage through his things. He threw clothes and bits of armor onto his bed. "Conquests…items…"

Athena kept by the door-frame, still bracing to run in case he launched a weapon at her. He'd never been violent, but…what if her request tipped him over the edge?

He reemerged with a traveling bag and hastened to yet another closet, where he filled said bag with supplies. More weapons, more armor, other items she didn't recognize.

"What are you doing?" She lifted to her tiptoes. "What's all that?"

He roamed over and dropped the rucksack at her feet. "Stuff we'll need for the trip. Provisions and potential bribes for the creatures we'll come across." He raked a hand through his locks, his expression oddly neutral compared to earlier. "They're all familiar with me, but you…your presence will shock them."

"Does this…" her jaw sank to the ground, "does this mean you accept?"

He laughed, but a twinge of bitterness bit through the otherwise seductive sound. "Father will strike me with his harshest bolts if I refuse you. And ignoring Hades is dangerous."

She couldn't believe it; he'd listened to logic over his arousing urges. "Well…" She wondered if she'd manage to pluck her jaw up from where it had collapsed onto the floor.

"I need his gratitude," he said, his momentary seriousness evaporating as he smirked. "So I will lend my sturdy arms and beauty to my dearest sister and take her to the Underworld."

She guffawed but stopped herself before she hugged him; he'd take advantage of her proximity to strip off her dress and grope her, she knew. "Thank you, Hermes."

Guilt gyrated into her heart. She'd lied to several Olympian gods now. A sickening sensation simmered in her gut as she imagined her punishment if discovered. But she had to hope Hades *did* want to see her and would play along.

Otherwise...I'm in trouble.

Flashes fluttered to life in her mind; horrible pictures of her fate should she fail. Hermes would abandon her in the Underworld with no way to return home. Hades would lock her up close to Cerberus and she'd live in a nightmare. Zeus would ban her from Olympus. Hera would cackle in pleasure.

She hiccuped as she redressed her slouching self and prayed her secrets would never spill. Prayed to prevent a civil war.

They stopped by her chambers so she could throw in a few of her own possessions, then trudged to the throne-room together, to announce their departure to Zeus. The King of the skies, though surprised at their alliance, wished them luck and good fortune.

Athena needed all of it. The willpower to maintain a lie, the determination to travel with Hermes. And the faith that she could solve this mystery.

‖ 11. SOME ‖
PSYCHE

Must keep traveling.

The next farm was only a mile away. Psyche padded forward, the soles of her feet fluttering over crunched leaves, plunging into muddy grass, slipping on cobblestone trails that sliced through her skin.

She wanted to rest, but the voice urged her onward. She wanted to stop at a small, abandoned house she'd passed an hour prior, to wait for its owners, to convert them. But the voice said no.

Her strides sped up despite her sore extremities. Pain flickered to her ankles and toes, and she winced.

Did other goddesses experience such agony?

Must keep going. I'm not far.

No time to relax; the next human awaited. It would have to share its dinner with her, so she could regain her strength. Replenish herself from the godly power she'd been losing. Draining. Drying up.

Then she'd move on to the next, and the next, and the next. Recruiting for her army, preparing for war.

The path became soil, and she sighed in relief at the sudden softness that seeped into her torn and tormented skin. The surrounding air reeked of manure and hay, a pinch of herbs and fresh grass. Another farm. She liked those; pigs and cows and sheep, dazzlingly delicious. All waiting to be devoured raw, worthy sacrifices for her cause.

Her temporary soothing faded as her throbbing legs reminded her she was far from done.

I need... ambrosia.

Nausea settled in her belly, crawling through her rib-cage, settling at the base of her neck, bracing to shoot upwards. She slowed her pace, racking her brain for probable locations to obtain the tincture that would keep her alive. Some lesser gods resided on earth; would they have ambrosia on hand? She only needed a few doses to control her suffering. A few drops to reanimate her, fill her with energy. Or she could send someone up to the palace for her. They wouldn't refuse her, right?

A pang in her lungs answered her question and prompted her to walk faster.

"No communications with gods. They'll reveal my location. Not yet."

The Olympians would detain her, interrogate her...and she had too much to finish, too much on her list. Too many humans to infect and transform before she permitted her family's involvement.

She cringed as the dirt turned to stone once more, cold and rough on her blistered feet. She yelped, yearning to stop, to breathe; but her limbs moved on, out of her control.

"Quit whining. Others have had harsher conditions, harder quests."

"And they didn't complain," she took over for her internal voice, "I know better. I do."

Though it was once docile as a lullaby, alluring as a fluffy sponge cake, the voice was now harsh and foreign to her. As her plot progressed, it shifted into something else. Psyche became scared of it, and scared of the ideas it whispered, yelled, inside her skull.

The voice wasn't her, it couldn't be. Were those *her* feelings, nestled deep in her soul? Had the poison brought out her real emotions?

She screeched to a halt—but not of her own volition. Her mouth moved and tones she didn't recognize slipped out. "Why must I question everything?" She sneered, but her tongue twitched as the voice within commanded her speech. "Why can't I move forward with my plans? The mad wandering isn't for naught. Neither is the suffering. I'm bringing humans to a cause that'll deliver them. Our second phase will strengthen them for the ultimate goal."

Tears swelled in her eyes—*her* tears.

I must accept it. I, Psyche, must remember my responsibilities.

She heaved one foot up, ready to resume her trek, but lost her balance as dizziness draped its heavy weight over her shoulders. Her other leg wobbled, and she fell sideways onto the chilly gravel and hit her head.

Her vision blurred as more tears drizzled down her cheeks. "*This*...is why I need...ambrosia," she said, addressing her controlling inner voice. "My abilities...are weak. I must replenish them, or I'll fail."

Jolts of pain pirouetted in her veins, causing her to seize. Her eyelids slammed shut, but she didn't lose consciousness. She heard a bird's wings flapping overhead, a gentle rustle of leaves, horses neighing faintly.

And then the voice; angry, searing, spilling through her like lava.

"You don't need it, Psyche. You must survive without it."

Bile rose up her throat and mingled with the acidic taste of venom on her tongue.

"You have few humans left. You're close. Don't give up. Rise. Pursue your goal, free the world, Psyche."

Wriggling about on the rocks, their sharp edges ripped through her tunic. She wailed as her eyelids fluttered, but no matter how hard she tried, her internal self declined to let her awaken. "Let me…get up…continue…mission…"

Visions zoomed through her; images of women popped in and out of her head like brief moments of dreams appearing in random order. First came Hera—majestic marriage goddess, a navy robe flowing around her curves, engulfing her, as peacocks circled her and screeched. She re-adjusted her crown, snarling at her surroundings.

Flash.

Hecate, divinity of witchcraft, long locks of auburn twirling around her head like deadly serpents. Dogs howled in the background, their claws creeping near the woman's near-ivory skin.

Flash.

Rhea, titaness, mother of the gods, clad in burned orange, two roaring and ravenous lions before her, prepared to pounce, hunger in their fiery eyes.

Lightning. Tremulous and threatening, dashes of thunder echoed in her scalp. Then came Mnemosyne; titaness of memory and mother of the muses. Psyche didn't know her at all but watched as she pranced about playing an unknown instrument. Giant monsters weaved around her, saliva dripping from their chins, mouths open to devour her.

"Stop! Why do you show me this?"

The lightning returned, intense and impossible to blink away from.

"Are they in danger? Must I help them? Are they…allies?"

Flash.

Styx—personification of hatred. Beside her was Lethe, oblivion. Two Underworld deities, running. Fear flickered in their expressions, but Psyche couldn't see who or what they ran from. She envisioned a massive tidal wave—

Lightning.

"What is happening?"

This vision sent shivers up her spine as she still slithered about on the dampened grass. *Gaia.* The mighty, primordial elemental deity. Goddess of the earth, mother of all creation. The ground beneath her erupted and she screamed and tugged at her skirts as it swallowed her—

"Stop!"

Psyche's eyes opened. Panting, her heart about to shoot out from her chest, she blew out a few ragged breaths. The images replayed in her mind, over and over, more and more confusing. The lack of godly energy was crippling her, and her internal self wouldn't permit her to fix it.

"Kill them?" She exhaled. "Save them?" She peered up at the sky above as ominous storm clouds formed and thunder rumbled in the distance. Real thunder. "Use them? What does this mean?"

The thunder grew deafening as it inched closer, drawn to her.

Before her inside voice said anything or prevented her from doing so, she sat up straight, eyebrows darting upward.

Thunder, lightning—*he* was coming. Had he heard her, found her?

"Zeus." She croaked, coughed, and cleared her throat. "*Zeus!*"

Her prior frailness festered, and she shot to her feet, swift as an eagle. The farm was close, and she'd need shelter if the king was on his way, because he'd unleash a deluge on her for her disappearance. He'd save her, but first he'd reprimand her with the force of a thousand storms.

She dashed, every bone in her body mending as her mind scrambled. Faces and names she didn't comprehend weaved into her thoughts, but she ignored them.

When the voice resonated within, it didn't paralyze her. It let her keep darting towards the farm-house as clouds continued to gather up above.

"I will understand these women in time. Some will help, some will escape. Some I will pursue, some I will kill."

Spotting the doors, she acquiesced. "Yes, yes, fine." The sooner she got inside, the farther she'd be from Zeus when he landed and screamed at her.

"There are others. Some will be allies, others will disappoint."

"Got it, *got it!*"

Zeus was coming.

"Everyone will understand."

"Yes, they will!" She threw the doors open and slipped in before the first drop of rain fell. Safe…but never safe from herself.

She stilled.

"I will punish Zeus…and all those he loves."

‖12. ARRIVAL IN THE UNDERWORLD, PART ONE‖

ATHENA

Athena's lungs filled with the untainted air of Olympus one last time.

"Lake Avernus?" She sucked in the freshness enveloping her home, charging with regrets about leaving.

Hermes sidled up to her. "Lake Avernus, southern Italy, yes."

They stood at the precipice of the palace, far from the massive golden doors. They teetered on the other side of the glowing gates that shielded them from the human world.

Athena cringed; she hated departing Olympus.

"Let's see who gets there first," said Hermes, snapping his fingers. In a puff of glimmering green smoke, he disappeared.

With a snort, Athena spun for a last glance at her breathtaking, marble-made home, then closed her eyes, imagining the place she needed to arrive at.

She lifted off the ground and floated, buzzing off the peaceful Mount Olympus and transferring to the human-inhabited planet below. She barely had time to detect the change in atmosphere before her sandals landed on a patch of dewy grass. A sultry breeze smacked against her cheeks. Hermes cackled from nearby, prompting her to pry her eyelids apart.

Delight warmed her soul. Lake Avernus wasn't large, but its waters, still and solemn, surrounded by vibrant vegetation, were isolated from the rest of the world. The location immediately inspired tranquility. The bustling city of Naples wasn't far, yet one never would have guessed it, with how quiet and sheltered this area was.

She watched as Hermes walked to the surface and waved her closer. He grinned from ear to ear as she approached, and he lifted his index finger in the air, rotating it. "Promise you'll keep this a secret?"

She nodded; if she didn't, he'd find some means to torture her.

Twirling his fingertip, as if stirring the wind, he whispered. The water's brilliance reflected in his eyes as it swirled, as if spiraling down a drain, disappearing into a black, endless well.

Once several square feet of the basin had vanished, a muddy pathway revealed, with a set of steep stairs leading into a dim tunnel under the lake.

Athena stared at the gloomy and magically dry entrance. There were no footsteps indented in the caked mud, meaning no one came this way often. If at all.

"I'll go first," said Hermes with a wink, "because I don't mind forcing you to admire my backside as we descend."

Sneering, Athena urged him forward.

Hermes guided her down the steps, then through the underwater passage. Their footfalls echoed, and the faint light from outside granted them some visibility. But soon, the water rolled over them again, taking its place as if it had never parted. It formed a sturdy ceiling overhead, leaving them in absolute obscurity.

She wasn't frightened of the dark. But stuck in a narrow space with her ever-flirtatious half-brother, unease coated her limbs and unbalanced her.

When they reached the end of the corridor, she noticed two torches in holders near an archway opening into a concave room. As they approached, she sighted another basin, this one's surface smooth and thick like tar.

A lake within a lake?

Hermes snatched a torch and swung it in front of him. The body of water was wide, covering a large portion of what appeared to be an underwater cavern. Several rivers were supposed to take off from here, but from her position, Athena couldn't see them.

"Welcome to the Acherusian Lake. Prime entry point for the Underworld." His arm grazed hers as he meandered in, and the motion sent goosebumps to skip up to her shoulders. "Most of the rivers resource themselves here, others only pass it by." He took another stride into the space, then pivoted. "Are you ready? The Acheron isn't far."

She grabbed the other torch, and despite her nausea, she proceeded after him. She squinted when, only a few feet from her and to the right, she spotted a fiery, lava-like trail flowing off to who-knew-where. Heat fizzled through the stuffy air, almost burning her skin. Her uncle had told many stories about the paths to his realm; but this one, she didn't recognize.

As if expecting her reaction, Hermes whirled to her. "Pyriphlegethon. Phlegethon, for short. The—"

"—river that flows to Tartarus itself," she said, recoiling. The name triggered her memory, all her history lessons. "I thought it was a ruse. A lie to scare souls. I had no idea it was actually on fire!"

Hermes shrugged. "Down here, you'll find that many rumors from upstairs are true. Some are preposterous, but there's some reality to them." He jogged to their left, to a dense, muddy body of water whooshing out of the lake.

Those murky waters she recognized; Acheron, the river of pain.

Otherworldly wails seeped into her eardrums. Her vision fuzzed when, as they neared the stream, transparent bodies popped up along the water.

Ghosts.

A few passed through her. She shivered as she set foot on the dilapidated, wooden dock that stretched almost halfway across the river.

Dead souls, waiting for the ferryman.

Odd sensations woke in her belly. Some of these poor creatures wouldn't have the proper payment to reach the Underworld; they'd be doomed to wander the river banks forever.

So distracted by the horror, she startled when a boat shimmied up to them from the shadows. A hooded man in a worn wool coat stood atop it, and his eyes were blazing balls of fire. His bony hand outstretched towards her, and she leaned away.

Hermes nudged her and slipped something into her grasp. "Give him this," he whispered, as Athena peeked down to see in her palm a rusty coin. "He knows me, so I don't need it. Right, Charon?"

The rugged Charon grunted, his dirty rags and soiled cheeks scarring Athena forever.

"Uh…okay." She tossed the coin into his hand, hesitating to climb aboard. She'd hoped the rumors about *him* would be exaggerated, that he wouldn't be so bleak and disgruntled…but she was wrong.

Charon stuffed the money into the pocket of his cloak and hobbled to the front of the raft.

"Go." Hermes poked her onto the cracking, close to breaking, flimsy piece of wood the gods of the Underworld called a boat.

She grimaced and put a foot on the board. Torches suspended from the cavern walls, lighting her path onto the floatation device. A few stone pillars lined the way along the water, some with sconces, some bare.

With nothing to hold on to, she bent her legs and widened her stance as Charon plunged his wooden staff into the opaque waters, and the ferry took off. It was quicker than she'd expected; she jerked backwards, but Hermes stopped her fall with a chortle.

"He'll get us to the gates fast, because we're wasting his time." Hermes' fingers paused on her shoulders a few seconds too long, lightly squeezing her. His heavy breath blew over her neck and she shuddered, shying away.

Fists bunching, desperate for a means to distract her disturbed thoughts, she looked around and located another Underworld river nearby. "Is that…Lethe?" She pointed at the stream; plain compared to the two she'd seen so far. "Lethe, river of forgetfulness. Next to the Acheron, no?"

Hermes smiled. "If you get a bit closer, you'll view Styx on its other side." He captured her arm and tugged her to the middle of the boat. "But it'd be best if you stayed over here, okay?"

She glowered at him, her skin ablaze from where he'd gripped her. "Why?"

He put a finger to his lips and shook his head. "Charon is strict, and not fond of visitors who are alive. Steer clear from him and speak little."

The dimmed lighting enhanced his features, and his serious, less scandalous tone almost wooed Athena into tolerating him. That human perfume he used *did* smell good, she had to admit…

She tore from his lustful aroma before he tried anything he'd regret. "Fine, but *let go of me.*"

He is my half-brother and my guide, nothing more.

Hermes batted his eyelashes. "Sure thing, darling."

As they drifted onward, Athena started spotting buildings along the banks. "Who would live here?"

"Several beings, believe it or not. These are permanent residents who don't wish to dwell in Hades' vicinity, but remain close enough if he needs them. Personification gods are to the right; Erinyes, overseen by Eris, to the left." Hermes' wince was barely pronounced as he spoke; were they in daylight, Athena would have been sure enough to question him about what made him uncomfortable.

But *everything* was uncomfortable, down here. Everything was eerie and otherworldly, and even someone as used to this place as Hermes was would have a hard time smiling through it all.

The ferry's speed kicked up a notch, dashing past the terrifying monster section. On one side, humid gusts whipped into Athena's hair as she rubbed her upper arms. On the other, the temperature chilled and caused her teeth to clatter.

Silence reigned as they hunkered on. Charon groaned every few minutes, and Hermes focused on his nails, once and again grinning at Athena in his deceptive, seductive way. She prayed for them to arrive soon.

Her prayers were answered when they swooshed through a thick vapor while trudging through coarse waters. Beyond the sinister veil, something shimmered up ahead—a gleaming gate. It was dozens of feet tall, sturdy and impenetrable. Attached to either side of it were fences of the same height, and made of the same glittering substance, to surround the actual Underworld realm. Other buildings—resembling houses—rested against the barricades. Guard posts?

No; the *real* guard was propped up to the right. Athena stilled and her jaw clenched at the vision.

Cerberus. The three-headed beast, its narrowed, yellow eyes on alert, snake snouts rising from its back to its tail. It opened its massive mouths—all three of them—and yawned.

She fumbled backwards, and Hermes caught her again. This time, he molded into her, his mouth inches from her neck, his cologne invading her nostrils, his member hard against her buttocks.

"He only bites if you try to leave against orders," he said, his voice melodious, murmuring near her earlobe. "And that is the Diamond Gate. Made of actual diamonds. Same with the surrounding fence." His hot breath cascaded down her spine. "Fascinating, no?"

She wrenched loose from him as the ferry came to an abrupt halt at another dilapidated dock.

Cerberus yawned again—scarier up close—but he didn't pay them much mind. He concentrated on something beyond the gates; which paralyzed Athena more.

He's giant enough to see over that high fence.

Hermes descended, and in gentlemanly fashion he aided Athena. His hand wrapped around hers and he wiggled his eyebrows; but she ignored him as she brushed off her skirts.

A rustle of leaves caught her off-guard. Following their movement, she sighted a hypnotizing, majestic elm tree that loomed beside Cerberus. It stood out in the dreary depths of the Underworld.

An inexplicable eagerness drew her to the tree. Questions, gentle murmurs in her mind, luring her closer. The leaves were so *bright,* so scintillating, they enraptured her, even from afar.

Hermes broke their spell by yanking her away. He tutted. "No, no, my sweet; those leaves are full of false dreams. Trust me, you don't want to touch them." He shoved her behind him. "And Cerberus? I said he only bites if you try to leave, but he's not a friendly puppy, either. You don't want to get within his reach." He shuddered, but it was so brief Athena wouldn't have known if she hadn't been scowling at him.

"Everything all right?"

His face fixed into its usual annoyingly attractive expression. "Don't go near the dogs, got it?" His lips twitched as he fought to maintain a smile. "Please?"

Fear dug into her abdomen. Did he worry Cerberus wouldn't let her leave?

Several figures emerged along the river bank, plodding up from the buildings Athena had witnessed along the way. Some slinked out from the houses in front of the fences. They walked, flew, wobbled; they held spiked weapons and muttered under their breaths and gawked at Athena. Some were full-bodied, some translucent, some with sizeable arms and legs that gave them the appearance of human-like spiders.

Hermes tensed as he seized her wrist and hauled her away from the beings, turning his back to them as he dashed towards the entrance to the realm. "We need to get in. Hades commands these things, but until he's seen us, they won't trust that we're not enemies." Before the Diamond Gate, he fidgeted, his grip tight.

The mumbling behind them grew louder, but a tiny part of Athena was curious. Who were these creatures? And if Hermes, a regular visitor of this realm, was afraid of them, how was she supposed to feel?

Steadying her breaths, she admired the intricate rainbow-colored patterns of the diamonds encrusted in the doorway. Though there was no light, they sparkled, stacked together to form a strengthened barrier against the upstairs world.

She raised a palm to graze near the jewels, and a wave of magic tickled her, crawling up to her fingertips.

The doorway shook and shuddered and rumbled, slipping backwards.

Athena jumped, and Hermes swallowed. He held on to her, and leaned in. "I have a confession to make," he swallowed again, "I've…never been inside." His voice was weak, nothing like his usual self. "I rarely get this far, though Charon does know me. So, once we pass this…we're on a new adventure together."

Athena breathed in, breathed out. Her heart braced to launch out of her chest, and choice words wormed into her mind.

That lying little thief. He can't be my guide—he has no idea where we're to go next!

The doors creaked apart, and a cloud of smoke whizzed over them, blocking their vision.

Beyond the haze, a lone figure appeared, its face concealed by a hood as it took a few steps in their direction.

It marched through the mist, stopping inches from Hermes. Once the hood dropped, Athena witnessed a man; black, bitter eyes gaped at her, and beneath a sizable beard, a set of thin lips moved. "Hello, Hermes."

He looks…familiar.

"A bit out of your comfort zone, aren't you?" said the being, his tone icy, but non-threatening. He switched to Athena. "And you brought a guest? Two Olympian royals, oh my. The king must be quite excited." He inclined his head and shuffled aside to grant them entry.

Hermes hopped past the limit. "I'm sure he is, Thanatos. I'd introduce you to my sister, but you have work to do, don't you?"

Thanatos.

Athena froze at the threshold. She'd heard many tales about the god of non-violent death, but never had a chance to lay eyes on him before then. "It's a pleasure to—"

Hermes heaved her into the area before she could finish. "Don't loiter. Let's go."

Thanatos took no offense and chuckled as he glided off to board Charon's ferry.

Athena broke free from Hermes again, and as the smoky fog cleared, she immobilized at the view unraveling before her.

Oh, what an adventure indeed.

‖13. MURDEROUS AND MAD‖

EROS

Thump, thump. Thump, thump.

Deafening. Familiar.

Thump, thump. Thump, thump.

Eros pressed a hand to his chest and waited, hoping his own heartbeats would match the sound.

He waited. And waited. And waited some more.

But as his pulse quickened, he understood his heart was beating faster than the thrumming in his head. Whatever he was hearing…came from elsewhere.

He raised his fingertips to his temples, pushed, and groaned. "A headache." He massaged the edges of his forehead and blew out his cheeks. "A darned migraine. Not a damned heartbeat."

Opening his eyes, he found that he'd fallen asleep on the floor. His vision was blurry, and he was dizzy.

He peered around his cell, drinking in its unwelcome yet homely aura. The tiny bed to his left was mostly bare, since the scratchy blankets were under him, and his leather jacket slumped near a corner of the cage. As he sat up, he spotted shattered glass and slowly drying liquid on the weathered tile. And a few droplets of blood—

"Whoa." He focused, and realized his pillow was at the opposite end of the enclosure, and the sheets dangled off the mattress, shredded and stained. "What in Tartarus happened here? Was I…in that much of a rage?"

He stood up and retrieved the salvageable pieces of blankets—apparently also ripped—and threw them onto the bed. He hobbled to the cushion and tossed it atop the sheets. He remembered none of this; none of the mess he had created.

With a huff, he kicked at the glass shards, making a neat pile of them off to the side. Whose blood was it?

Mine? Or…

"No…I couldn't. I *wouldn't*. Someone…must have put me to sleep." He lowered onto his hardened mattress, breathing in and out to calm himself. Had his slumber been meditative, restorative, for once?

Whatever this fit had been, it wasn't like his others. Someone had seemingly neutralized him before he became gruesome.

He applied pressure to his temples again, struggling to remember.

Murder.

He'd wanted to assassinate them. All of them. In the depths of his core, that desire lingered. Though he'd rested, he sensed it brewing. Worse than usual.

Whatever had happened after his rampage, whoever came in and sedated him…had saved everyone. They'd spared Olympus from his explosive fury, his thirst for death, caused by his sadness at missing the one he loved—

"*Psyche!*" He shot up, tingling from head to toe. "Is she here?

She must be close. Only she can soothe me." He raced up to the bars, and despite the zap of energy that threw him back, he didn't recoil. "*She* stopped me, didn't she?"

Squeezing his eyes shut, he concentrated, searching for her heart. He'd sense her if she was in the palace; he'd sensed Aphrodite and Athena in the dungeon, regardless of all the enchantments put in place to block his powers. Their hearts weren't connected to his like Psyche's was.

"Come on, my love." He pinched his lips. "You're here, *you must be*." He pictured her voluptuous silhouette and her savory smile. "Why else would I be so calm?"

Agonizing seconds passed. Grueling minutes. But the only heartbeat echoing in his eardrums was his own. Faster, throbbing, screaming at the realization that…no, Psyche wasn't in the palace. She was still missing.

"But then why did my rage fade?" He shrugged and spun to slouch against the prison's metallic delimitation, sliding down until he reached the ground. "How did I lose all my tension if she wasn't here? Who lulled me into a semi-peaceful slumber and drowned my murderous intentions?"

Sweat oozed through his pores, sleeking over his hairline, his chin, the back of his neck. He veered around and, while on his knees, he jammed into the bars and shook them, wincing at the zaps charging through his hands.

"Let me out! Please. Psyche…is in danger! *I* am in danger. You can't leave me here alone!" His voice reverberated to the dungeon door, fizzled under its threshold; but no one would listen. The living space was high, much higher up.

For them to gather his pleas, he'd have to screech.

"Gods of Olympus! *Listen to me!*" He rattled the bars and grimaced at the pain. "My wife and I are in peril! You haven't found her! Do you not understand? *It's a sign!*" The electricity pricked him like thousands of needles clawing into his skin, but he pushed through the agony they caused. "Let me out, *let me out* and I will find her! Only I can!"

He recalled that during the moments when he provoked humans and made them murder one another, he couldn't feel Psyche. But now, with the poison weaker, with his consciousness partially restored...he could. He knew he could. If they'd release him, he wouldn't roam about and kill—he'd rescue her.

"Come on! I'm better! I don't want to slaughter you!"

A low moan slithered out from him, but he hadn't unleashed it. It was uncontrolled, unhinged. It was demonic.

"Whoa." Something shifted in his belly, as if his intestines were moving. "Is there...something inside me?" He doubled over and gagged. "Wait, *wait!* Are the savage intentions still hidden? No...." His guts churned, twisted, burned. "Stop!"

The poison was alive, like a snake sneaking out from a bush, uncoiling, opening its mouth to show its fangs painted in venom.

His stomach gurgled, and the disease within shot to his nerves, his neurons, his muscles.

Fuck! No...I was fine. I was fine! What's happening?

Gripping the bars again, he growled. Yelped like a puppy. Then roared, yanking the bars, ignoring the zapping along his skin as it sunk into his veins.

"Help...please..." His voice contorted, turning raspy, deep, disturbing. "Quick...I need...to get out...going...crazy..."

Flashes flickered in and out of his mind. He fought them,

grasping the cage, but they wouldn't cease.

Human hearts. Blood. Drops drizzling into puddles, expanding into lakes. Squelching, slurping. Drinking.

"No...stop!"

He sank sideways and cupped his hands over his ears.

No...I don't want to see this...don't remind me of what I did.

Teeth sinking into flimsy flesh. Blue veins. Red veins. Shiny fangs. Chomp, chomp, *chomp*—

"No! Enough." Wobbly, breaths hitching, he lugged himself to his knees again and wrapped his fingers around the cool metallic bars, praying for relief. For death, even—if that would stop the hurt, he didn't care.

Golden arrows. Slicing through skin, ripping organs. Glowing in the sun.

Think of Psyche. Think of Psyche!

Only *she* would be able to coax the images out of him.

And there she was; a vision of purple velvet, lounging on their scarlet satin sheets, in their luxurious quarters. In a flash, she was naked. Her delicious curves called out to him, her gleaming figure taunted him. She patted the space beside her, and her luscious lips parted in a daring smirk. Dazzling curls of gold pooled over her breasts, and she concealed her womanhood with fanned out fingers. She giggled, a sound so heavenly, so enticing, Eros became aroused—

The picture blurred. Fuzzed. Fogged over. Once the smoke cleared, Psyche was still there. She stood, cackled, and marched up to him. Without a word, she stuffed her fist into his torso and tore out his beating heart. She tossed her head to laugh louder, each guffaw curdling his blood. When she returned her neck to normal, her eyes glowed crimson, violet, sapphire, ebony. She sank her teeth into the throbbing organ and squealed in satisfaction.

What is the matter with me? Why am I seeing this?

This nightmarish Psyche spun him around and pointed at the dead bodies sprawled on the floor behind him. Blood covered their bare limbs, splattered beneath their crushed skulls, and their bellies were open with guts spilling out. From deep gashes more blood gushed out, and chunks of flesh littered the spaces between them.

One being had strawberry blonde hair and a bosom he'd recognize anywhere. Another near her had a copper helm falling from its dark-haired head, a gashed, muscular torso, and features matching Eros' to perfection—

His parents. And ten others. Twelve beings total, dead.

The Olympians.

Psyche susurrated in his ear. "This is what you want, my love. Don't let your fears stop you. Don't let these bars stop you. Fetch your arrows." Her tart breath raised the hairs on his arms.

No…it's not. That's what the infected part of me wants. Not me…not me!

"Not me!" he repeated, his voice weak as tears streamed down his face. The rumbling in his abdomen continued; the poison was a beast coming to life, aching to be released, to create chaos.

He knocked on the bars, but his strength had depleted. He wasn't positive how much longer he had, his consciousness slipping back and forth like this, wavering between despair and white-hot madness.

In his crazed state, he heard footsteps. Faint at first; then quick, loud, *louder.*

The prison door busted open. He tried to adjust his posture, to glimpse the person who came to his rescue. In his haziness, he saw a handsome, beardless young man.

"Oh dear." The dashing fellow sprang forward, his medium length light locks falling to his shoulders as he kneeled before the bars, reaching for Eros' hand. "Eros," he said, his voice a sweet song, a tune of the heavens. "Are you having another episode? Let me grab Father—"

Eros recognized that youthful, glowing face, that tone. "Apollo," he begged, "help me."

Fire licked at the linings of his stomach. Pang after pang, the deadly snake manifested itself, creeping up to his lungs, constricting them. It lodged into his throat and swelled near his tongue.

A metallic flavor lingered in his mouth.

The poison is about to consume me again...

"Father turned off my mind-reading skills. He did so for all of us to aid Athena. So you must speak, Eros." Apollo's squeezing drew him to reality, if only for a few seconds. "I've been trying to help you...but this substance is so elusive...I can't crack its code."

Eros' godly energy swelled, pushing to flutter out.

No...he can't see this. He can't—

He drowned under the weight of the toxins. His emotions were no longer his own, his thoughts turned ravenous and wild. If Apollo figured it out...he'd silence him to halt the bloodthirsty demeanor from settling in again.

He couldn't be silenced anymore.

Think...think.

Biting his lip to hold in his urges, Eros blinked at the god crouched before him. "I...thank you...for all you've done." His gaze darted around the dungeon, desperate for inspiration, for answers on how to escape.

He needed his arrows, his poisonous invader had said; so how could he somehow fool Apollo into retrieving them?

He glanced at the deity of healing, whose golden eyes welled with genuine concern. "It's my job. We're family."

The deeper Eros stared, the deeper his resentment became. Apollo—ideal of perfection, his touch soft, yearning to be of assistance. Always handsome, always courteous, hiding his true nature behind his good looks and charm. Eros knew of his truth, of his catastrophic exploits, of how many times he'd gotten in trouble because of his sexual appetite. Eros knew, because *he'd helped.*

Apollo owed him.

As the poison continued its expansion into every cavity of his body, Eros craved to rip Apollo's arm off, to yank him into the cell and spit in his face and break each of his bones and watch him suffer.

"Ah...I'm back. Transformation complete."

He wanted to snarl, to gape into Apollo's soul and devour him—but for his plans to work, discretion was key.

"Here I am. The Eros who takes no bullshit. Not the blubbering idiot anymore; I'm the angry Greek god who wants hearts to feed on."

He understood what he had to do.

Whimpering, faking his pain—that had dissipated when he accepted the return of his true self—he jutted his chin towards the door. "My...arrows. What if...they can...cure me?" He coughed. "The blood...Cerberus' blood..." He pretended to drift off, his eyelids fluttering, his mouth drooping.

"The antidote," Apollo's singsong timbre nearly tipped him over the edge, "it could come from something so dark, yes. You infected others with it, but used on you…" He let go of Eros and clapped. "Yes, *yes,* it might have an adverse effect. No guarantees, but it's a start."

As Apollo stood, Eros wailed again, his eyelashes flapping like a butterfly's wings. "Bring them…here. I want to…watch…must be sure." He slumped, but internally he cackled, persuaded his ruse was working. "Want to…destroy them…myself. Bad arrows." Panting, he plopped onto his side.

Apollo hesitated. "Well…" He inhaled, tapped a finger to his chin, then nodded. "I'll see what I can do. Stay awake, all right? I'll hurry to grab supplies and locate those arrows. Father locked them up." A flush spread over his cheeks as he hurried off.

Once his footfalls were out of earshot, Eros perked up and grinned. "Stupid fool." He shoved a matted strand of hair from his forehead. "Go on, snatch my weapon, help my vision come true." He snickered. "Psyche won't eat my heart, but she'll feast on yours. All of your hearts…you sniveling, slimy deities."

He wiped the perspiration from his brow and gathered enough saliva to appear to be drooling, preparing for when Apollo would return.

With the magic contained in those arrows I'll break the cage, finish Apollo off, and go find Psyche.

"I'm coming, my love. Don't worry."

||14. ARRIVAL IN THE UNDERWORLD, PART TWO ||

ATHENA

Nothing appeared real once the Diamond Gates sealed behind Athena and Hermes. Before them stood a tall, multi-colored house with large metallic doors and no windows. A sign at the top, lined with mahogany trimming, said *AWAIT YOUR TURN FOR JUDGMENT.* The edifice barred the route farther into the Underworld…and Athena had no doubt who it belonged to.

The three judges.

Her eyelids fluttered as she drank in the panorama on either side of the building. To her right, a massive field of fog—of spirits. The misty figures roamed in circles aimlessly, and their moans tugged at her heartstrings. Past them, she sighted another gate, likely enclosing one of the main afterlife realms.

Craning to the left, she glimpsed a meager body of water, resembling a dried out lake. Faded vegetation surrounded it, and beyond it she heard bubbling and popping noises, and a few unidentifiable whispers. It was a marsh—perfectly fitting in with the atmosphere of dread.

Past the swampy pond, she discerned a tall manor of shiny black marble, rising up higher than the fences barricading the Underworld limits. Even from afar, she spotted its enormous entry doors—but before she could ask if that was Hades' home, the door in front of her opened.

She slid backwards; Hermes puffed his chest and stepped forward. "Hello?" he said, his gaze locked on the man who'd surfaced before them.

The man was familiar, with an odd resemblance to Zeus. A chunky beard, curly hair, a dignified and snooty demeanor, a scepter in his right hand—

"Oh, dear." Athena dropped into a curtsy, but Hermes didn't budge. Did he not know who this person was? How revered and important? "King Minos," she said, tugging at Hermes' arm to make him bow.

Hermes wouldn't bow, unaffected by this dead royal's appearance.

When Athena looked up, she saw Minos analyzing Hermes, eyes narrowed. "Hermes. Pleasure. As you know, no need for formalities here in the Underworld." His sight switched to Athena and his eyebrows elevated. "Is that *the* Athena? Well, what an interesting day this has become." His scepter clinked on the ground, helping him keep his balance. "I just had to send a terrible politician to Tartarus, and now you show up? My, my." He smiled, but it wasn't a heartwarming, sincere gesture. "Here to visit our ruler, I presume?"

Athena straightened up and peered askance, her cheeks heating with embarrassment. For someone who'd never visited Hades' kingdom, Hermes sure knew the rules well; and he *might* have told her about them.

Thankfully, Minos, the judge of the *final vote,* couldn't read her mind and detect her shame. Her father's powers of concealment still worked down in the Underworld, and yet she hesitated to look him in the eye; one could never be sure. Minos couldn't be aware of her ruse.

Minos ambled towards them but slipped to the right, to pass by them instead. "His palace is that big black blob back there." He threw his thumb at the building Athena had been observing. "Hop over the two bridges, pass the Stygian Marsh, Mnemosyne's hut, and you'll be on the royal path." He came within inches of stepping on Athena's toes, but took a sharp left, sneering at Hermes.

"Thank you, sir," said Athena, her arms tense, her breaths choppy. To her astonishment, Hermes seemed to experience the same fear as he shivered beside her.

Minos wandered out of sight, towards the fields of moaning spirits.

"Come," Athena moved towards the bridges Minos mentioned, "the sooner we reach Hades, the sooner we can get out of here."

A shiver skipped down her spine. Everything here was the opposite of Olympus. Darkness and shadows replaced the luminosity of the heavens. Instead of a sky, an endless obscure ceiling loomed overhead, sprinkled with fake twinkling stars. Torches lined the pathways to further illuminate the way.

They trudged on in silence, passing the judge's building—black marble veined with a graying mélange of sparkles and glints of diamonds. The cobblestone passage was sharp ebony, and rotting, dying grass peppered on either part of it. Everything was dead.

Well, everything except for the occasional ominous vegetation the likes of which one would only conjure up in a nightmare. No flowers, but *moving plants*. One such plant had limbs—stunted legs, Athena assumed—and it ran into the wilting herbs in the distance, squeaking in some foreign tongue.

Holding in a squeak of her own, she sped up to the first bridge and read its sign.

"The Acheron," she said, relieved at finding a landmark she knew.

Hermes, less fazed by the dreary surroundings, leaned a smidgen overboard. "Not as murky as outside the gates."

"Murky or not," Athena snickered at the rushing waters below, "this place gives me the creeps. Come on."

Between the bridges, and off to the side, was an eerie wooden cabin. A modest structure, with boarded windows and an ajar door, it fit in with the scenery, yet something about it made it stand out. Athena couldn't pinpoint if it was its polished yet rusty brown shade, or its energy; but its sign said **Mnemosyne's Hut**, and that quickly explained her discomfort. Mnemosyne, the titaness of memory, was a discreet deity no one knew much about. Athena had forgotten she lived down here, and didn't wish to disturb her. No noise came from the hut as they passed it, so Athena presumed it was empty; but she wouldn't wander closer to be sure. A titaness as powerful as Mnemosyne wasn't one to mess with.

She'd trifle with our memories and make us forget why we're here.

Insides churning, Athena patrolled to the second bridge. The Lethe flowed below it; she noted its clear, glimmering waters. Calm and attractive—a perfect trap for unknowing visitors.

The river of forgetfulness.

At the end of the bridge, the path veered left, nearing what

Minos had referred to as the Stygian Marsh; a mythical area often spoken of in tales. She glided onward with caution, her focus on the swamp and its overgrown, hickory-hued grasses. Colorful creatures hopped in and out of its transparent waters, rippling the surface up to the slushy bank. A few nymphs in flimsy clothing bathed in the shallower parts.

On instinct, Athena pivoted to Hermes, and rolled her eyes when she spotted him tiptoeing to the marsh, licking his lips.

"Oh, I don't think so," she growled, snatching him by the tiny blond hairs on the back of his neck. He moaned in discontent, but she didn't care. "We're not here for your pleasure."

She only released him once they were at a safer distance, and he'd wiped the drool from his chin.

Another river rushed to their left; quick-paced, loud like a waterfall. Treacherous. Athena gulped; it had to be the Styx. Its waters represented the goddess that all deities swore oaths on. So many promises made and held, so many wars started because of *this* stream. Though Athena hadn't sworn on Styx to locate Psyche, she might as well have. She'd let nothing deter her from solving the mystery, from returning the beautiful deity to her husband, saving her family.

The path widened into a road big enough to fit two earthly vehicles. The stone became a polished concrete, bits of rubies and sapphires encrusted within. Athena lifted her gaze to the palace ahead. Intricate carvings of myths were woven into the marble, along with precious metals and jewels, glimmering under the fake Underworld stars. Floating sentences in ancient Greek surrounded the structure, like a faded golden halo. They were only visible for an instant; an invisible barrier, a spell against threats, Athena assumed.

"Whoa," Hermes whistled, "Uncle Hades has it good, doesn't he?"

Athena counted four stories in height. She *was* impressed, but she wouldn't show it. "Father's palace is nicer. More welcoming." She snorted. "He doesn't need to flaunt his wealth. Power and position are more important, anyway."

The white structure she called home wasn't as high as this dwelling; it stretched out, where this place stretched up. But she would have preferred to stand before her father's gleaming gates than to feel the doom in her belly at the sight of *this*.

Hermes wrinkled his nose. "Should we knock?" They halted their progress a few feet from the doors. Multi-colored lights from jewels beamed down on them. "There are no windows…no idea if anyone is home."

"And no guard, either," said Athena, gloom growing in her gut, as if storm clouds had rolled in to obscure her vision, and poison had spread into her veins. "Shocking. Hades is a king, yet he has no security? And us," she grimaced, "we are royalty, showing up to visit him, yet no one offered to accompany us? No one stopped us but Minos, who merely pointed us in the right direction? What *is* this? Where are these people's manners?" She spun on her heels, eyeing the rivers, the marsh, Mnemosyne's empty hut. "How did we get in so easily?"

Hermes shrugged, still fixed on the polished palace entrance. "In Olympus, we have the winds, the sun, Gaia on constant alert of all who enter. Our fences are sealed from the human world. But Hades…" he pursed his lips, "well, he does have Cerberus. Charon won't let just anyone on his ferry. Thanatos wouldn't have granted us passage. And Minos wouldn't have—"

"—okay, yes, we were allowed in, but it wasn't easy." Athena combed her fingers through her curls. "Still...isn't it fishy? Our presence surprised Thanatos and Minos, yet they never questioned it. And they didn't bother to guide us." She side-glanced at her half-brother and saw his expression shift from wonder to worry. "Is this a trap?"

The palace doors burst open, prompting Athena to widen her stance and summon her sword. Hermes reached for a scabbard hidden in his belt.

No one exited, and the doors didn't widen much. Only a small, feminine-shaped hand slid out and waved them closer. Inviting them in.

Athena remained on alert, but Hermes cocked his head, perked up, and advanced.

"Hey!" Athena tried to seize his wrist, but he was too fast. "Stop! Were you listening to me? What if this is a trick?"

Hermes grumbled something as he neared the door, and the hand beckoning them over.

Clasping the hilt of her sword, Athena crept up to Hermes, preparing to grab him and run.

The doors wrenched farther apart. A violent breeze whooshed out, whirred around her, tickling the skin of her back—then shoved them both inside.

The door slammed behind them, leaving them blanketed in darkness.

"Hermes, dammit!" she whispered, narrowing her gaze, desperate for her vision to adjust to the obscurity.

Lights flickered on. Bright flames flew up from sconces on either side of them, exposing a lengthy but narrow entryway cloaked in hues of deep aubergine, glistening ebony, and rich charcoal. Large-framed doors lined the walls, and ornate paintings and framed jewels the size of Athena's fist littered the spaces between light fixtures.

Standing before them, her mesmerizing metal-blue eyes reminiscent of Demeter's, was an auburn-haired maiden, scowling at them. Her majestic mahogany tunic shimmied over her legs and trailed on the floor behind her. A crown of wilting flowers rested atop her head.

"Queen Persephone," muttered Athena, in awe at the woman's resplendent demeanor. She tugged on her too-short dress, feeling exposed. "Is that you?"

"Athena, Hermes." Persephone's lips twitched, yearning to smile though she continued to scowl. "Why are my royal, Olympian half-siblings in my underground palace?" Her voice was stern yet pleasant, stiff yet light.

"Surprise!" Hermes giggled and his cheeks reddened.

After a quick curtsy—Persephone was a queen, after all, regardless of the Underworld's ominous traditions—Athena ran up to embrace her. "I should have recognized your hand," she said, ruffling the young woman's curls.

Persephone returned the embrace, but pushed her off with a half-hearted smirk. "Yes, and you're lucky Hecate hasn't let out the dogs today." She switched to Hermes. "Don't even think about stealing anything here, you rascal. I know you. There are eyes everywhere in this palace."

Fingers fanned out over his heart in feigned offense, Hermes laughed. He'd been ogling a dazzling necklace in a framed box, and Athena could have sworn she caught saliva drizzling from his lips.

Persephone's touch was cold and tingling as she gripped

Athena's hand. "No, but seriously. Why are you here? It delights me to see you, but Hades didn't warn me of any visitors today." She was paler than Athena was used to. In her summers in Olympus, her skin shifted to tanned copper. She wore bubbly oranges and graceful greens, resembling a grand tree, a flower in bloom. Demeter's double, in every way. But here, she was a dying pomegranate, a blackened rose. A queen of the dead. Beautiful, nonetheless, but in a horrifying, deadly way.

She'd left Olympus only a month prior, and she already looked more like Hades' wife than Demeter's daughter.

"Odd," said Hermes, strolling up to Athena and clapping a palm on her upper back, "because he's expecting Athena. He summoned her."

Athena's spine tensed. She prayed her uncle would play along with her ruse. If he questioned her, and in front of Persephone...the young queen would tell Demeter, who'd tell Hera, who'd tell Zeus—

"Oh, did he?" Persephone's sculpted brows raised. "I would have appreciated a warning, but..." She whirled around and shouted into the never-ending hallway. "Hades! Your guests are here!"

Pounding footsteps punctuated the silence, followed by a door nearby creaking open.

A majestic man in a discolored cloak stepped out, expression contorted in confusion. "Guests?"

Under other circumstances, Athena would have grinned, curtsied, and laughed at Persephone's inconvenient manner of requesting her husband's presence. Instead, she rooted to the spot, pleading with her cheeks to not overheat, to not turn red.

Hades swept farther out into the hall. "What guests?" He froze and blinked at his niece and nephew. A semblance of a smile slew across his lips. "Athena? Hermes? How lovely of you to visit." He closed the door behind him and didn't seem to view Athena's subtle head shakes to warn him against revealing the truth.

Please, please *say nothing.*

"Uncle, you—"

"—a wonderful surprise," Hades said, still ignorant of Athena's less and less discreet glares to quiet him. "We never get Olympian visitors. Even you, Hermes, have never come this far—"

"—you summoned me, Uncle, remember?" Athena hustled up to Hades and put her face so close to his he had no choice but to gape at her. *"Go with it, please,"* she mumbled, then returned her voice to normal, "to discuss things in private?"

"Ah, right." Though a touch surprised, Hades winked at her. His mouth was down-turned, clearly taken aback, but he didn't denounce Athena's ruse. "Yes, apologies. I did."

"We have little time," said Athena, her intestines twirling into tight knots. "May we speak?"

Hermes snuck up to her, and she sensed his gaze on her; probing, pondering.

He heard my whisper, didn't he?

A playful air danced in Hades' expression. "Yes, please, follow me, dearest niece and nephew." He gestured at the room he'd exited. "You must have much to explain."

"That, you do," slurred Hermes as he and Athena marched after Hades.

"Explanations forthcoming," Athena said, addressing both her uncle and her brother.

She flipped around for one last glance at Persephone, who'd crossed her arms, her head tilted as she watched them go. "We'll catch up later?"

Persephone shifted her weight and sauntered by, her features unreadable. "Perhaps. But for now, go. The king doesn't like to wait."

‖ 15. THE POISON, AGAIN ‖
ATHENA

Hermes' stare continued to graze Athena's cheeks as they wandered into Hades' dreary chamber.

"Get comfortable," said the king, hands clasped, marble-like eyes studying his niece and nephew.

The hardwood floors didn't creak beneath their weight as they took their spots. Hermes strode to a plush burgundy chair, grumbling. Two similar chairs rested nearby, and an oak table separated them from an emerald-hued divan that Hades collapsed onto. Athena lowered beside him.

"Nice," said Hermes, looking around, then focusing on Athena, his bushy blond brows scrunching.

"My secondary Parlor." Hades waved at the cool crimson walls coated in shimmering rubies. "Excessive, I know, but I entertain many privileged guests in here." He frowned as he twisted to Athena. "So why are you here? And in such a hurry?

"Wouldn't we all like to find out," whined Hermes, pressing into his seat cushions and pouting.

"Wait." Hades cocked his head, his gaze flipping from Athena, to Hermes, to Athena again. "*He* doesn't know?"

"He does." Athena swallowed as she fought the flashes of the screaming match to come. But she had no choice; Hades had played along in front of his wife, to spare the drama to come if she were to know the truth and reveal it to her mother. But he wouldn't lie behind closed doors, away from curious ears. Hermes, though he played stupid, wasn't daft enough to not figure it out eventually. "He knows why we came. He had no clue we weren't summoned."

Hermes spat out a few choice Greek curses, so foul they made Athena shiver.

Hades huffed and ignored him. "Fine. I won't scold you, Athena, because I've always trusted your judgment. So," he massaged his short beard, "to what do I owe this visit?"

"Psyche." Athena crossed one leg over the other, peering at anything but her ruminating brother. "Tell me what you know of her disappearance. And of Eros' carnivorous situation. The truth."

Hades tapped his pointed chin with a slender fingertip. "Ah." He slanted into the divan, stretching out his long legs. The gray streaks in his blackened curls shimmered in the candlelight. "What urges you to wonder if I'm aware of anything you're not?"

Athena bit her lip. "Aphrodite told me." Hades blinked. "She mentioned your discussion, before Father's meeting after they captured Eros."

"I didn't realize you and she were close." Hades stood up and spun away from Athena's questioning glances.

"Yeah, neither did I," added Hermes, still sulking, but his gaze fixed on a golden plaque on the other side of the den, seemingly distracting him from his anger.

"Interesting." Hades' head angled back as he peered at the ceiling.

"We're not close, but..." Athena sighed, "Zeus made me lead

investigator on this case, and Aphrodite had key intelligence, being the mother of Eros, and all."

Hades marched off to a hutch at the edge of the parlor. He opened a cabinet and extracted a cherry-tinted cup and a bottle in the shape of an hourglass. He unscrewed its top and allowed a vibrant orange liquid into the goblet. He took a swig as he paced. "Please…never inform your father of the informal way I approached our dear goddess of beauty. He and his manners…it'll displease him."

Athena had her leverage; she smirked. "Fine. Then you mustn't tell him you didn't beckon me here."

Hermes groaned, but neither Hades nor Athena cared for his attitude.

"Deal." Hades sipped again; he wasn't one to waste time. "Aphrodite…yes, we spoke. I had to warn her." His fingers fumbled to hold onto the cup, trembling as he sped up in his pacing. "I *do* have leads, but…I'm still developing them. I would have summoned you for real if I had something concrete, but I don't."

Athena jumped up. "Developed or not, I need those leads. Anything will help." She dared a peep at Hermes who, to her amazement, had straightened up, intrigued. "She claimed you mouthed something to her, but she had no notion what. I assume it was of some importance?"

After rapidly draining his drink, Hades poured himself another. Athena ambled to him and caught a whiff of pomegranate and ambrosia-filled liquor. She glared at him, demanding a reply.

"What did I say to her?" He gulped. "I said *Hecate.*"

Hermes gasped, and Athena froze. "What?"

"Hecate." Hades held the rim of the goblet near his thin lips. "I kept quiet because I feared someone spied on us. Hecate…has answers. She is linked to all this, but *not* as a suspect."

"*The* Hecate?" Hermes hiccuped. "She's not responsible for all this, is she?" He got up and skidded to Athena, his shoulders tight, his demeanor different than earlier. He was evidently tense, and out of nowhere.

Did he have some issue with the all-powerful witch-goddess?

"Hecate…the perfect suspect." Athena pinched the bridge of her nose.

Hades mumbled and shook his head as he forced more liquor into his mouth. "I *just* said—"

"—No…no." Hermes grimaced and backed away. "Not her."

"No?" Athena swiveled to her brother. "She isn't a suspect, you say? Goddess of magic and witchcraft with a bloody past and a reputation showing her as merciless? I'm sorry, but it is plausible. I'm mad at myself for not considering this sooner."

"No!" Hades' shout bounced about the room, sending Hermes tumbling onto a chair. Athena shielded herself with her arms and winced before whirling around. "I mean," Hades spilled some of his beverage on his feet and scoffed, "no. It's not conceivable."

Her uncle was always the strangest of her family members. Always wore black robes, never combed his chin-length mane, often appeared scruffy despite his majesty. But she always trusted him, always heeded his words. Yet today…she doubted him. He hid something, and she had to figure out what.

"Why not?"

"Because Hecate is a witness." His tunic trailed through the puddle of alcohol at his feet as he meandered to the opposite end of the space. "I would never consider her at the head of this violence."

"I agree," piped up Hermes, stuck on the seat he'd fallen onto.

Hades flashed a sudden nasty glare in his direction. "Don't."

"What?" The god of mischief attempted to glare back but lacked the intensity of Hades' dark eyes. "I *do* agree. Athena," he pointed at her and snarled, "is the one who doesn't!"

Hades' nostrils widened, as if to spew smoke, if not fire. "You have no right to speak about Hecate, you—"

Athena dashed between them before Hades struck Hermes. "I have no inkling what your issue is, but this isn't the moment." She nudged Hermes further into his chair, shivering at the electricity in his aura. "Sit and wait. And *you.*" She rotated to Hades, coming so close he smashed the cup to his chest, surprised at her motion. "Calm down. I'm not saying I disagree, but I do need to speak with Hecate myself, so that I may assess her guilt, or lack thereof."

The door swung open, slamming into the wall. Two maidens stumbled in, falling on top of each other in heaps of frilly petticoats and muffled squeals.

"Ladies?" Hades swept over to them and with one wave of his hand, he lifted them to their feet. He glowered at them both, and again his nostrils prepared to expel fumes.

One of them was Persephone, brushing off her dress, muttering apologies. The other adjusted her posture with the grace of a snake, throwing back her jet-black hair streaked with scarlet as she set her frightening violet eyes on Athena.

"Talk, then," said the latter, her voice mature, sultrier than Athena had expected. "I'm here. Assess me."

Is that...Hecate?

Athena had met the sorceress-goddess before, but it had been centuries, eons, and she tended to change her appearance with her moods.

Hades looked ready to hurl his cup at the intruders. "Were you eavesdropping?"

Persephone peeped at the tips of her shoes in shame, but Hades wouldn't scold her in their company. Anyone here could report to Demeter about mistreatment. Especially Hecate, because according to rumors, she was the queen of the dead's fiercest protectress. The king could do nothing but gawk and groan.

The goddess of witchcraft flapped out her skirts and offered Hermes a quick nod of recognition, her cheeks tinting the faintest shade of red. "Hermes, hello."

Hermes had hopped up when he saw her, straightening up like a statue. He produced a bashful, lop-sided grin. Everyone and everything else seemed to fade from his vision, as he only had eyes for Hecate.

Excuse me?

Athena's jaw dropped.

Does he have a crush on her? Or does she have him under a spell?

"So," Hecate veered to Athena, "as Hades said, I'm a witness. A victim. But I have information that may help you."

Athena had to admit that Hecate, though reputed as dangerous, was intimidatingly beautiful. She had a youthful countenance, womanly curves, and an intriguing glow around her silhouette.

Still, Athena yearned to smack Hermes' head, to snap him back to reality.

"A victim?" Unease clawed into her abdomen; she didn't trust Hecate. Not after the gossip of her extracurricular activities. And less so if Hermes had a *thing* for her. "Victim or foe, that is up to me to decide."

To Athena's surprise, Hecate grinned. "Smart as expected."

"She's not a suspect," said Hermes.

Hades growled at him but nodded. "Yeah, what he said."

Persephone squeezed between Athena and Hecate. "Listen here, dear cousin…sibling…whatever. You and I are friendly, but Hecate is my closest friend. My savior, remember? Mom trusts her. I trust her. So if she says she's a victim, then she is. She healed me. Why would she do that if she plotted to use me to destroy the Olympians?"

Hecate seized Persephone's forearm and yanked her out of the way, whispering in her ear, soothing her. Hecate had helped Demeter search for Persephone and was later entrusted to watch over her in Hades' kingdom…which meant she was respected down here. Athena would have to secure other means to frame her.

Screams resonated in her skull, her nerves pinched, her rib-cage hurt. Every inch of her body begged her to *not* believe the witch.

"You're still doubtful," said Hecate, more perceptive than anyone else in the room. "Perhaps if I show you my crypt I can better explain and prove my point? Permit me to fight for my innocence, Athena. You owe me that much."

"I owe you nothing." Athena glimpsed Hades, then Hermes, then Persephone. "But I owe those who vouch for you. They heed your words like prayers. Fine, let us visit this crypt of yours."

It was most definitely a trap, but it was three against one. Hades obeyed Hecate's predictions, Persephone loved her like a sister, and even Athena's moronic brother was love-struck by the sorceress' sharp tongue.

Athena had no alternative.

* * *

Hecate's crypt was, as expected, in the basement.

At the end of the main hall, a set of steep stairs led them down. Athena's skin littered with goosebumps as they approached. The slippery steps and gloomy, water-coated ceiling didn't reassure her; and the basement entrance was drearier than she'd imagined. An ominous stench of despair and death warped into her nostrils.

Hecate guided them down the torch-lit corridor, passing a few battered thresholds with odd whimpering sounds coming from behind them.

She opened the third door to the right. "My potion room." Athena made a move to follow her inside, but the witch blocked her. "Beware; entering this place is a privilege. Only Melinoë and I are allowed here."

Refraining from rolling her eyes, Athena acquiesced. "Melinoë?"

Hecate let them in, and as if on cue, a frightful, veiled creature popped up beside the door, garbed in black and white, hair sticking up as if it had seen a ghost. Straggling slate locks lined its paler-than-the-moon skin, and it was missing a few teeth. It bypassed the visitors and ran to the large cauldron in the center, dropping something in, giggling at the splashing.

Persephone sidled up to Athena. "My daughter." The being slunk into the shadows in a corner. "Couldn't bring her out into the real world, so…Hecate keeps her down here as her special assistant."

This was a tale Athena had never heard.

Uncle Hades has an offspring, and he tucks it away beneath his palace?

Intercepting the disdainful glance Athena threw at Hades, Persephone grabbed Athena's wrist. *"She's not his,"* she whispered, squeezing, quivering.

This piece of the tale was even juicier; but it would have to wait.

Hecate cleared her throat, pointing at a copper cabinet at the rear of the chamber. Shelves of potions and awkwardly shaped bottles and mystique books surrounded it. "This locker contains dangerous drafts. Experiments. Recently, someone broke into it."

Only she and Melinoë had access to this cabinet; so did this mean Hecate was accusing Persephone's wretched daughter?

"No, Athena." Hecate's tone tore through Athena's suspicions, as if she'd read her mind. "Not Melinoë. Powerful enchantments bar this cabinet's doors. Ones she can't trifle with. Only I can. Or so I believed."

Hermes tiptoed over to the shelves of exotic brews. "Fascinating," he said, inspecting the surface, sniffing at the liquids within.

Athena pursed her lips. "So there's a thief in the Underworld? One with heightened abilities? Great; what does this have to do with Eros and Psyche?"

Persephone and Hades huddled close, and Hecate cringed. "The stolen potion was the one used on them. And on Persephone." Her prune eyes flashed like lightning, fueled with fury.

From his hunched position near the cabinet, Hermes grunted. "What?"

"You made that poison? It belongs to you? And you feel this will make you less guilty?" Athena's temples throbbed, ached as

images interlaced and jumbled and exploded in her brain.

She staged a break-in? Passed herself as a victim to evade her crimes?

Persephone ripped from her husband's embrace and flew up to Athena, poking at her breastbone. "Don't you dare accuse her!" Hades hastened after her, yanking at her waist to draw her away, but she wouldn't relent. A fierceness flowed about her features; one Athena had once seen in Demeter. "She cured me, we told you." A burned pomegranate scent escaped her mouth. "Why would she do such a thing? As a ploy to rile Mother up, infuriate Hades? Really?"

Though he finally pried Persephone off Athena, Hades acquiesced. "She speaks true, dearest niece."

Hermes, having whooshed to Athena's side during the commotion, pressed a hand to Athena's shoulder. His touch was jarring, jolting. "She's right." He stole a glance at Hecate, whose lips itched to inch up into a smile. "Why would Hecate go to such lengths? Why would she encourage anyone to walk up to Cerberus and take his blood? Come now. Hecate rubs you the wrong way, but—"

Athena dodged him before he could harden his grasp on her shoulder. "Fine. *Fine.* Because I'm outnumbered, I'll give you the benefit of the doubt." She refocused on Hecate. "When did you notice someone had forced their way into your things, and how did you know what they obtained?"

Slouching, Hecate gaped at the secret storage. "A few days before I got wind of Eros going insane. I was interrogating a few folks down here, but I didn't put two and two together until Persephone came to me and appeared off. So I mentioned it to Hades, and he told me what happened upstairs. We extracted whatever was in her, I analyzed the contents…and recognized the ingredients as my own."

Athena moseyed to the cauldron and scanned its swirling liquids. Glowing golds, simmering silvers, a smell of woodsy herbs and metal filtering into her nose. She knew nothing about potions, but this one smelled foul, evil. "Which ingredients? What persuaded you that Persephone wasn't herself?"

"She was robotic. Kept uttering half-assed sentences that made no sense. And the ingredients are secrets I can't reveal." Hecate tossed her ebony mane as she leaned over the other side of the cauldron. "But I can say there were a few drops from the river Lethe. How the mixture blended with her immortal blood, slowly shifting it to something else…I couldn't mistake it. *I* created it; a terrible concoction. There was a reason I sealed it up tight."

"Then why did you create it?"

The liquid from whatever brewed in the cauldron reflected in Hecate's eyes, gleaming in them like multi-layered jewels. Her fingertips curled around the pot as she averted her gaze. "I intended it as a potion to help one forget their fears. But when I tested it on Melinoë, I discovered it also affected one's deepest desires, or wildest thoughts. It provoked irrational behaviors and savage attitudes. Persephone showed a tiny twinge of that. And when Hades mentioned Eros spoke with her and he came here, to the Underworld, and neither he nor Persephone recalled any of it, I understood."

Hermes padded over to her and, as he had with Athena, he set a hand on the witch's shoulder. But she didn't reject the contact; she smiled at him, relaxing, accepting his touch.

Something was going on between them, and Athena's investigative nature shrieked on the inside, desperate to interrogate them.

"To our luck, Persephone only received a slight dose, so her treatment was easier. But if consumed in heftier doses, as I suspect for Eros, and likely for Psyche…it'll drive the victim to craziness. They'll have varying reactions and actions, based on what's lodged in their hearts. It would cause unexplained urges, driven by voices in their heads commanding them to do unspeakable things."

||16. TRUST IN ME||
PSYCHE

"Not much farther…go on, go on."

Rain splattered across the muddy pathway and trickled under Psyche's tunic. She padded onward, ignoring her aching limbs. She'd kill for a godly massage; for rose petals and ambrosia oil and her husband's hardened hands pressing into her skin.

But the mission messed with her sanity. The more she thought of her bed, her silk sheets, the crisp cocktails she shared with Eros before their love-making, the more she suffered.

But the grumble in her tummy reminded her to focus, to shut up.

"I get it, sheesh," she said out loud, her toes sinking into a puddle. She winced as the filthy water fizzled into the cuts and scrapes in her feet. "Eros has his own objectives. You'll let us reunite when we both succeed."

The cruel voice within moaned in agreement.

"Yes, my pet. Do not worry. Obey, and you'll be rewarded."

Psyche slowed her trot at the picture of Eros in her mind; her sweet-faced, tart-tongued, beloved spouse. "But he…he's worried, no? Searching for me? I sense it. Smell it." She paused, though her legs screamed at her to continue. Droplets drizzled down her shoulders. "Should I wait? All I do is wander…leaving a trail of dead animals and zombies in my wake—"

Growls germinated in her core, vibrating out of her pores, seeping out into the atmosphere.

"He doesn't pursue you. He's busy."

Her legs reanimated against her will, carrying her forward.

"He's locked up, searching for how to break free. His goal is in Olympus, now; you are here, you protect the humans."

The voice was shrouded in a soft velvet covering, yet it screeched inside Psyche like a miffed up cat. It was foreign; *too* foreign. A part of her recognized it, as if having heard it before; but when it roared and squeaked, she had no way to decipher it, to put a face to the sound. Whoever this was, she didn't enjoy their intonations, recoiled at their exclamations, and hated their vocabulary.

Suppressing a shiver as her feet splashed on the sodden ground, she cringed. "I've gone insane." She snorted. "Yes, I have. Talking to myself, fighting my own movements, hearing voices in my head, blithering nonsense as I provoke humans into eating live animals. I *love* animals! What is wrong with me?" Again, she sought to cease her strides, and though her limbs slowed down, they wouldn't stall. "This *stuff* in me. Liquid courage. It's poison, isn't it? You…*you*, whoever you are, in my mind…you're using it to make me inflict harm on others, to infect them. You're using me to drive mortals mad!"

She came to an abrupt halt, but not of her own accord. All her organs slammed against the linings of her stomach, her rib-cage, her arms. Her muscles tensed, her veins knotted, and she was nauseous. The internal tone screeched; piercing, powerful, fiercer than ever.

"YOU WILL STOP ASKING QUESTIONS."

She blew out a shaky breath, unable to move. Her extremities were numb, and the bruises on her feet raw, as if reopening and bleeding.

"You ask who I am?"

"Y-yes," she managed, though her lips barely parted to permit her to speak.

"I am your subconscious. I am you, deep within. Someone who knows what's best."

"S-sure," she said, unclear on why she was speaking to herself, why she was having a conversation with her own mind.

"You're poisoned…but this is a good toxin, and it will help you save the world."

It claimed to be her, but Psyche forced her face into a grimace, because it wasn't. It didn't sound like her; not her melodious timbre, her harmonious words, her silky sentences. She'd sung and hummed with Eros every day since their wedding; and *this was not her.*

Again, her legs took off without her command. "How…how will I save the world by driving humans to folly? By not being with my spouse? My d-daughter? In the skies, with the gods, my family—"

"THEY ARE NOT YOUR FAMILY."

She picked up speed and raindrops smacked into her cheeks, drenching her blonde curls. "O-okay."

"You'll understand, I promise. It's necessary…to build an army."

"Build an army," she gulped, "save the world."

"Yes. Eros is doing the same, trust me. My voice helps him, too."

"The voice in him? He has one?"

Her internal captor didn't care to answer her queries anymore; it had its own agenda.

"You'll be together again. We will be. When the world is a safer place. Soon."

The clouds above thickened, cloaking the road in obscurity. As if someone had turned off the light and left Psyche alone in the dark. The drops multiplied, transforming to hail, and in the background thunder echoed.

"You're not me. You can't be." She flinched as a drop the size of a cashew crashed into her shoulder. "I…don't talk like that. I don't crave such cruelties. You're not my subconscious."

Her belly lurched, throbbing and swelling. She gagged, bracing to vomit up whatever lurked inside her, tormenting her, torturing her thoughts. But nothing came out, and her pace didn't slow. Instead, sharp pangs banged in her intestines.

Her toes were frozen from the icy liquid shooting from the sky. She massaged her abdomen—somehow allowed to do so—but found no comfort. No soothing.

"Why must your conscience mimic your exterior?"

The words wandered from one end of her brain to the other as she pondered their meaning.

"A conscience must differ from one's exterior self. To urge you to pay attention to it."

"I suppose, but…"

"No buts, Psyche. I want what's best for you. For us. I dislike hurting you to get my point across."

She bit her lip as rain spiraled down her cheeks. No, not rain; tears. Tears of confusion, of conflict. She'd completely lost her mind, parading about some abandoned pathway in a country she didn't know.

"How can you hurt me? Why?" She sniffled, dodging a drop the width of a strawberry. "This makes no sense. I…am a goddess. You're not me, you're…a ghost. You're possessing me. And I refuse you. *I refuse you!*" Her speech played out to the heavens, and liquid sloshed into her eyes, drowning her, but she didn't budge.

It didn't care.

The discomfort from her gut traveled to her chest. It skidded up her neck, stiffening it, as if an invisible hand forced her head into place.

She peered ahead, and her heart stopped.

"Pain is the only way for you to comprehend."

This time, when she tried to speak, her consciousness snapped her lips shut.

"No. Hush. No one whispers in your ear. I am *you."*

She moaned, desperate to pry her lips apart, but they were sealed.

"You are a madwoman on the outside, yes; but a determined deity within. Quit your questioning."

As her fists tightened and she prepared to claw at her own mouth, a sense of calm infused her. Lavender and lily scents loomed in her nostrils. The tone turned honeyed, laced with a desire to compel, convince.

"I want to help. Let me help."

Psyche's gaze darted back and forth as she walked. The trail became concrete. She expected to lose her balance on the new terrain, yet she kept steady.

After a few minutes, her lips loosened. "Thank you." She blew out heavy breaths, with no intention of obeying this voice. "I don't want to be a madwoman, nor wander about this unfamiliar place." A jab in her thighs made her reel, but she wouldn't relent. "I can't push mortals to insanity. I can't eat raw meat, become sick. That's not saving them!" Her knees buckled. "You're destroying them! What kind of twisted army do you seek? You monster. This...won't end well."

Thunder roared above her. The sky was opening. Below, the ground shook, rocking her like an earthquake. She gasped as the concrete split straight down the middle, hungry to devour her.

She toppled backward as the path crackled. A muggy, humid breeze barreled up to her and she choked on it.

"This ends when I say so. How I say so. You will obey. Listen, or you'll die."

She hiccuped, praying for oxygen; but the more she worked to inhale, the more rugged and rough her breaths became.

"Listen, or you'll die!"

"O...kay..." she cried, grabbing at her throat. Her body rolled closer, closer, *closer* to the precipice—

But she didn't fall in; she immobilized. The quaking stopped. The cracks mended, gluing back together as if they'd never separated. The sky cleared—enough to provide a slither of light. The rain continued, but it was no longer hail; now it caressed her cheeks like a husband's warm touch.

As she rose, her internal wounds healed. Her external scars sewed shut. Everything reverted to normal, as if her life-force hadn't been slipping out.

She resumed her voyage to another barn house...thirsty for flesh.

"Yes."

With one word, the voice no longer masked its coarseness, its cruelty. It was enough to wrap around Psyche's heart, to burn her eardrums, to inflict surges of suffering.

Psyche couldn't care anymore. Her facial muscles didn't spasm, and she didn't batter the creature with questions. She ate the agony and accepted her punishment.

"Trust in me. Our goals are aligned. I'm in charge. All will be resolved."

"Of course." Her saliva was sour, sickening. Poisonous.

"Humans will play their part, gods will sacrifice themselves, and the world will be at peace."

She nodded. Somber, subdued, an odd serenity in her silence.

"Trust your gut, Psyche. Trust me."

||17. SECRET AFFAIRS||
ATHENA

"Stolen." Hecate's molten tone burned Athena's eardrums. "Not misplaced, as I haven't moved it since I created it. I knew how lethal it was."

Athena crossed her arms. "Then why not report it at once?"

"I was afraid. The fiend took other secret ingredients too," said the witch-goddess, her violet eyes brimming with scarlet. "Of no importance to the case, as they weren't in the potion…but stolen, nonetheless." She extracted a quill from the folds of her gown and snapped to produce a piece of parchment out of thin air. "Here," she scribbled a few words, then handed the paper to Hermes, "Apollo will recognize these. He's your healer, no?"

When her hand touched his, Hermes stilled, gulped, and sucked his lips in as he tucked his chin. Hecate blushed and turned away.

Athena gagged; since when did Hecate show emotions, any hint of affection? As the witch batted her eyelashes, Athena felt it in the air, heavy and intoxicating; *desire.* As if Aphrodite or Eros lurked nearby and had shot arrows at them.

She ignored the horrid amorous atmosphere as best as she could and glared at Hecate. "Fine, but how did someone get it? And who? If not Melinoë, who else would dare sneak down," Athena's nostrils wrinkled as she eyed the cobwebs in corners, "here?"

Hecate didn't reply at first, too busy trying not to brush her hand against Hermes' again. Hermes shuffled his feet like a shy, innocent boy. Which he was not, never had been.

If they'd noticed the flirtation, Hades and Persephone said nothing.

At last, Hecate shrugged. "I don't know. I interrogated everyone in the realm. My methods aren't kind. I brought Mnemosyne along, too. As a titaness of memory, I presumed she'd help, but she obtained nothing, either. *Nothing*. The culprit isn't from the Underworld." She peeked at Hades, who nodded; and then at Persephone, who winced. "I'd never poison my queen, never use her in a ploy to render Eros mad and kidnap his wife. Psyche is *wandering*, I'm sure of it. I have no interest in harming other gods." She gaped at Hermes quickly, surely hoping no one would notice, but Athena did. "I no longer go above ground unless..."

"...unless you're having a *frenzy.*" Athena groaned. "Has that happened recently?" Her throat pinched, which coated her voice in spite, in suspicion.

Too bad—I've never trusted Hecate.

"No, they're rare these days. And even so...my frenzies are only to scare humans, shake them up. No death or blood. I'd never hurt them." The witch walked over to her cauldron and stared into its depths. "As for my other whereabouts, well...I'm not allowed in Olympus unless Zeus invites me, so...I've been here, always."

Hermes strode forward, blocking her from Athena's view. "She wouldn't have had the access needed to poison Eros and Psyche."

"Right, you made your point." Athena was sick of everyone defending Hecate, but this was true, she couldn't deny it. Zeus cared for Hecate, but most Olympians didn't.

She hasn't been up there in centuries.

"But…" Four pairs of eyes glowered at Athena, and she flinched. "What if she has a spy upstairs? An accomplice?" She squinted at Hermes, waiting for him to understand what she implied.

When he did, he squeaked. "Me?" He waved his arms frantically and stomped. "Come now, because I exchanged a few glances with her? I'm too busy to run around Olympus poisoning my family!" His nostrils flared as he approached Athena, his forehead inches from hers. "I was out on business most of the time Eros was on his rampage. You know, helping to reap the souls he killed?"

"Athena." Persephone's pleading tone interrupted Hermes' growling. "Please, don't do this. Remove her, remove *us* from your list of suspects. I vouch for her, for Hermes, for Hades—and you'd believe *me*, no?" She sidled up, her skirts swishing over the grime on the floor, her tamed eyebrows lowered and desperate. "Mother trusts her, *I* trust her. Would you distrust your aunt? One who never stirred conflict or caused chaos and who ensured humans remained alive?"

Hades grumbled in agreement, Hermes made a *"see what I'm saying?"* face and folded his arms, and Hecate continued to gawk at the contents in her pot.

Of course Athena trusted Demeter, but her judgment was always off regarding Persephone. She'd do anything for her daughter, including trusting a reformed witch-goddess who transformed into a three-headed sorceress when angered.

"And," Hades waded over to Persephone, "*I* vouch for Persephone. Meaning for Hecate, too. Everyone here is accounted for, Athena." He slicked back a few strands of his longer-than-usual ebony hair. "She lives in my realm, in my palace. Shares my food, my counsel. She's done nothing to warrant such accusations."

Four against one—Athena was caged in, cornered, outnumbered. In this dank dungeon-like room, she couldn't think straight.

"Fine." She threw her hands up and veered away from their glowers, her focus on the peeling walls and the chipped bowls on uneven shelves.

She'd been wrong to come here. They were all prepared for her, alibis galore, retaliations and reasons pouring out like a wine fountain. She hated being wrong.

"Let us return to the parlor to discuss this further." Hades' smooth tone drew Athena from her thoughts. "We'll be more comfortable there, to go over ideas, debate, decide."

Ah, so Uncle dislikes these crypts, too?

She consented, but in truth she didn't want to talk to them. They were all suspicious and had spread nothing but doubt since she'd arrived. Were they all working together? Or were they separate, but joining forces now, to trap her, and by default Zeus?

Hermes grabbed her shoulders and spun her to him. Her skin tingled. "Stop overthinking. Hecate didn't do this. I've bumped into her enough times down here to be sure of her innocence. She's not your culprit."

"You *bump* into her, do you?" Athena would have laughed if his touch didn't repulse her so much. "I thought you never came this far into the Underworld?"

He grunted and released her to rub the back of his neck. "Stop it. You're unfocused." He pivoted to Hades. "I think we need to retire to bedchambers, if you have any available, Uncle. A few hours of rest to…clear our minds."

Hades set a hand to his heart and inclined his head. "We do. Lovely guest accommodations, which I can take you to now, if you wish." He glided over, the hem of his charcoal tunic turning brown from the dirty floors. "I've been a horrible host, haven't I? Of course the journey exhausted you. The air is different here, unfamiliar for you sky dwellers…come, follow me."

Athena sent one last glance at Hecate, whose eyes twinkled with mischief as she glimpsed Hermes, her lips twitching into a grin. Hermes didn't see it, or if he did, he pretended not to, urging Athena out of the crypt.

As Persephone and Hades led the way to the stairs, Athena seized Hermes by the elbow and, despite her disgust for him, leaned in close. "You have some explaining to do," she whispered, rage rolling off her tongue. Rage at what, she wasn't sure—his gross affection for the witch, everyone's defense of her, the gritty grime of the area, if not all of those facts at once. "You're hiding something."

They climbed the steps, and Hermes snorted, but didn't fight her grasp or proximity. "Am I?" They arrived at the burgundy entryway, its pomegranate smell a reprieve from the dreary downstairs. "*I* have to explain myself? I thought it was the other way around."

Persephone excused herself, and Hades motioned at them to go with him up the wide, black marble steps to the first-floor landing. This corridor was identical to below, with the same torches and polished hardwood floors beneath their sandals and the delectable sweet, fruit-filled aroma; but it was wider, easier to navigate, and with twice as many doors lining its auburn, jewel-encrusted walls.

Hades stopped in the middle of the corridor and pointed at two doors across from each other. "My finest guest rooms for my finest guests." He smiled and backed away. "I sleep little, so I'll be in my parlor when you're ready to chat. I want to finish this discussion without interruptions." He winked at Hermes and brushed his knuckles over Athena's cheek-bone before slithering downstairs.

The instant his tousled black locks disappeared, Athena rounded on Hermes. "So you say *I* have to explain myself?"

Hermes scoffed. "Uh, yeah, for lying to me? Doesn't that call for an explanation?" He smirked, but his eyes were narrowed, nefarious. "Your wisdom title seems to be erasing from your resume. You may want to consider adjusting it to the goddess of lying—"

"—oh, you conniving little rat! You dare speak to me like that?" She resisted the urge to grab her spear and shove it through his chest. "I had my orders, and I had to lie to get us here. Would you have voyaged with me if I advised you I lied to Father? That step-mommy Hera threatened me because she found out?" Fury fumed out of her like an uncontrolled fire, but she couldn't stop. "I had no choice. I *had* to come here, and since Father wouldn't let me without a guide…you're here, too."

His back against the wall, Hermes shook his head. "I'm the trickster god, sis. I would have helped you lie, had you informed me of this plan."

Athena's irritation nearly dissipated. Her facade nearly tumbled. But she was waiting for the other shoe to drop; for Hermes to show his true cards.

And he did; he smiled a smile so wicked, so foul, she wanted to smack him *and* herself for believing he'd ever help her.

"For a price, of course." He passed his tongue over his lips as he wiggled his eyebrows. "A hefty price."

"You wretched, filthy thing." Athena wagged her finger in

Hermes' face, yearning to wipe off his revolting grin. To throw jolts of energy into his stupidly broad torso and weaken him, teach him a lesson. But she wouldn't. She was the goddess of wisdom, composure, and self-respect. So she lifted her chin, huffed, and fixed her ruffled tunic. "I should have never accepted your guidance into this realm."

Hermes snatched the finger she'd waved about and brought it to his mouth, pressing its tip to his lips. They were plump, soft, wet. "But Father wouldn't let you leave without me, remember?" He slowly licked the sides of her finger, languorous and sensual, rousing flutters in Athena's belly. His pungent, human cologne wrapped around her, as if pulling her closer, begging her to mold into him.

No...I have never given in, and certainly won't now.

She despised her family's appalling frolicking amongst themselves; Hermes' out-of-place seduction wouldn't sway her.

Breaking free from his trance, her wit and strength overpowering his muscle and ardor, she spat. "You have the vilest of minds. Worse than Aphrodite." She wiped off the finger he'd assaulted, grimacing in offense. "Does Hecate know this about you? How disgraceful you are? Does she enjoy it when you do such things, say such things?"

"Hey!" He combed his fingers through his mane and his lopsided grin disappeared as he stiffened. "Don't mention her. Don't bring her into this. Ever. She's innocent. Pure." He averted his gaze, but there was a fiery energy about him that Athena didn't like. "Leave Hecate alone," he hissed, reaching behind him to grab at a door-knob.

Athena refused to allow him to scamper off so easily. "So it's true. You like her, don't you? You care about her. Oh, this is good." Hermes scowled, but it didn't halt her. "She's a maiden, like me. She protects her virginity fiercely. Dear brother, does she have any inkling how horrible you are to women?"

She didn't recognize herself. Maybe the atmosphere in the Underworld had unhinged her, provoked her. But to witness Hermes squirming, eager to hide in his room, was revenge on his years and years of taunting her. This was knowledge to use against him, to keep him in line if he had a mind to reveal her to Zeus.

His discomfort shifted before her eyes. He clenched a fist and raised it, as if to punch her; but Athena anticipated his move and blocked him, thrusting him off with such force he flew several feet down the hallway.

"What the…" He stumbled to maintain his balance and scratched his chin. "You've gotten stronger."

Athena flipped her hair—in true Aphrodite fashion. "I've always been strong, brother. So don't test me again."

"Whatever." He plodded up to her, snickering. "Dangle this over me if you must, to ensure I don't rat you out to Dad. But don't tell anyone of my feelings for her. Got it?"

She craved to howl at the moon like Artemis and shame him, but…she'd gone far enough. If he held his tongue about her lies, she'd safeguard his. For the sake of their shambled family.

"Deal. But *you* must leave Hecate alone. She's not one to be trifled with, and if you pet her the wrong way…"

Hermes returned to the door he'd been about to open and pushed. "Sure, deal. Oh, and don't forget," he loomed in the doorway, his earlier amusement flickering to life again, "don't eat or drink anything from this realm. I wouldn't want you forced to remain here forever."

Before Athena could protest that he would, in fact, prefer it if she stayed, he slammed the door.

"I'm the goddess of wisdom, dammit." She grumbled, slipping into the other chamber, breathing in its fresh linen scent.

Hermes and Hecate *together*? What an off-putting idea. A witch and a scammer; a maiden and a whore. With a chuckle, she sank into the plush bedding and rested her weary head against the soothing pillows.

She revised her board of names, mentally dragging Hecate to the left—the suspects. With a sigh, eyes squeezed shut, she shoved Hermes…next to her. Culprits in unison, plotting together.

"Could it be?" She yawned. "Would they?"

She fell asleep dreaming of poisoned ambrosia nectar and crazy heart-devouring creatures roaming all over Olympus.

‖18. A NOT SO FOOLPROOF PLAN‖

EROS

Eros fidgeted.

Why is he taking so long?

Twitching, his foot tap-tapping to the floor, he waited. Flashes of glorious gore tore through his thoughts, and he waited. And waited.

He'd lost his mind. The moment he shot the first blood arrow into a human, he'd driven himself insane. There was no cure, was there? It worsened as he yearned for the fair Apollo to return.

He was ashamed of lying to the sun god. A sweet thing, he was; Eros had lusted after him more than once but remained faithful to Psyche. To see him and his cute curls parading about Olympus, bedding all the handsome men, and a handful of lovely ladies, often stirred Eros' jealousy.

But today, Apollo was a fool. He volunteered gladly to retrieve what Eros wanted; his freedom. His golden, bloody, magical arrows that he couldn't wait to snuggle, kiss, and use to pierce the skin of all his godly siblings. How had that idiot not sensed the madness coursing through Eros' blood?

Eros smirked. It was to his advantage, yet he wondered how the deity hadn't perceived something off. Apollo's inadvertence would be Eros' gain. Soon, he'd sneak out of his enclosure, finish his goals, reunite with Psyche, and await further instructions.

Glaring at the dungeon door, he was desperate for footsteps, heartbeats, something to signify Apollo's return with his objects of desire. But nothing came. The room remained cloaked in darkness, not a flicker of oncoming torches, not a sign of anyone swooping in to deliver him.

Had he been caught? Compromised? Was someone on to Eros and warned Apollo? Or…

He did *read me. He saw through my stratagem, used his acting skills to persuade me.*

Such ruse was more Hermes' domain than Apollo's. Was Hermes nearby, pulling the strings, spying?

Eros' breaths sped up and he smacked a palm to his chest, praying to steady his nerves. If anyone grasped his distress, guessed he'd succumbed to his frenzy again, that he was thirsty for blood…it would fail. It would all fail.

Things had to go according to plan. Apollo would bring the darts. He was gullible—there was no faking that. But Eros' heart thumped and rattled, erratic and impossible to soothe. Why had it been so easy to convince Apollo?

Eros leaned against the stone walls for support, wincing as a drop of sweat slithered to his cheeks and tickled them. If he got too worked up, everyone would see it. Whoever deigned to visit him next would denounce him.

His life rested in Apollo's hands. It depended on if Apollo bit the bait, believing Cerberus' blood was part of a cure. Eros planted that seed in his mind, and if he didn't have faith in it…it would never grow.

And I'll never get out of here.

Licking his lips, he tasted the delicious blood on his tongue. He smirked; oh, the hearts to devour, the humans to sacrifice, the tricks, the plots, the mess. He loved it.

First, he'd dispose of the delectable Apollo. Then make quick work of Aphrodite, Athena…and then he'd return to his real role: to eradicate the selected soulmates, to cause a ruckus confusing enough to rile up the gods.

Soon after…the ultimate showdown. He squealed at the prospect—

Thump, thump. Thump, thump.

A heartbeat?

Light footsteps, faint breaths—someone was coming. Finally. Each step was musical, airy; it was Apollo. Eros smelled him, the flowers and cotton-candy and cocoa.

Another muffled sound accompanied his footsteps, but Eros dismissed it as being his own heart hammering in trepidation.

He got into character and threw himself to the ground, cheeks pressed to the bars, drool drizzling from his mouth, like before. As his eyes rolled back, the door creaked open. He feigned a struggle to twist his neck to the arrival, and found Apollo sneaking in, a torch in one hand, a bag in the other.

Eros flinched. *The* bag, with the arrows. He'd discern it anywhere, even with his eyelids half-closed.

My salvation.

"Apollo…you came," he murmured, doing his damndest to kill the smile seeking to scrape across his mouth.

The sun god set the beacon in its spot by the door and rushed forward, crouching before Eros. "Yes, and I brought supplies. Apologies for the delay, I had to find something to dilute the blood in, so it'd be easier to digest. Less potent." He gulped. "I fear the effects, but you might be correct."

Eros moaned. "Fine, *fine,* then…let me touch one. I…must…break them."

He watched Apollo extract a vial from the thin tunic barely covering his manly parts. A clear liquid scintillated within the glass, and he snatched an arrow from the sack and tipped its extremity towards the substance. Eros fought the urge to squeal as a few scarlet droplets blended into the concoction.

"I know you want to heal, but…" Apollo screwed the vial shut and shook it, to mix its contents, and replaced the arrow into the bag. "Touching these now isn't a good idea. Once you're better would be best."

"Apollo." Eros suckled on the spittle he'd produced, playing his role as a defeated, weakened mad-man with perfection. "I must…avenge my behavior. Must…and this is how." He coughed and opened his palm, waiting.

Gaping between Eros and the bag of shining arrows, Apollo scrunched his nose. "I don't know."

Eros battled the growls in his throat.

Do it. Do it, to help me heal. I'll murder you quick, save you from suffering.

A coppery curl curved over Apollo's perspiration-covered forehead as he bent down. He lifted one arrow, squinted at it, twisted it to and fro, analyzing it. Eros' breaths quickened, his thoughts turning vicious, ravenous for Apollo's blood to splatter all over the floor.

Never mind—I'll torture you for how you're torturing me.

"I suppose." Apollo straightened up, his shortened tunic molding to his perfect waist. "Yes, you're right." He leaned to Eros and began to thrust the arrow forward, to clink its tip against the cage. Eros reached for it—but Apollo yanked it away and slid it over his shoulder.

"What…are you…doing?" Eros hacked again, more violently than he'd meant to.

"He's giving it to me," said a tremendous voice, coming from the shadows. A large palm snatched the arrow from Apollo, and a figure morphed out of the obscurity.

A figure with a familiar and fearful outline of a mature frame draped in a robe so golden it brightened the entire dungeon. With luscious gray locks cascading down either side of his stern face, and eyes so icy they might have been made of icebergs.

Eros' jaw dropped so fast it was painful.

No…of all the ways for this plan to go awry…

"Thank you, son," said Zeus to Apollo, though he set his stormy glare on Eros. He steered the musical deity aside as he strolled up to the cage.

With a bow, Apollo slipped something into Zeus' grip, then batted his lashes at Eros. "I don't blame you for trying to trick me, Eros. Madness consumes you. Thankfully, I read all your thoughts, as opposed to what I said. Glad to know I've intrigued you." Eros could have sworn he winked as he sauntered off. "We'll fix you, I promise."

Eros swallowed, his chin giving in to gravity. Zeus' enormous shadow towered over him, and from the corner of his eye he spotted the king's thick blue veins glowing up and down his muscled arms.

Crawling backwards, Eros shielded his vision. "Could you...turn that crap off?" He dropped his act; there was no point using his energy if Zeus had figured him out.

But he'll feel my wrath. He'll be the first.

"Oh, will I?" The god of thunder cackled. "I hear you, Eros. Every sordid thought that travels through that messed up mind of yours. The enchantment on this cage makes your mind open to everyone who wishes to listen to it. So, pray tell, how might I feel your wrath when you're stuck behind those bars?"

Though the king's illuminated aura burned his retinas, Eros peered up, unafraid of the ever-menacing ruler of Olympus, leader of the gods. He didn't grimace, didn't wrinkle his nose, didn't move his lips.

"I hear heartbeats, Zeus. My powers grow despite these *enchantments* you set up to contain me."

"Ah." Zeus scratched his chin through his thick beard. "Well, *that* I can fix. I'll strengthen the spells. There's no way I'll allow you and your insanity to escape." He picked up the other arrows protruding from the sack.

"You..." Eros got to his feet. "You demonic piece of shit."

Zeus' chortles only grew louder. "Demonic? Me?"

Eros' snarl intensified. "Yes, you are. I want you dead. *Dead.* You fuel my anger, Zeus. You, the king of everyone and everything, deciding for us all."

"Clearly you *need* a king." Zeus pricked his thumb on the tip of an arrow, but not hard enough to draw blood. "I decide because I can. Because my family voted me as the head of all gods. I wanted to set my lightning upon you, boy. After your mother found you...I wanted you to die. For you to fight the constant echoing of thunder in your ears, for you to burn in the hell-fires of Tartarus. In the pits." He tsked. "I didn't want to give you an opportunity to explain yourself. You harmed my humans, so I'd harm you. You call me snide? Well, you're a vile, spoiled, disgusting little bug I wish to crush. To assassinate right here and now and end all our problems." His voice was scarily steady, never faltering.

Though his belly rumbled, overcome with the desire to rip Zeus to shreds, Eros gritted his teeth. "You don't frighten me, almighty king."

Zeus caressed the tip of the dart against the base of his neck, in true defiance, worsening the squirming of Eros' insides. "It would be to everyone's benefit if I ended you. We extracted some of the venom in you and we don't need you anymore. Athena will locate your wife, and *she'll* cooperate with us." A gust of glacial wind seeped through the cage. "I've convinced myself. That's it, I'm disposing of you this instant."

Pushing against the breeze as it prickled his skin, Eros curled his lip. "After everything you forced me to do for you? Every mistress I acquired, every distraction I provided, every arrow I wasted?" He slammed into the bars, his guts yelping at him to bite Zeus' head off. "Mommy dearest wouldn't like it if you offed me without a trial. You'd start a civil war. Daddy Ares will back Mommy, and Daddy's siblings will team with him. And Hera…oh, sweet Hera, she'd never let her baby Ares come to any harm, would she?" Zeus didn't move, and Eros grinned. "There you go…turn the gods against you. And Mother…she's more powerful than she's allowed to divulge, isn't she? Daughter of Uranus and all—"

Zeus interrupted Eros' speech with a surprising bout of laughter. "Oh, Eros." He sniffed at the arrow and recoiled. "Ever the spontaneous one, aren't you?" In one swift movement of his hands, he shattered *all* the arrows, shredding them to pieces.

Eros' knees buckled as bits of his beloved darts fell to the ground. Ruined, forever.

Zeus snapped his fingers and any trace—wood, gold, blood—zapped out of existence, turning to a pile of golden dust at his feet.

"You…" Eros' fists tightened so much he no longer felt them. "You devil. Cruel, crippling monster!"

"*I'm* the monster?" Zeus scoffed. "Look at yourself, at what this toxin has transformed you into. A blood-thirsty, heart-craving, human-killing machine. Those arrows stimulated you, so to watch them break was a necessary step to curing you. Did you not say that yourself?"

The dust swooshed out of the dungeon, sliding under the door.

Eros crumbled, his temples pounding so hard his vision blurred. "I don't want a cure. I want to *murder you.*"

Zeus kneeled to be level with him. "Obviously. That's the unfortunate part; many want to kill me, for many moronic reasons. But that won't reveal who poisoned you, who still controls your mind. Nor why. So we must heal you." He pulled out a vial—the one Apollo had given him before hastening out. Its contents bubbled, tinted red, about to overflow.

"No…" Eros gagged. "No, absolutely not."

He wants me to drink Cerberus' blood? It was a ploy! A trap! He…would poison me further?

Uncorking the bottle, Zeus tensed. "Yes, I would poison you, a thousand times if it meant getting answers. Without hesitation. After your behavior? You deserve nothing less than to be poisoned to death. But contrary to my claims, I won't finish you off." He jiggled the vial. "This virus mixture won't kill you. But it's experimental, so…it might hurt."

Before Eros had a chance to protest or move out of reach, Zeus jammed his arm through the bars and snatched him by the throat.

"Open your mouth, or else I'll injure you more than I wish to." He shoved his other hand, holding the vial, into the cage.

"You—" Eros snickered and tried to steer away from the flask as it approached him, "—overpowered asshole!"

The voices inside screamed, begging him to attack, throttle the king, bite his fingers off. But the tiny, lucid part of him reminded him Zeus wanted to help. His lips parted, and Zeus tilted the liquid into his mouth. A cold, bubbling substance coated his esophagus, spiraled into his belly…and *exploded.*

A pop in his abdomen, a firework, it pushed him onto his back, where he gawked at the ceiling as he writhed in pain and seized.

"What…the fuck…"

He had no weapons, no defense. Only prayer; and he prayed this would fail so that his true self, the carnivorous beast within, might continue to plot his escape.

The liquid sloshed from one extremity to the other, charging through his veins. As his head lolled to the side, he witnessed a blurry silhouette enter the dungeon, lining up beside Zeus; and both observed him, eyebrows raised.

"Did it work?" Eros recognized Apollo's harmonious voice.

Curse you and your stupid sister and your stupid mother, you prick. Die, die, die!

From slitted eyes, Eros saw Zeus releasing a deep breath. "Only time will tell, son."

||19. MESSAGES FROM DEATH||
ATHENA

"Princess."

Her fingers clasped around its wrist; *the culprit*. Its skin silky smooth, its spicy, herbal scent twitching her nostrils. She couldn't envision its face, but it was there, *it was there.*

"Princess."

The voice was so close, so clear, but it didn't match the blurred features before her; those belonging to the wrist she'd snatched.

"Athena! Goddess of wisdom, please wake up!"

Her eyelids thrust open to view the mauve canopy above. To encounter a feminine face with pale cheeks and delicate eyes, and hands shaking her awake.

"Wh-what? What is it?" Athena shot into a seated position, her forehead warm, the sheets beneath her damp and itchy.

Inclining her head, the youthful girl who'd woken her muttered muted apologies. "It's urgent, Princess. But you sounded like you were…"

"Solving a crime?" Athena snorted. "Yes, I was…in my dream." She threw aside the velvet covers and blinked. Her eyes fought to adjust to the semi-permanent darkness. "What is so urgent?"

The girl held a torch in one hand, her other bunching at her side. "He did not say, only sent me to fetch you."

"He?" Athena stretched her legs, her feet, her toes, and slipped off the mattress.

"The king." The girl's features were panicked. "He summons you, now."

Nose scrunched at the rude awakening, Athena scrambled to locate her sandals. She ruffled her chestnut mane before scurrying after the serving girl. She was far from presentable and had no clue how long she'd slept, but Hades was adamant on seeing her at once.

Halfway down the hall, Athena paused. "Wait," she said, and the girl spun around, eyes wide and worried. "What about Hermes?"

"His Majesty only asked for you, Highness." She waved at Athena to hurry. "He's not a patient man."

Athena tucked a few impossible-to-tame strands behind her ears. "Right, but why now, why only me?"

The girl skidded up to Athena so fast, like a strike of lightning, and almost as painful as one as she snagged Athena's forearm. "I don't ask questions, and neither should you." She yanked, and Athena flew after her.

Once downstairs, the girl nudged her towards a rounded wooden door, across from the parlor.

"He waits for you inside," she said, and after a hurried curtsy, she disappeared back upstairs.

With a sigh, Athena knocked and crept in. The décor and atmosphere in this space was identical to the parlor, but instead of a sitting area it had a massive fireplace and an ornate desk. The table was covered in paperwork, quills, piles of documents, but Hades stood off to the side, staring into the fumes.

"Uncle?" She closed the door. "You wished to see me?"

He swirled to her and smiled, his raven eyes warm, reflecting the flames. "Welcome to my study, dearest niece." He motioned at a chair before the desk.

She waddled over to the ruby-red cushions but didn't sit. "What's going on? Where's Hermes?"

"He doesn't need to be here." He gestured at her to sit, and as he prepared to do the same, someone knocked. "Yes, come in, come in." He rolled his shoulders, cracked his neck; he was tenser than usual.

When the door creaked open, Athena understood why. In the threshold stood the cloaked deity she'd encountered the day before.

Thanatos.

"Majesty." He bowed, then spotted Athena and his lips fluttered into a semblance of a smile. "Athena, pleasure seeing you again."

"You've met before?" Hades urged him in.

"Yesterday, upon her arrival." The god of death sealed the door and slithered up to them.

Athena peered between them, sensing distress in them both. A negativity she hadn't been prepared for.

Had Hades revealed her ruse to Zeus? And Zeus ordered her punishment; her death? Such a command would be exaggerated, impossible to believe, but it explained Thanatos' presence—he'd come to reap her.

"What is it?" She arched her spine, pressing her feet to the ground, bracing to run, if she had to. She wouldn't die before meeting with her father one last time.

"Thanatos is my most trusted reaper." Hades flinched. "I told you I had information, but actually…*he* has it. More than what I initially thought."

Thanatos took the chair beside Athena's, his expression concealed by his hood.

So…I'm not dying today?

The god of death crossed his legs and set his gloved hands atop his thighs. "I reap many souls. Though I have a dedicated team of underlings, and rarely go farther than the general southern Italy region, I've been drawn out. I sniffed out an irregular stench of doom in the air, and out of curiosity, I hovered near it." He glimpsed Hades, who nodded at him to continue. "A mortal soul came to me for reaping and…it spoke. Told me things that might help your case."

"My case?" Athena's brows bristled up as she peeked at Hades. "He knows what I'm here for?"

Hades said nothing, and Thanatos tapped on the desk to regain her attention. "Under such extreme circumstances, I was forced to reap Eros' victims. No need to tell me what's happening. I figured it out." He leaned close to her, his aroma of dirt and freshly mowed grass filtering into Athena's nose. "Do you not think my king would warn me of another god on the loose, wreaking havoc, under a spell? I've been on the alert for Psyche. You need not distrust me. I'm death, yes…but a peaceful being. I seek no violence, never have, never will."

"Fine." Athena allowed herself to relax into her seat. "Go on, then. What else?" He gave off a more trusting vibe than Hecate, so she assumed he might be of use to her.

"This man I reaped informed me he had been driven mad. Forced to feed on wild or farm animals…*raw* farm animals. Some wild, too." Athena gasped and covered her mouth. "To devour them whole, which would bring strength, power from the uncooked flesh. He claimed a voice inside him instructed him to carry out these orders, else he'd die."

Hades reached for a goblet at the corner of his desk. "Disturbing."

Any part of Athena that had been hiding under a blanket of slumber woke. "By Zeus…by Olympus…raw animal flesh. Father mentioned something like that. That is blasphemous, no?"

Thanatos frowned, and even under his hood, she noted the shadows skidding across his tanned skin. "He alleged that once…*satiated*…he wandered. Aimlessly. He deserted the carcasses and roamed in circles, waiting for further orders." The cloth covering his head slipped, showing his crow-colored eyes. "Have you ever seen any human horror movies, Athena?"

"No. I prefer not to partake in the technological devices humans invented." She cringed. "But I've listened, and I understand most references from said movies."

Thanatos squinted. "Do you know what a *zombie* is?"

She stilled; the word disturbed her, prompting monstrous images to flood her mind. "Brain-eating reanimated corpses? Most earthlings fear they'll come to be from some virus or other and take over the planet. Zombies, yes." She bit her lip. "Those theories often reach us at the palace. Father mentioned some mortals have gone as far as hoarding supplies, learning essential fighting skills to prepare. But…no such poisons exist on earth. So…what do zombies have to do with my case?"

"That man," Thanatos grabbed at his throat, "he said *that's* what he felt like. A zombie. But he craved raw animal meat and was confined to a specific area. And heard voices."

"Zombies. Heavens." She massaged her temples. "Who caused it? Who drove him mad, and how? Did he know?"

She at once regretted asking the question because she already had the answer, and hated it.

Thanatos pulled out a notepad from his coat. "He encountered a woman clad in a pale pink tunic that clung to her body. Frazzled blonde hair, bright blue eyes, deadly white skin, barefoot."

Hades' eyes widened as he became rigid, hanging off the edge of his chair. "Oh, no."

"She approached him, grabbed him by the shoulders, and breathed something into him. A mix of a sweet purple haze and a foul green smoke that seeped into his lungs. He remembers little after that." Thanatos lowered the pad onto his lap.

"*Psyche,*" whispered Athena, recalling the woman's last physical description, what she was last seen wearing. "Father acknowledged the animal deaths…so she is responsible for them?"

Did Father know it was her? Is that why he wanted me on earth, first?

"It's taking place in the south of France, the countryside. My spies report that the victims are isolated farmers and their families, sometimes random passersby." Thanatos fidgeted, the notebook ready to fall from his legs. "They all have the same behavior, ignorant to the surrounding world, but at a distance from civilization, meaning they go…unnoticed."

"Strengthening humans by poisoning them. Isolating them so they only eat animals…" Athena stood and rubbed the back of her neck. "Someone really thought this out." She pinched her lips with her fingers and a delicate rose scent weaved into her nostrils; one that would usually soothe her, but today it made her sick. "The toxin strain…it reacted differently with her. So does this mean there are two culprits? Or was Hecate right about the effects varying from god to god?"

Thanatos glanced at Hades, who shrugged; neither had a decent enough reply for her.

"So," she pushed the chair and moved out to pace behind it, "if we assume whatever got Eros got Psyche too…it's *that* poison she spreads to humans?"

"If that's her," Thanatos swiveled, scrutinizing her every move, "then yes. Her motive seems to be to infect isolated mortals. But why?"

"It *is* her." Athena tipped her head to glower at the jewel-encrusted ceiling. "Zeus suspected this, I'm certain of it. And instead of heeding his commands, I listened to Aphrodite and her silly hunch. She made me come here." She towered over Thanatos, who nearly fell backwards from her bold presence. "What else did the man say?"

The deity of death's hood dropped lower, revealing his sleek and surprisingly well-kempt raven mane. "Nothing more than what I've reported. That voice threatened him with death, and when he stopped marching about, too exhausted, his belly churning…it ordered him to commit suicide. I'll spare you the gory details, but when he came to me he was bloody. It was a nasty sight, and I've seen a lot. His poor soul begged not to be sent to the pits for his crimes."

Suicide—a first-class ticket to the depths of hell, according to some.

Hades, once glorious and composed, now shivered—and not discreetly. "What kind of sick individual would do such a thing?" He rose and meandered to the hearth. "Appalling."

Athena's limbs were restless once more. "Did any other infected humans perish?"

"As far as I'm aware, no." Thanatos got to his feet and pinched the bridge of his nose. "I've seen much madness in my career. But this is peculiar. This infection inhibits the usual confused ambling and the internal orders from voices, but the animal killing, the zombie tendencies? Those are new. I'm not sure what to make of them." He tugged his hood over his hair, showering his features in obscurity.

"Well…lucky for you, Father put me in charge." Athena perked up, imagining her helm atop her head, her sword in one hand, her shield in her other. Yet the picture of herself in warrior gear didn't help; there would be no physical fighting in this mission. It would be a battle of wits. "It's up to me to comprehend what twisted creature is capable of such horror."

Thanatos excused himself, leaving Hades to gape at the fire, and Athena to resume pacing.

"This is bad," she said, fumbling with her dress, wishing she had something to squeeze, to work out her stress.

Hades' timbre, so unusually soft, disrupted her. "*Is* Psyche causing this? Or is there more we're not seeing?"

Athena twirled to him, and his expression was grim; more so than ever. "Oh, Uncle." She gripped the top of her chair. "Both. Psyche is the one provoking the killings, but who provoked *her?* My main duty, as of now, is to stop her…but I have no notion how."

‖ 20. YOU'RE SAFE ‖
EROS

Though leaden and crusty, Eros' eyelids finally pried apart.

Had he died? He blinked, and his stuffy dungeon room came into view—but sideways. His cheek was pressed hard onto the cold, stone floor, and he noticed a set of sandals in the distance, pacing in the darkness before his cell—

I'm in the pits of Tartarus, aren't I?

A groan echoed from above the feet he still stared at. "You're alive. Groggy, I'm sure, which explains your delusion." Zeus—his tone powerful as ever, pinched with irritation, a tad raspier than usual.

Eros sat up, his scalp on fire as he rubbed his forehead. "How…" He vaguely recalled their last conversation, and how it was cut short. But a pang in his chest propelled whatever he couldn't remember into his brain. "Oh. *Oh…*"

I tried to trick Apollo, threatened to kill Zeus, and drank poison.

Zeus set his back against the enclosure, but craned his neck to the side, studying Eros. "Not poison. Something to ease your nerves. It worked, though you fought it at first." He sighed, and a few of his silver-gray locks curled around the bars. "You fell asleep, and though you're awake now, I'm not convinced of your state of mind. Don't rush through the process, don't force yourself…or you'll revert to your bad ways."

"So, is this," Eros hiccuped as he pulled up his pants that had apparently drooped to an inappropriate level, "a cure?"

After all I did, he saved me?

"Not a cure." Zeus spun, his nose pushing against the bars, his eyes a deep, stormy blue. "How are you feeling? Any burning fires I should be aware of? Lurking rage? Belly pain?"

Eros gawked at his hands, then flipped them to view his palms. They weren't covered in blood, as he'd become used to. Flashes of his prior crimes cramped into his cranium, but they didn't trigger him. Didn't cause him to shiver, cringe, growl.

"I'm okay, I think." He glimpsed Zeus and his breaths quickened, his body tensed…but nothing happened. "I'm unsure for how long." He tested his legs, shaking them out, checking his balance by jumping up and down.

I'm me? Not the raging monster?

Zeus focused on the shards of glass from Eros' previous outbursts. "It'll always be hard to be clear. You had quite the explosion earlier. Faking illness and weakness, seeking to corrupt Apollo…" His chin snapped up, and electricity laced up the metallic bars as his features obscured. "You could be faking your demeanor now, too, though I'm not sensing imminent danger in your soul."

Such a shift in attitude would have provoked the bloodthirsty Eros, and Zeus surely knew it. But if that vile creature still loitered within, it slept, or its muzzle was shut.

"No…I'm not pretending. I can't control it, but right now, I'm me. I'm here…and almost normal."

The visions vibrated somewhere in his mind, but they didn't interrupt him like before. They didn't coerce him into letting loose and screaming for blood. He could breathe.

Zeus crossed his arms, shoving them firmly against his broad but for once covered torso. "Almost?"

"Because I'm still unstable, right? That…voice…inside; it *is* me. I can't make the difference between my regular thoughts as the god of love…and those of the carnivorous killing machine echoing through my head." He paced up to the bars, and Zeus considered him, squinting, lips twitching. "I'm unclear what's good or wrong. What opinions are real or fake. What's in my heart or forced into my brain from the toxins. It's exhausting."

When Zeus relaxed his stiff shoulders, part of his tunic slid down his biceps. "Have you figured out what triggers you? Or…" he grimaced, slanting closer, "will discussing this incense the voice you speak of?"

Fixed on Zeus' bare shoulder, and on the silky fabric that glided to the crook of his elbow, Eros chewed on his lip. "Do you have more of that elixir, in case it does?"

Zeus fished the vial out of a pocket as he readjusted the wandering strap. "Not much." He held it up, shaking it. "And unfortunately, I cannot spare any more of it, as we need some for Psyche, once we recover her."

Eros stilled.

Psyche.

He closed his eyes as jolts of energy raced up and down his arms, legs, spine, and exploded inside like a savage firework.

Oh, darling, what have we done?

"She…if she's poisoned, like me, then the voices…" He collapsed to his knees and cupped his head in his clammy hands. "She hears them too, yes? Which means she's suffering, she…" He jerked up as tears swelled in his eyes. "What is this monster forcing her to do? Where is she?"

"Is Psyche," Zeus lowered to Eros' level, "a trigger?"

It was odd to see the King of the gods crouched in front of a dungeon, speaking to Eros as if he hadn't plotted to murder their entire family.

"I…" Eros' scalp throbbed, and his heart drowned in despair and guilt, twisting in fear. "Yes, she is. Certain facts about her…the danger I sense her to be in…my worry for her well-being. The intensity with which I miss her. These have triggered me." The silence in his gut and the quiet in his mind worried him; would the beast awaken again if he continued to mention her?

His stomach gurgled, and it was so loud, Zeus shot up and strode backward, his thick eyebrows elevating. "Eros?"

Eros wagged his finger; there was no rage in him, no thirst for death. "This…" He pressed his hand to his abdomen. "It's not resentment. It's sorrow. Pain. Agony at having lost my wife."

Zeus let out a heavy breath, his posture shrinking.

"When I'm threatened or reminded of what I did…the voice animates, but at this moment, it hasn't." Eros brushed trembling fingers through his matted hair. "But it has said that I'm not done. That I have more to do and must escape this cell to do so."

Zeus tapped his chin, approaching the enclosure once more. "So that voice, that *other* you…it isn't finished killing humans?"

Calves cramping from how he hunched, Eros stood up, his stance wobbly. "Yes. He…*it,* is proud of the results, saying it'll lead to something more, reunite me with Psyche. That there's a reason for it, but I never get farther than that. I usually pass out from exhaustion, black out as *it* takes over, or…my normal self returns."

Clouds hovered over Zeus' eyes. "The magic in this metal," he knocked on the bars, "is an enchantment to induce calm, remove evil ideas. Yet those toxins in you resist it. This potion by Apollo," he shook the vial again, "isn't a remedy. It's temporary. Your mood will swing again. Your monstrous thoughts will return...but I have no idea when. So remember this whenever the violence awakens: *yell for me.* Scream my name, and I'll come to help."

"Majesty?" Eros gulped. "How?"

"I'll cross that bridge when I get to it." Zeus' lips tugged into a frail smile. "We've had our differences, and I may have egged you on to test the extent of your fury, but I wish you no harm, Eros. You are family."

"Me?" Eros jabbed a thumb into his rib-cage. "But I don't deserve this blessing." He sniffled as liquid inundated his lash-line. "Poison or not, I must have had all this inside before, right? Anchored deep within where that wretched shit found it and drew it out, made me conscious of it?"

"You're not in command of those thoughts." Zeus' expression softened, and for an instant, Eros prayed he'd squeeze through the bars and hug him. How he yearned for physical contact, for affection, even from the mighty king of the gods who'd not that long ago wanted him dead. "I only wish we had more of the concoction to keep you stable."

"What was in it? Aside from Cerberus' blood, if I didn't hallucinate that part."

Zeus massaged the back of his neck. "I can't tell you. Not yet. But Apollo is reaching out to other healer gods for more assistance. He hopes to get answers, but he lacks the more obscure skills and forbidden ingredients that we'd need for a more permanent, potent potion." His earlier softness dissipated as he narrowed his gaze. "Psyche will return. Athena is on her trail, I'm certain of it. I imagine she received much intelligence in the Underworld."

The image of Athena navigating the murky Underworld sent chills up Eros' back. How had *he* traveled down there unscathed? And he hadn't asked for permission, too; so how had Athena convinced Zeus to allow her there?

"I hope she knows what she's doing," said Eros, still shuddering at the blurry recollection he had of the area. The fake stars overhead, the atmosphere of despair, the stench of death.

"She always does." Zeus stepped back. "I have no doubt she'll locate Psyche and once she does and brings her home, the truth will piece together."

"Did she go alone?" Eros flinched. "I'd hate for her to risk her life like that. I wanted to slay her, so I hope I didn't send her packing—"

A pleasurable sensation tingled in his belly as he pictured himself strangling the goddess of wisdom. He crumbled to his knees again, coughing, fighting to erase the horrid image.

"Eros." Zeus flew up to the bars and rattled them, desperate for Eros' attention. "Breathe. Rest your mind. Forget your tendencies."

"I...is she..." He cracked his neck and knuckles and expelled a weighty breath. "Is she alone?"

"She's not." Zeus gripped the bars, charging them with more juice before rising and backing to the exit. "Hermes is with her. So be at ease. You're safe here, and soon Psyche will be as well."

As Zeus snatched the torch and slipped out, the prison saturated in darkness once more. Eros fumbled over to his bed and sprawled out, inhaling and exhaling, searching for inner peace.

"Zeus isn't so awful," he said to himself. "So why does my evil side want to murder him?"

‖ 21. TIME TO GO ‖
ATHENA

The Underworld's irksome aura had sufficiently crept under Athena's skin—it was time to leave. She had Psyche's location—southern France—and not another second to lose playing guest to her beloved but weird uncle.

She urged Hades to send someone to wake Hermes, and as she exited his study, to wait in the hallway, her heart skipped a beat. Would the King of the Underworld grant them permission to take off?

Hades' disappointment flickering to life on his face when she informed him she had to flee…it haunted her mind. His gaze drooped, he frowned, his shoulders slumped. And though he didn't plead with her, it was clear he was reluctant to let her go. Upon arriving here, she'd ignored the rumors she grew up with—that Hades had a reputation for entertaining guests but never letting them leave. He had so few visitors…and now, she understood why. His world was a solitary one, despite his wife's warm comforts and all his obedient—albeit awkward—subjects.

The worries she'd had the day before resurfaced. The dread of this obscure realm, its odd beings, its strange customs, and its food she wasn't allowed to eat. Thankfully, she'd stayed away from any kitchens or dining halls, but her stomach grumbled for ambrosia.

She paced, vision locked on the auburn walls that reminded her of pomegranates, and the sparkling jewels that made her think of sprinkles on a cake.

A groan came from the staircase, followed by uneven footsteps. She spun to find Hermes, his blond locks twirled into a messy bun, his signature winged sandals half-laced over his dark ankles.

"There you are," she said, skidding up to him, her loose-fitting tunic shifting about her and exposing her thighs.

He smirked. "Well, that's a nice vision to wake up to." He licked his lips as he scanned her from head to toe; if he'd been sleepy, Athena's presence now woke him. Aroused him.

Gagging, Athena moved away and knocked on the study door, to warn Hades. "We're leaving."

When the door opened, Hades' sorrowful expression worsened as he loomed in the threshold. "Come in," he said, his voice more of a wail than a regular tone. "And good morning, Hermes."

"Yeah, yeah, morning." Grunting, Hermes plopped onto the first chair he found and stretched. "How can we leave? Did you get all you needed?" He yawned, but stopped in the middle of it, eyebrows swishing up. "Wait, did something happen while I was sleeping?"

Hades waddled over to his desk and sat with a pained sigh. "Yes."

Athena remained standing, peering at Hermes, whose eyebrows wiggled. From his lower level on the chair, he could likely see all the parts her dress was meant to conceal, so she chose to keep her distance. "Thanatos delivered news of Psyche's wandering. She's in France. I must confront her at once and get her home. Willing…or not."

Hermes sat up straight, turning serious. "He found her? We're certain it *is* her?"

Another desperate puff of breath escaped Hades' mouth; exaggerated, like a cry for attention. "Yes."

Athena ignored him—all he wanted was to convince her to stay longer. "I wouldn't doubt Thanatos' description of her. Blonde, blue eyes, barely-there dress, barefoot, mumbling all sorts of nonsense…it's her. But she's mad, under a spell. Poisoned, I'm sure."

Hermes lurched to his feet. "So what are we waiting for?" He swept back a few loose strands and adjusted his creased tunic. "I mean, I have a quick stop to make first, it'll only be a minute—"

Athena snatched his arm before he raced to the door. "No." She didn't want to read his mind, not in front of Hades, but she didn't need to. Hermes wanted to say goodbye to Hecate.

I don't trust her, and don't want her grubby hands all over him, figuring out our next destination.

He fought a pout, his nose scrunching. "Please," he whispered, tugging out of Athena's grasp.

She grabbed him again. "You can't." She twisted to Hades. "Uncle, make sure none of your subjects depart the realm. Especially Hecate. No frenzies or disappearances, as those might jeopardize our mission, understood?"

Hades' disappointment faded, replaced by irritation. "You still don't believe her, do you?"

"What I believe doesn't matter," said Athena, returning to Hermes to avoid Hades' scrutiny. "But if she were to choose now to seek one of her outside dances with the moon, it would compromise everything. This is essential. When I give my report to Zeus, I have a hunch that he'll summon her for a testimony. *Keep her here.*"

Hades mumbled some sort of half-hearted agreement, and Hermes tensed. She released him, wary he might strike her in anger.

"May I at least see you out?" Hades gestured at the door.

Athena agreed, and Hermes grumbled.

Once they slung their bag straps over their shoulders, Hades led the way down the hall. Once they reached the imposing threshold, he halted, rotated, and barred the path.

"You don't want an in-depth tour, first?" His tone was desperate, his face paler than it had ever been; and it was usually sheet white. "You only saw this side of the realm, but I must show you Asphodel Meadows, the gate to the Elysian Fields." He smiled. "I could take you inside. Perks of being the ruler. Heracles dwells there, I'm certain he'd be happy to —"

"—Uncle." Athena hated to interrupt one so powerful, to decline his offer, despite how much she abhorred his realm, but she had to. "We cannot. I must apprehend Psyche before she moves on from France or gets wind of my arrival. Whatever controls her may have spies everywhere." She gasped—Zeus had warned her of this.

Nowhere is safe. I don't trust Hecate, I doubt Hermes, and Hades is mad with grief. Foes all around.

She swallowed and pushed a few hairs behind her ears. "We must go."

Hades veered around and snapped, and the door opened at his command. He waved at them to follow him down the gem-encrusted pathway, but his strides were slow, tipsy with sorrow.

Hermes trailed along next to Athena, his flirtatious nature under wraps, hidden beneath a veil of solemnness. She dared a side-glance at him to find him battling a grimace, eyes twinkling in the light of the fake stars, shoulders slumped forward, each step a stomp on the ground.

She felt a pinch of sympathy; did he truly have feelings for Hecate? She should have pitied him, yet…she wouldn't. He'd broken so many hearts, stolen so many virginities; it was fate that he'd fall for Hecate, a fiercely virgin goddess. The big slap in the face that he'd needed for centuries.

They marched on, and Hades stopped to point out landmarks, explain histories. He was wasting time, capturing his niece and nephew for as long as he could. He even tapped on Mnemosyne's door, though it was obvious she wasn't home, insisting on introducing her to Athena.

"Uncle." Athena huffed, exhausted from his pointless gallivanting from spot to spot, greeting servants, howling at passersby to present themselves. Hades was stealing from her the precious moments she needed to locate and save Psyche. "We must go, please." She grasped Hades' hand, halting him from rushing off to some nymph that Hermes had raised his eyebrows at. "We have much to do and cannot dawdle about in your company, as much as we'd like to."

Hermes snorted, and she nudged him, giving him the *play-along* look, at which he sneered. "Yeah, Uncle, we're sorry."

Only when they approached the Diamond Gates did Hades speak up again. "I regret letting you hurry off so fast." He flicked his wrist, and the barriers opened, creaking as they parted. Before them were the mysterious, misty rivers, the foggy fumes surrounding the grounds, the aura of unknown, of occult. "Aside from Persephone, I have no family here. She doesn't enjoy my company as I enjoy hers."

A stab of guilt poked at Athena's insides as she studied Hades, his black tunic's hem swaying in a gentle breeze, his chin tipped to hide his quivering lip.

"We're grateful for your hospitality," she said, forcing the bulge in her throat to drop. "But I have a duty to my fellow Olympians, and *that* comes first."

Why is he so insistent? This is most unlike him.

As they passed the diamond-filled threshold, Hades sulked. Hermes sauntered towards where the boat would greet them, but Athena hesitated. A blast of heat came from her left, and she slowly turned to see Cerberus' three heads directed their way. Its yellow eyes wavered on Hades, and it sniffed the air, growling at the sight of her and Hermes. Its mouths were so large and its bodies so giant that its breath billowed all the way over from where it had been standing guard.

On instinct, Athena seized Hermes' hand. He made no foul comment, as he'd also twisted towards the three-headed beast, his fingers trembling between hers.

"Uncle?" they both said, fixing Hades, waiting for him to call his dogs off.

Hades, still as a statue, stared at his pet. He had to give the command for Cerberus to stand down, or put it asleep, to fool it. So...why did he delay?

One of the heads opened its massive mouth, showing a row of glistening and surprisingly white teeth.

Athena squeezed Hermes' hand. "Uncle Hades? Would you please let us exit?"

Hades seemed to float in a faraway land, his expression neutral, his eyes vacant. "Rethink this," he said, still focused on his beast.

"You could live here, both of you. My beloved niece, be of use to the family here! And you, nephew dearest…you need not station upstairs to perform your obligations!"

Cerberus took a thundering step towards them, the chains around its three necks rattling.

Athena's extremities numbed. She'd been in millions of battles, and yet the idea of fighting this giant, dog-like monster terrified her to the core. "Hades, be reasonable."

The Underworld guardian stormed a few more feet forward; the ground shook under their feet.

"Someone else may absorb your job as lead investigator." Hades batted his lashes. "This task hasn't made you happy, has it? All the stress…you've been through enough, no?"

Another step from Cerberus further rocked the ground, testing Athena and Hermes' balance. "Please—"

"—be one of the judges!" Hades' neutral lips swerved into a sick smirk. "Join Minos, Rhadamanthus, Aeacus. Help them sort the dead. They need aid, and who better than you?" His eyes were black like tar, like pits of doom, like endless wells of murky water. As if he hoped to hypnotize Athena; as if he was *someone else.*

Cerberus barked; a deafening roar that brought Athena and Hermes to their knees, their bags tumbling to their sides.

This was not *supposed to happen.*

Racked with convulsions, she gaped at her uncle's ebony hair swishing on either part of his strong jawline. That sinister smile, so foul, so frightening, ripped her heart to shreds. She'd defended him for centuries, she'd loved him. But was he, the King of the Underworld, the culprit? Had he drawn her here via Aphrodite, to distract her from finding Psyche, discovering the truth? Was he the voice controlling the poison in Eros, Psyche, and *his own wife?*

Athena sucked in a breath, and the muggy air, ripe with dread, burned the hairs in her nose. A slobber droplet splashed in front of her, reminding her of Cerberus' fangs and how close they now were. The creature towered behind Hades, its sets of nostrils flaring, two of its mouths open, its viscous tongues lolling out, thirsting for godly flesh.

Athena grabbed Hermes' arm and hauled him up, yanking him farther away. They kept low, crouched, submissive. Fearful for their immortality.

When she braved another glance at Hades, the evil she'd perceived swarming around him was gone. She saw fear in the whites of his eyes, in his faltering grin, in his weakening posture.

"Uncle?" She gulped. "You're afraid, yes? Of this culprit, of losing us, your family?"

He said nothing, but cringed, and the angst undulated over him like a blanket, cloaking him in uncertainty.

He's not our bad guy. He'd never harm Persephone, would let no one take Cerberus' blood without payment.

She let go of Hermes, realizing poor Hades was as wary as them all. No need to fear him.

With a hissed whisper, Hermes urged her not to move, but she strode up to Hades. She took one small step at a time, shuddering whenever Cerberus snarled. It remained looming over its master's shoulder, but it wouldn't attack her unless Hades ordered it; and he wanted her alive, didn't he?

She placed a palm on Hades' shoulder, doing her damndest to not crumble as the dog yapped, its slimy saliva drizzling on either side of her.

"Stop. This is madness. Hermes and I didn't eat your food, nor did we do anything to displease you. You cannot trap us here. We belong in the upper world. You're a righteous king, not an evil old man who needs to take prisoners because he is lonely."

Hermes popped up beside her, a shield in one hand—hers, she recognized it; he must have extracted it from their bags while she crept up to Hades. His teeth gritted as he spoke, "listen to her, Uncle. Be reasonable. Our place is in Olympus!"

"I…" Hades blinked, his cheeks twitched, and he recoiled from Athena's touch, as if she'd dug her nails into his shoulder and shocked him with her power. "What the…"

Skin drenched in cold sweat and curls sticking to her forehead, Athena teetered on her heels. "We'll visit more often, yes?"

Hermes scoffed. "We will?"

Hades peeped between them, as if waking from a nightmare and having no clue where he was, who they were. "I…no, no, I'm sorry."

He lifted his hands, and a golden thread escaped his fingertips, splitting into three, and sneaking into Cerberus' bodies. Cerberus froze, its mouths stuck as its groans evaporated.

Expression cold, but not unkind, Hades motioned towards the river. "Something got to me. I'm not sure what, but I'm normal again. It made me…hesitate. Something isn't right down here, Athena, Hermes…but to be safe, you must go. I will handle this."

Athena's eyes widened. "You…were you poisoned? When? How?"

Hades shrugged. "I don't know if it was poison. Something was in my head, yes…but I have no idea what, nor how. Never mind that right now; the spell I put on Cerberus won't last long." He waved dismissively at Athena's worrisome features. "I'm fine, I promise.

Temporary insanity caused by sadness. A bit too much alcohol. The air out here, near the rivers…it always brings back my senses."

Unconvinced, Athena attempted to press her palm to his forehead, to check his temperature. "Are you sure?"

Hades shoved her off. "Yes, now get out. You cannot wait for Charon, he's too far. Hermes," he snapped at the thief god, "I permit you to use your sandals, but don't make it a habit."

The three-headed beast's bodies pulsated, fighting the enchantment. So, despite her distress at Hades' eerie mood swings, Athena knew they had to hasten; their window of opportunity was minuscule. She wouldn't die by Cerberus' massive fangs.

Hermes kneeled and activated the white fluffs on the sides of his sandals. "Ready?"

Hades tugged them both into a brief embrace. "Good luck. And you, niece," he kept her in his arms a few extra moments, "you'll succeed. Uncover the plots. But remember, please," he drew his lips to her ear, "Hecate is our ally, not our enemy. She's innocent and may be of great use to us."

Hermes slid his arm around her middle, turning her rigid with disgust as he heaved them upward. "Thank you, Uncle," she said, unable to relax in Hermes' grasp.

"Fulfill your duties. I *do* expect a visit soon, is that clear?" Hades snorted. "No more stopping at the gates, Hermes, got it?" He walked backwards through the Diamond Gates, saluted them, and the fence sealed itself.

"Time to go," murmured Hermes, pulling Athena closer, his lips an inch from hers. "You won't enjoy this ride, but I will."

Athena fought the bile rising up her throat as he hoisted higher, the wings beneath them fluttering excitedly. One last glimpse at the insane realm she didn't understand, and off they went, zooming down the Acheron, soaring to the Underworld entrance.

||22. YOU FOOL||

PSYCHE

The agony shooting through Psyche's body had become her. She acknowledged it, like a minor side ache from running too fast, but didn't let it ruin her. The voice—that she had no doubt wasn't her—took over her consciousness. It commanded her every move, decided her actions, chose where to roam, and who to contaminate.

She had no choice, and on the outside, in her numb, isolated bubble, she accepted it. But deep within, beneath the horror and screaming and agony, she knew something was wrong.

It was something she couldn't fix. She could only obey.

The rainy weather subsided, leaving a few gray clouds overhead, and faint sunlight pierced through, nearly raising Psyche's spirits. She hadn't come across an inhabited farm for miles, and the voice inside wondered if she'd turned every villager into one of her militants.

So she hobbled on, her bare feet so sore she couldn't feel them. She no longer hissed at the pain, even when sharp rocks tore her skin or dirty water filtered into her bloody bruises. She passed a few abandoned buildings, old barns, empty forests…and paused.

A cabin stood alone, off in the distance. Shining like a beacon, in a spotlight, whispering at her to come closer. She sniffled, gauging the horizon, checking for inhabitants.

She concluded the home was vacant, but it didn't stop her from approaching.

"Relax. Regroup. Figure out our next spot. Conjure a map."

"Relax…"

"Rest, Psyche. Rest."

She smiled weakly as she plundered on, rejoicing at the idea of letting her muscles unwind. At the prospect of soaking her feet, drying her bones, closing her eyes. Would the voice turn off once she entered dreamland? Would her soul receive an ounce of soothing for an hour or two?

"Peace and quiet…"

The being inside cackled from somewhere in the confines of her brain, but she wouldn't let it spoil her hopes.

A yard from the building, she stilled. Footsteps echoed nearby. Or perhaps they were far, but the world was so tranquil she heard them, anyway. They were loud, pounding, fast. Running quicker and quicker…coming from behind her.

"Your imagination. Keep going."

"No…" With a bit of reserved strength—the less she challenged her demons, the more energy she conserved—she whirled around.

A girl ran towards her. A familiar girl, bouncing faster and faster, with no intention of stopping.

As her insides growled, Psyche realized this poor girl, eager and excited, was at risk if she came too close.

"Wait!" She cringed, her throat painful from speaking up. "Come no closer!" She raised an arm. "I'm…dangerous."

The girl froze, maybe ten feet away. "Psyche!" Her breaths were so loud, Psyche sensed them raising the hairs on her arms.

Her arm trembled the longer she worked to hold it up. "Who...are you? What do you want?"

She squinted at the girl. All her wandering had rendered her vision blurry, but the fog lifted now. This girl was no mere girl. She had to be in her late teens, early twenties. Fully formed in the bosom area, long caramel tresses framing a porcelain complexion, exuding a radiance Psyche winced at. A...*godly* radiance?

Could it be...someone from Olympus?

As Psyche studied her, the young woman dared a tiny stride forward. "Psyche?"

Psyche snarled—or the being inside did, at least—and stepped backward. "Halt! I warn you—"

"—but do you not recognize me?" The teenager's boots were brown, worn, covered in soot. She wore a tunic—a trait of ancient Greek civilization. The same cut, the same fabric as those sported by Olympians, Psyche could tell. It was peach-colored, torn in places, soiled in others, swaying back and forth to reveal bloody knees beneath it. Her figure was feminine, and similar to Psyche's. Hourglass shaped, voluptuous, inviting, but frail.

And that tone...melodious, sweet as honey.

Psyche's gaze zoomed in on the young woman's warm, hazel eyes. They swirled with positivity and kindness.

Recognition hit Psyche so hard she lost her balance and grabbed at the air for stabilization. "That's...you're...you're my..."

The voice's growl vibrated in her skull, gnarling, gnawing at the few non-fried neurons as if cutting them to pieces.

"She wants to draw you home...so leave her be!"

Its snarl was loaded with rage, disdain, disgust at whoever this young lady was.

"I should have known she would catch up."

"She?" Curiosity infused Psyche with a few more ounces of energy. She overpowered her internal monster and managed three steps forward. "Hedone? *Hedone?"* She croaked, fighting to spit out the words before the voice stopped her. "Daughter, dearest daughter, is that you?"

An invisible force shoved her backwards, and she fell to the ground with a violent thud.

"Not your daughter. A trap... a mirage. They want to block your progress. Don't let her, don't let them."

Psyche forced her neck up, keeping her gaze on her slowly approaching daughter.

"Mother?" The young woman's face lit up, as if the sun shone only on her. "I've been following you for weeks! Tracking you, baiting you." Her chest heaved up and down, her arms twitching at her sides. "Finally, I see you. *You."*

Psyche wanted to smile, to take her child in her embrace and squeeze; but she couldn't move. Her captor had slammed her to the ground, keeping her flattened against the pebbled path, banging her head onto the dampened concrete.

"You're protected, Psyche. I've got you."

Her fingertips dug into the muddy grass beside her. She couldn't get up, but she had to move away. With a push, she hauled herself back; inch by inch, distancing herself from her daughter, wary of harming her.

"Your body is enchanted, shielded from any tracking devices or powers. She's lying—or she's a witch."

"No," Psyche hissed through gritted teeth, "no, I smell her, she's my daughter—"

"—she diverted the spell. Broke you. Her scent ruined it. This explains so much."

Psyche forced her neck up again. "Explains…what?"

"Mother?" Hedone had gotten nearer. "Are you all right?"

Psyche held her palm up and shook her head. "Stop." She tipped her head back and glared at the sky. "*You,* beast in me—it explains what?"

Something crawled up her throat, causing her to gasp, hiccup, choke. And whatever it was fought its way out of her. Was it the poison? Had Hedone's presence expelled it at last?

"No," she said, but not in her own voice. It was *the* voice—the one inside that had now taken over her vocal chords. "It explains why you doubt me, *us,* our causes. Why you think I'm not you. Because I am. I'm everyone, Psyche." The tone was harsh, strained, morphed in ways that made Psyche's skin crawl; but she had no way to muffle it. "It explains why you don't recognize that." Her head lowered and her chin jutted at Hedone. "She messes with your mental balance! Prevents the scales from tipping to victory! She can't be here." An animalistic roar breached through her lips. "You must get rid of her."

Hedone lept away, but remained focused, not letting Psyche's captor frighten her. "No. Mother…you're ill." She blanched. "Whatever drove you to this…it's weakening, I can sense it! If it were strong, I wouldn't have found you. I wouldn't be here. The barrier…it is lowering, your madness is fading!" Flinching, she extended her hand, her fingertips so close, coated in ambrosia and amber, enticing as ever. "Let me help you. Let's control it before it consumes you!"

Psyche screamed; a deafening, earthquake-inducing screech that she had no means to prevent. *She* was on the inside now, begging, pleading.

Not her, not her! Don't hurt my daughter!

Her eyes watered and tears streamed down her cheeks as she attempted to speak for herself. "I...can't..."

Please...please...

Hedone's warmth was close, so close. "I can help. Get you home, safe. We'll bar this insanity from ever commanding you again. From provoking you into doing these unspeakable horrors." Her filed and dirt-ridden nails were millimeters away. Psyche squirmed, ready to be whisked off to Olympus. "Take my hand, Mother. I'll rescue you."

The voice retreated to its shell—Psyche's brain—but its intensity didn't lessen.

"Go with her and you'll regret it, you fool."

Another yelp slithered from her half-closed mouth, its sudden force thrusting Hedone backwards and onto her knees. Bursts of wind swirled up and around Psyche like tornadoes, surrounding the two goddesses like a bubble of wrath.

"No more bullying," bellowed Psyche. "You," she clenched her teeth, "will not," she tightened her fists, "call me," she held her breath, "a fool." She rose to her feet, pushing the breezes aside as if they were lightweight curtains.

Hedone braced for the whipping gusts and reached out once more. Psyche took her palm, which created an electric shock to rush through her. It weaved around her arms, wrapped around her veins, tightened every organ—and wrenched her upwards, floating feet from the ground.

Hedone's body flew also, and together they hovered for a moment, before being ripped apart. Their bodies dashed in opposite directions, like a zap of energy separating them. A crack of thunder, a flash of lightning.

Landing at the end of the field, Hedone struck her head on a wooden pole; Psyche banged into the facade of the cabin she'd been aiming to visit.

Woozy, she tried to stand, to hurry to her child, encourage her to go; but the voice, that damned voice, it wasn't subdued. Ever-present and powerful, it rumbled, rummaging through her intestines, twisting them.

"I lowered my guard, I gave you a chance to retreat. Permitted you a moment of control. You disappointed me. I warned you, you fool. You immense, mortal-born idiot."

It was worse than before. Croaking, gravelly, evil. So strong it misted over Psyche's eyes and sped up her heartbeats.

"You will ignore Hedone. Do as I say. No resting. I'm angry."

Whatever strength Psyche had mustered moments before had vanished. The being within had won, gluing her lips to prevent her from complaining.

"You'll pay. But for now, you march. We have more stops. I sense humans nearby."

A renewed vitality brewed in her belly, but she disliked it. It was foreign and fragmented, its sharp edges slicing at the insides of her stomach. It screamed.

Stolen energy; *Hedone's* energy.

"Yes…your daughter's essence. It doesn't belong, so it hurts. One touch was enough to steal it."

Psyche wriggled about, as if an invisible rope bound her to the spot. She fought it, but it was no use; she elevated above ground again and abandoned her ailing daughter. The girls' pleas plowed into

Psyche's heart, but the overpowered voice directed her as far as possible from her only salvation.

‖ 23. RESCUE ‖
ATHENA

The flight to the Acherusian Lake was painless, and yet Athena was more than relieved when Hermes released her at the staircase leading up through Lake Avernus.

He made the swirling motion with his finger, and the watery ceiling parted, forming a passage out of the Underworld, and back to earth.

Athena sighed once she set foot on the muddy banks of the lake, and warm sunlight bathed her, bringing her to life.

"I suppose that'll teach us to better enjoy our time in the sun, won't it?" Hermes watched the water slither over the opening once more, burying the entrance. He turned to Athena, concern sketching over his face. "This is where we part ways, sister dearest. I can't apprehend Psyche with you." His eyes gleamed, and his lips tugged downward, for a change.

Athena fought not to jump for joy—his presence had been far too intoxicating for her taste. "Fine. Inform Father of what we found out and have him ready more cells in the dungeon. I expect Psyche will be hostile and difficult to deal with until we cure her."

Hermes bowed, and as he rotated to walk away, he glanced at Athena once more. "You'll keep this entrance a secret, yes?" He tucked a few stray hairs behind his ears. "And all the other secrets you discovered in the past twenty-four hours?"

She would have guffawed at his sudden sweetness, his shyness, as the sun beamed down on him, giving him an angelic, innocent air. "We had a deal," she said, waving him off. "You keep mine, I keep yours."

Snapping his fingers, he produced a bag out of thin air. From within it, he extracted a vial and tossed it at her. "Here," he said, as she caught it. A bottle of clear but thick, slushy liquid. "Pure ambrosia, undiluted. You'll need it."

Before she could thank him, he disappeared in a cloud of sparkling yellow smoke. "Oh, Hermes." She slid the vial into her satchel of weapons and gear that she prayed she wouldn't have to use today.

Squinting, she imagined the location Thanatos had given her. The southern French countrysides, fields of lavender, crops, rickety cabins surrounded by lush trees.

Her feet lifted, her body trembled, and with a *pop* she was off.

She landed in the heart of a vibrant, humid forest. Almost immediately, she detected the familiar coppery stench of blood. And a horrific stink of death.

"Oh no," she peered around, neck muscles tensing, "am I too late?" She gaped at the bushes and trees surrounding her, locating a muddy pathway between them.

She scampered over to it, crouched low, and moved through, ears on alert. After a dozen paces, she came across an animal carcass—what might have once been a deer. Flies buzzed about its rotting bones, and a trail of blood drizzled from it, leading her farther down the dirt passage. It was worse than she'd thought—only an intoxicated monster would leave such remains behind to rot.

With every inch she patrolled, more scents gathered in her nostrils. Those of sweat and confusion, mingling and creating acid on her tongue. Anger, pungent and deadly. And another scent; a refined, near godly ambiance that never diluted, despite the poison infecting the atmosphere. *Immortality*—syrupy nectar and velvet perfection. But mixed with the acidity, the death, this usually pleasing aroma made Athena gag.

Psyche was here.

Athena retrieved her helm from her bag and set it atop her head. One inhale, one exhale, and she took off down the trail. Her limbs moved at inhuman speed, swifter than a cheetah, coursing onward like an eagle zoning in on its prey. Here and there she slowed to sniff out more carcasses, all abandoned and decaying. Rabbits, foxes, even skunks; they'd been licked clean but for a few morsels remaining to stink up the forest.

She also unearthed an ominous trace of mortality in the air, cloaked in toxins and panic. *That* smell prompted her to stop and look—and she gasped.

There they were, amidst the foliage, like sulking shadows in the woods—wandering, blabbering, shrouded in mud and blood.

Humans.

They marched on like corpses, colliding into one another, no purpose, no destination. They mumbled, but their words made no sense.

"Zombies...so, Thanatos was right." She stared at the lifeless, hungry beings, yearning for raw animal meat.

Psyche did this? Who would order her to create these monsters?

Ignoring the disgust unfurling in her gut, Athena traveled past the walking corpses, following the godly scent as it grew denser; so astringent it masked the odor of deterioration.

Soon she came upon a large, grassy field. A small cabin loitered at the end, across from the woods where she arrived.

The godliness ended there, replaced with an eerie static, a stifling electricity that had nothing to do with the electric poles surrounding the area.

Athena's skin coated with ice, and she shivered. She'd never forget that sensation—the terrifying aftermath of war. The frigidity that lingered after a battle between deities.

Had someone else been here? Someone who'd fought with Psyche?

What does this mean? What happened?

A tiny voice, mellow, muted, came from her left. "Athena?"

Athena jolted to it, and found a body propped up against a pole, shriveled, suffering. That caramel hair and those sharp hazel eyes and that peachy tunic—no matter how dirty—were unmistakable.

Athena rushed to the girl's side. "Hedone?" Fear whizzed to life in her rib-cage as she collapsed to her knees, helping the young goddess sit up. "How…what are you doing here? Where is your mother? Have you seen her?"

Wincing, Hedone planted her feet. "She…" Her legs wobbled as she heaved up, and she toppled into Athena, who caught and stabilized her. "She is not herself." She leaned into the pole and let out heavy breaths.

Pressing a hand to Hedone's forehead, Athena groaned. Her immortality had drained, and in a considerable amount. "What happened? You are weak, my friend." She thought of the ambrosia in her satchel, but hesitated; she wouldn't have enough for Hedone and Psyche, and the latter was her priority.

"I've…been following Mother…for weeks," said Hedone, teeth grinding as she stretched an arm out, revealing red blotches and violet bruises along her skin. "Our collision left me a bit on the mortal side."

"Collision? And are you…" Athena tipped backwards, as if the air itself might contaminate her, "poisoned? Like her?"

Hedone's eyebrows scrunched. "Poisoned? No, of course not. What are you talking about? I—"

Athena grabbed the girl's face between her hands. "Did you cause all this?" She jammed their noses together. "Did you provoke your mother and all this disgusting insanity?"

"Athena!" Hedone ripped from her grip, but not without cringing. "What is this?" She brushed off her tunic, but couldn't remove the dirt, grass, and bloodstains. Her brown riding boots had come apart at the soles, and bruises marked her lower limbs, punctuated with deep, oozing gashes. "I'm sane. Wounded, sure, but not infected. If Mother is sick…well, whatever she's got, I didn't get it. Thank Zeus."

Athena relaxed, but her heart hammered in her chest; something was off. "So she's not herself, you say?"

"She's nuts." Hedone snorted, and a bit of blue ichor—godly blood—dribbled out of her nostrils. She wiped it and tried to stand up straight. "I've been tracking her since…well, since she slipped out of Olympus. She ate something odd, I saw it. No clue what it was, though. She had an adverse reaction to whatever it was and didn't seem normal when she went to bed that night. So I watched her, and I was right to do so. It keeps getting worse."

A glacial shiver undulated up Athena's spine. "Have you

spoken to her?"

Hedone shrugged. "Not until a few hours ago. I didn't want her to see me. She freaked me out. Puffs of toxic clouds were all around her...it was so eerie. A maddened goddess on the loose, spreading a bizarre disease that prompted humans to eat animals *off the bone,* just like that?" She convulsed. "Getting close to *that* would have killed me. So I lingered...but Mother isn't the only one who has lost her mind, no?"

"She isn't?" Athena cocked her head.

"I viewed things on that entertainment box that mortals use...the television?" Athena nodded, and Hedone flinched. "Bloody stuff. Someone rampaging across America. They said the case was solved, but I don't believe it. Was that Mother, too? Is she duplicating herself?"

Biting her lip, unwilling to cause Hedone any more distress, Athena lowered her chin. "No...though it is possibly a strain of the same virus Psyche ails from. I'm unsure how you witnessed it. Apollo and Artemis and Zeus were supposed to cover it up."

"Wait." Hedone narrowed her gaze and her eyes glowed gold. "Cannibalism, blood, hearts..." She stilled, stiffening as if struck by lightning. "Oh, please, no. Don't tell me—"

"—Eros, yes." Athena's soul hurt to see Hedone's courage evaporate, her frame vibrating as she dropped to her knees. "I'm sorry, but your parents were both poisoned. *He* is detained, thank Olympus, in the dungeons. But your mother..."

"My parents are lunatics!" Hedone pounded her fists onto the ground, reopening scars that had started to heal. "Poison. I thought I smelled something eerie on Mother, but Father, too?"

"It's true, but I'm here to—"

"—she's on the brink." Hedone seized Athena's wrists and dragged her to her level. "She's spinning out of control, and I tried to stop her, but…"

"But what?" Athena tumbled beside her. "Tell me. I need to find her. All of Olympus and mankind are in danger if I don't."

With a trembling arm, Hedone pointed to the middle of the field. "Did you feel that energy?"

"Battle remains…yes." Athena redressed herself and took hold of Hedone's shoulders. "Did she attack you? Is that why you're so frail?"

Hedone recoiled. "Our energies…collided. The moment I attempted to touch her, take her away, teleport…we were thrust apart. Thrown in different directions. Something disturbed her aura, and then she disappeared. That something…it protects her. Like an enchantment cloaking her, making her nearly impossible to track."

"Good and evil clashing." Athena massaged her temples. "The venom forced her to forsake you and move on. Hurt more animals, turn more humans. Zombies…" She spun to the field. "That residue is powerful. It's what drew me here; that godly energy permeating the air. She stains everything she touches."

Every strand of toxic immortal power polluted the atmosphere and the vile odor flicked on a light-bulb in Athena's brain.

Stains everything she touches…

"This residue…it follows her. It *is* her. So with it, I can find her." Athena used her fingertips to manipulate the oxygen particles. As she did, a scene took form before her. Shadows composed of wisps of air, glittering purple, playing out what had happened between Psyche and Hedone. Then showing Psyche's trajectory— her landing across the way, against the cabin, then getting up to wander into a continuation of the forest on the other side.

"How are you doing that?" Hedone stood and hobbled over, watching the scintillated oxygen, in awe at the replay of what had occurred.

"Artemis taught me to follow scents," said Athena, daring a few steps into the misty air, intent on following Psyche's trail. "I'd forgotten about it. It's meant to help her locate prey she wounded and that escaped. Granted, I'm not as good a huntress as she is, but this'll work."

Hedone leaned against Athena, struggling to breathe. "Go, then. Go after her."

Athena snatched her hand. "You're coming with me." Hedone had no opportunity to protest, as Athena *whooshed* into motion, whipping through the field, past the cabin, on the hunt for Psyche.

When the scent stopped, Athena halted, and Hedone sank beside her, about to faint. Few were able to tolerate Athena's ease with running with such speed.

"Here."

They'd arrived at another clearance, another meadow, this one sprinkled with lush lavender and purple tulips. At the center, a woman draped in a soiled gown paced back and forth.

Athena kneeled next to Hedone, focusing on the figure ahead. She stormed, rambling incessantly as her feet smashed into the flowers. Golden blonde tresses floated behind her as she stomped, stomped, *stomped;* and for a second Athena glimpsed her face.

Psyche!

The poor goddess flailed about, arguing with herself. "No, you cannot make me! Not anymore!" Her gown was ripped, tainted with crimson and dirt and grass. "Stop! Stop this!" She clawed at her cheeks and pulled at her hair.

Hedone crawled backwards, terror in her eyes. "I can't…*we* can't get any closer."

Athena grimaced. "I didn't come all this way to let Psyche's madness stop me. I will get closer, and I will succeed."

It was the confidence Athena had lacked, the push she'd been desperate for. On a whim—with Hermes' sickeningly seductive voice echoing in her mind—she pulled out the vial of pure ambrosia. One glance at it and she understood why he gave it to her—not for Psyche, but for *her*.

That shield of magic around Psyche…I can't break it with my regular powers.

He'd been aware she'd need to amplify her strength, harden her abilities, become powerful enough to jam through the enchanted barrier circling the slurring, tipsy Psyche.

Athena uncorked the bottle and unleashed its contents into her mouth. A surge of vitality warped up her limbs, wrapped around her organs, pumped into her veins, filling every cavity in her body. She couldn't see it, but she sensed the glow growing around her silhouette, the pulsating shock-waves rippling over her skin, infusing her. The strength—delicious, delivering, titillating her in ways she'd long forgotten about.

Athena, goddess of war, had returned, after centuries of being confined in a tiny portion of her brain.

As if summoning another piece of her personality, as if shifting into her true self, Athena sucked in a deep breath as her outer transformation continued. Her helmet formed over her curls, and she adjusted it. Then she secured her satchel and lowered into a stance of preparation. Grabbing Hedone's arm, she concentrated on Psyche's footsteps.

"Athena—"

"—hush. I'm going to take hold of her, and we'll teleport. Brace yourself."

Not giving herself any room to hesitate, to wonder if she'd fail, Athena puffed out a breath, peeped at the sky, prayed for luck—and dashed up to Psyche.

The savage and intoxicated goddess pivoted in time for Athena to bump into her and knock her to the ground. The poisoned goddess screeched, but the deafening noise did nothing to mess with Athena's victory streak. She encircled Psyche's wrist, dug her fingernails into her clammy skin, and fought off the bursts of venom trying to break her, weaken her.

Gritting her teeth, Athena pictured Olympus in her mind.

Home, get us home.

Everything swirled, images jumbled together, landscapes melted. The three goddesses shot into the sky, vanishing in fumes of peach, lilac, and blue.

||24. I HEAR HER HEART||
EROS

I'm okay. I'm okay.

Eros gaped at the cell's stone ceiling, his breaths regulating with difficulty. There had to be a cure; a way to end all his internal struggles.

He found solace in the silence, away from heartbeats that triggered him and the demons that once dominated his mind. From the horror that convinced him those troubling thoughts were his own.

He prayed Zeus had it all under control; that he'd locate a specialist, someone with knowledge to extract the poison, permanently. And that that specialist would be able to do the same for Psyche—if anyone ever found her.

Trust Athena...the goddess of wisdom will deliver my wife...and my daughter.

Every crack in the old plaster reminded him of his flaws. Were *they* the reason he was infected? Had he asked for all this?

His wife, so perfect and pretty, a pleasing deity that never disobeyed...who would want to harm her? What terrifying creature would seek to torture their souls, wreak havoc in the world? Who would want to use them to weaken and disarm Olympians?

I transformed soulmates into cannibals...watched as they

feasted on one another…

Why would anyone wish for that?

He squeezed his eyes shut, willing the fleshy flashes away. Far away. He thought of positive moments, determined to keep the demons at bay.

A low pounding interrupted his attempts at remaining calm. He used his elbows to lean up, to glare towards the dungeon entrance.

Footsteps?

The sound was rhythmic, familiar. Curious. Less of a stomp and more of a *thump*.

"Oh…" He sat up completely. "No, not footsteps."

The rhythm was too steady, too consistent, each beat close together.

"It's a heartbeat."

The thumps turned erratic, pumping, loud. Frantic, fearful. He crossed his legs and pressed his palms to his temples. Focusing, he analyzed the sounds, seeking to recognize them.

The heart's owner revealed to him, its depiction blurry at first, then the curtain obscuring their features unleashed like a bright, blisteringly hot sun.

His eyelids parted and he stared at the darkness behind the bars. Each pulsation intensified, drawing close, close, *closer*. So blaring it generated a migraine. And yet…he smiled. He knew that heart and would never mistake it for anyone else's.

"Psyche?"

As if responding to him, it sped up—then stopped. As he held his breath, it started up again, but with a deadly tempo to its pattern. Feeble, sick.

"Psyche? My love?" It thumped too quickly to be normal. It

became uneven, frightening him so much his belly ached. "What is wrong with your heart, dear? *Where are you?*"

The harder it thrummed, the more pangs he sensed in his chest, as if a fist wrapped around his own heart and compressed the life from it.

"Are you ill?"

He slipped off the bed like liquid spilling from a glass. Slamming onto his knees, hands over his ears, he cringed. The pulses turned so excruciating he moaned out in agony.

"Zeus...*Zeus!*"

The beats approached him. He smelled her—the delicate, powdery substance that coated her cheeks, the cherry-scented plumpness of her lips, the pleasurable toxicity of her floral perfume. She was *there.*

But how was he hearing her? Zeus had enforced the enclosure; he shouldn't have sensed Psyche at all. Yet he was forced to bear witness as her life-force drained. As she died. Was it some sick joke from the poison that still kept him captive? Somehow enabling him to know the exact moment his wife perished, by giving him long-needed access to her heartbeats—but too late to help her?

The pounding continued its irregular song, sending him into a panicked frenzy. Had Athena found her? Or was her dying heart calling out to him? Transcending all magic for a final goodbye?

His breaths were choppy, and he choked for air. "Psyche...my love...what is happening?"

The cell's walls seemed to cave in on him, as if the spell on the facade wanted to eat him. Her heart was so soft, so weak, so contaminated...yet it beat, on and on, refusing to let go.

Was there a message in those uneven thrums? A secret note to divulge her location to him? He winced, ignoring his dizziness as he listened, desperate to decipher a pattern, coordinates, a code.

Something bubbled in his gut, disrupting his frail focus. "No…" The bloodthirsty anger yelped for attention; the hunger for murder woke.

He growled and pounded his fists to the ground, rattling the surface in his fury.

"Not now, *not now!*" His knuckles melted into the concrete. "I need my wits, no rage, *no rage!*" Tears swelled in his eyes. "She needs me! I must be lucid for her!"

Thump, thump. THUMP, THUMP.

His blood thickened, transforming his fear to outrage. Swirling around his organs like a tornado. Taking his love for Psyche and crunching it into a ball, shoving it to the bottom of his abdomen.

Not now. NOT NOW!

Despite his reanimating fury, the beats continued like a drum declaring a battle. Psyche was in peril; yet he had no means to aid her, as he approached his own version of danger.

He didn't want that danger. "I…am…Eros." He panted, imagining himself ripping his torso apart, discarding the infected flesh that rendered him savage and sinful. "Not…*you.* Not…the creature…"

I want to find my wife!

His temples seared with pain, every extremity became limp, and he seized. Wriggling about on the ground, he battled the bubbling irritation, praying to erase it. No more visions of shredding through muscle and snapping veins. Enough with the fangs and the coppery taste on his tongue.

"I can't!"

Adamant on zipping his evil alter ego into a deeper part of himself, he heaved up to his feet. He reached for the bars, drool drizzling from his drooping mouth as he warred with the monster that tried to tear out.

Psyche was the trigger, yet he had to hear her pulse until the last moment.

"Zeus." His throat was on fire, but he cleared it and groaned. "Zeus. Hey, *Zeus!*" He laughed—or perhaps *it* laughed, he couldn't tell. "Zeus, help!"

A ringing roared into his ears.

"You can do better…especially if you wish to trick him into letting you out."

Hadn't he sealed that thing up? "No…" He rattled the metal. "No, I don't want to. Zeus! I need you, now! You told me to yell for you, so I'm yelling!"

The ringing amplified, burning his eardrums.

"She's wounded. She's close. So get out, Eros. Take her and resume your goal. Regain your strength."

Electricity spiraled down his biceps, tiptoeing to his wrists, weaving around his fingertips. "No…stop." He refused to let his inner self take control, so he slammed into the cage, to knock himself out and no longer have to deal with the enemy within. "Zeus! The bad me is back! Please!" His voice had softened, quiet as a midnight meadow, tiny as a particle of oxygen.

"Use the fury I give you. Build your power. Escape!"

His legs gave out and he collapsed, wailing as the pain went from excruciating to unbearable. "No, no! You lie! Killing humans doesn't make me strong! It doesn't bring me closer…to her!" Salty liquid poured down his cheeks, some of it sneaking into his mouth.

"Giving in solves nothing! I am the god of *love!* Not violence! I'm no match for these enchantments!"

He fell backwards and chuckled.

"No, you're no match for me."

"You?" He sniffled, wishing to sit up, but his body glued to the ground. "Who are you?"

The inner voice didn't miss a beat.

"Your true self. You can't contain me, no matter what they make you drink. There is no cure."

The icy surface below him calmed his turbulent headache but didn't stop the creature's communication.

"You're meant to make humans mad, Eros. Drive them to eat hearts, to be wary. To blame…the gods."

"You're disgusting!"

"I'm YOU, Eros. The sooner you accept it, the sooner you'll reunite with Psyche."

A new wrath awoke in him. But not the creature's; it came from *him,* his heart, his angst, and provoked by the being inside. "Not my Psyche. You won't hurt her. Won't hurt us."

He kicked his feet, hoping to stand; but the beast that controlled his mind now controlled his limbs.

"She's dying! Intoxicated, insane. We'll both die!" He pressed both palms to the floor and pushed; but to no avail. "I won't listen to you!"

He kicked and kicked, berserk, squealing, yearning for freedom. But the pounding resonated in his mind.

No…*in the cage.* Out loud. It was healthy, alive. Weakened, but steady. Not poisoned…but anxious. And it wasn't the monster in his mind.

Who is that?

He had no trouble understanding it was a heartbeat this time.

Intrigued, the being within allowed him to sit up and twist towards the bars. One sniff, two sniffs, three…and he figured it out. A pleasurable cadence, a whiff of sweetness—it was Hedone.

"Daughter? Is that…you?" His spine stiffened. "Have you found Psyche? You are together? You're bringing her to me?"

The irregular heartbeat from earlier and this new one were interlaced, forming a third thumping, and getting closer by the second.

Somehow, he crawled to the bars, though his arms and calves were sore. A distant grumble echoed in his brain, but he silenced it. It became fragile with the approach of the heartbeats. "Zeus? Zeus, help!"

The third thumping he heard wasn't the mix of the first two; it was another altogether. This one was powerful, wise, mature.

"Athena?" He melted against the bars. "She found them?"

He slumped backwards and cackled. The noises—all the heartbeats, the commotion, the tension—reverberated around him.

"Yes, Athena. She'll open the cage, let us out. The mission…can resume."

His conscience teetered between rising ferocity and hopeless panic. He rolled onto his stomach, rocking back and forth as he held his head.

If Zeus didn't show up fast, before the rage overflowed, he was done for.

||25. LOCKED UP||
ATHENA

Clutching Psyche's wrist in one hand, Hedone's arm in the other, Athena landed, sandals pressing to the marble floors of the Olympus Palace. She wobbled, but the women on either side of her helped stabilize her limbs.

By some miracle, Psyche had stopped fighting her grasp halfway through the trip, but she squeaked, muttering under her breath. "No…not here, *not here—*"

Skin coating in sweat, Hedone peered at her. "Athena…is she all right?"

"No." The toxin stench resided in Athena's nostrils, bringing bile to her mouth. They'd luckily arrived in the corridor containing the prison entrance, but she worried they were running out of time. "It's overflowing, drowning her organs." She released Hedone but kept her close—there was no proof she hadn't inhaled some of the hazy poison herself. "Help me get her to the dungeons."

A young girl carrying an empty silver tray rounded the corner and nearly fell over at the sight of them. "Highness?" She redressed herself, but the tremble in her tone showed she wouldn't be of much use. "Do you need—"

"—Zeus." Athena jutted her chin at the girl. "Fetch him. And

Apollo and Ares. Have them meet me in the dungeons at once."

The young and frightened cup-bearer bowed and scampered off.

Whirling on her heels, Athena thanked Zeus for temporarily lifting the rules about teleporting into the palace and sought after the portrait hiding the entrance—the painting of Zeus, holding a lightning bolt, about to send it thrashing through a cloud. Once she spotted it, she scaled the ivory walls to reach it, and dragged the writhing Psyche with her, Hedone following.

With a deep inhale, she touched the dusty surface of the canvas, and a faint *click* signified she'd triggered the system. The picture pried itself from the wall, opening to the dingy, dim stairway.

Hedone peeked in, awed. "I never knew…"

Athena pressed a fingertip to the girl's mouth. "And you'll never tell a soul, understood?" Hedone nodded. "Hurry; it's a long road down, and we have to lock her up before the venom consumes her…and us."

Once the door closed behind them, Psyche grew surprisingly quiet, as if unconscious.

Hedone grabbed a torch and lit the way. "Is Father down there?"

"Yes." Athena took a few steps, and Psyche moaned, but didn't resist.

Unfortunately, her zombified state didn't last. After a few flights, her muscles contracted, and she refused to move. "Stop," she groaned, her voice a low, demonic growl that made Athena's hairs stick up. "They…want to help me…you cruel thing. You torturing creature—"

Something is talking inside her mind.

"Hold her," said Athena, urging Hedone to assist her.

The girl obeyed and tugged Psyche to her. But Psyche hissed

and snapped her teeth at Athena. *"Let go of me you wench!"*

"Whoa." Hedone shuddered, almost falling as she tried to restrain her mother.

"It's the poison," said Athena, taking the torch from Hedone, in fear that she'd drop it and set them all aflame.

Hedone gulped. "It talks to her, in her head. I saw it happening before our confrontation."

"That makes sense." Athena pursed her lips as they attempted a few more paces downwards. "But you should have told me sooner."

Why would she hide that?

Wariness woke in Athena. Why had Hedone trailed Psyche for so long but only approached her today?

"But they saved us." Psyche's melodious tone broke Athena's thoughts. "So stop. Stop this! Your plot…against the gods…the gods are good!" She teetered to the right, then to the left, jamming Athena into the stone walls and almost tripping Hedone.

Too many times Athena's grasp on the torch loosened. Hedone seethed, troubling to keep hold of her mother.

Psyche interjected every few strides, never making sense. "No…the gods are wretched, wretched fools!" Her timbre turned sharp, obscure, unlike herself. "Disgusting bags of dung, all of them! Embarrassing filth!"

Busy fighting to focus on the steps and not stumble, Athena's grip slackened, and Psyche rounded on Hedone, yapping at her like a rabid dog.

"And that one, a disgrace of a daughter! No offspring!"

Will we make it down there before she eats us whole?

"It's worsening," said Hedone, shrinking.

But the poisoned goddess' next words were for Athena. She

rammed into her, drooling, her gaze vacant. "You daft, dimwitted, daughter of a titaness whore." There was such certainty, such a regal allure to her speech, it shocked Athena into silence. "Shame, shame on you. Release me, I must finish what I started. Proceed with my apocalyptic scenarios so I may dispose of you. All of you. You power-hungry, human-loving monsters. It was not meant to be like this, it was not—" She shook, twitching like a madwoman, warring with herself.

Taking advantage of her distraction, Athena managed to tighten her grip again, and hurried downward.

When at last they reached the bottom, Athena kicked the door open and hastened in. She set the torch in its spot, and on instinct, her gaze searched for Eros.

He was huddled, rocking back and forth, muttering to himself. Crying.

"Dad?" Hedone freed Psyche and stumbled forward.

Eros' neck snapped up, and he noticed them. He paid no heed to Hedone but zoomed on Psyche with a smile. "My love." His eyes darkened, like black marbles, shiny and obscure and dangerous. He lowered his head and resumed his rocking.

Athena cocked an eyebrow.

I deliver his wife, and that's his reaction?

With a wave of her hand, she illuminated the darkness to the right of his cage. As she'd requested, another cell awaited, and she waved again to open it and stuff the goddess inside.

"Here you go," she said, snapping to seal the doors and keep the crazed deity from escaping.

Psyche took two strides inside then flipped around, banging into the bars. "You will let me out, you virginal waste of immortal blood!"

An urge to spit onto Psyche's pallid complexion took over Athena—such low, ill-thought insults irked her. But she refrained; it would do no good.

"I will not, and that tone will get you nowhere. You're locked up for your own safety, Psyche!"

And for everyone else's.

That poison, and whoever used it to control gods, was potent.

"But I'm not Psyche, you idiot. I'm—" Psyche moaned, cutting herself off at the opportune moment. "No, not happening!"

Hedone meandered up to Eros' cage. "They're the same. He's talking to himself, too. We won't get anything out of them until they're cured." Sadness swelled in her eyes and her cheeks turned a rosy pink. "Which one is worse off? Mother, causing animal deaths and creating zombies? Or Father…cursing humans to eat hearts? What is the link between the two?"

"Hard to say." Athena snuck behind Hedone and flicked on the lanterns on the other side of Eros' enclosure. One more cage awaited, and she unlocked its metallic door before seizing Hedone's upper arm.

"Hey!" Hedone fought her, but it was no use; she was still weakened from her confrontation with Psyche.

Athena used that to her advantage and tossed the girl into the third cage, latching it before she could crash out. "I'm sorry, Hedone."

"*Let me out.*" Hedone crammed her nose into the bars. "Why?"

"Because you're not safe either. Until I'm positive you aren't intoxicated like your mother…this is for the best." Athena backed away, staring at the small family, unease unfurling in her gut.

Psyche's frantic curse-hurling stopped as she twisted to notice her husband next door. She watched him for a moment, then collapsed. "No, stop it!" She crawled backwards and huddled against the farthest wall.

Eros' head was still buried in his hands. "Hedone isn't sick," he said, his voice lucid, calm. Normal. "Her heart is wounded, but she's not mad. Only a weak goddess. A weak offspring."

Hedone turned to him, her jaw dropping. "Father?"

"But Psyche," he cackled, lifting his chin, revealing a smirk from the depths of hell, "oh, she's psycho. Ha! That was funny!" His bone-chilling laughter stilled Athena, twisted her stomach into knots. "*Psycho Psyche!* Psycho poisonous Psyche! Do you like it?" He threw his head back and chortled louder.

Athena couldn't move.

He's insulting his wife?

"What is wrong with you?" Hedone tapped on the bars between her enclosure and Eros', seeking his attention. "Mother was missing…now she's here, and you call her names? And what's this about you turning your charges into cannibals? What kind of sick crap did you two ingest?"

Between erratic sobs, Psyche gasped for air. "Help!"

"*Help, help!*" said Eros, morphing his tone to mock Psyche. He glanced at Hedone. "Devouring soulmate's hearts. It's specific, you fool. I did it to anger the gods, get attention, and frustrate humans. To lead me to Psyche. And look! I was correct! She's here." His gaze was glossy, focused on Hedone, though he didn't seem to *see* her, as if he stared right through her. "But we have work to do, so you and that pompous wisdom fraud of a goddess need to let us go."

An orange glow drew around Hedone's figure. "You will not speak like that, whoever the heck you are. *Get out of my father!*"

Eros ignored her, slowly shifting his view to Athena. "Oh, hello." He licked his lips. "*Wisdom bitch.* Remember me? I fantasized over ripping your heart out."

Athena grunted. "Do not lug me into this." Tiptoeing backwards, she reached behind her for the door.

Eros never wavered, studying her movements, his nostrils flaring. "You're all useless." He snorted. "Psycho Psyche knows it too, that's why she's lost herself. Preferred to wander instead of staying here. This palace is the real poison. Her disappearance pushed me to this rampage, and I'm glad it did. The gods…Olympus…it's not our true cause. You have tarnished our genuine reputation." Fire flickered in his voice as he stood up, glowering at Athena, striding forward.

"What nonsense is this?" Hedone again knocked on the bars, and Eros twitched as he flipped his lower body in her direction but maintained a firm gaze on Athena. "Fight it, Father. Push this thing down. You're the god of love…so fight it with love! Remember your good days with Mother, with me. Your accomplishments."

She's trying, I'll give her that.

Eros' neck muscles tensed. "I don't want to be the god of love. I want to be the god of hate, like my father. He'll die, though. You'll all die. To restart the process, to cleanse the immortals, my parents must die. And you, Athena. Psyche will help, since she and I…are one and the same." He completely twirled to Hedone, cracking his knuckles.

Hedone skidded away, eyes wide in worry. "What?"

"Kill, *kill*, we must kill everyone," echoed Psyche, still folded in two on the other side, torn between howling in agreement and yelping for help.

Eros flung a thumb behind him, at Psyche. "I feel the poison in her. It's the same that flows within me. We want the same things—"

"—*kill, kill!*" Psyche's hands banged on the concrete. The ground shook beneath her, as if her touch caused earthquakes.

"What she said." Eros whooshed closer to Hedone's cage. "We want to kill the gods."

Panicked, poor Hedone flattened against the opposing wall. "Father, stop!"

Eros chortled, Psyche squirmed and squealed, and Hedone burst into tears.

What sort of mad-house is this?

As her back collided with the dungeon door, Athena's heart quit beating. Eros and Psyche's cages scintillated, the bars shivering, the magic fizzling out, fading. "Oh, no."

Athena never cursed, and less so in the human's preferred tongue. But here, only one expression came to mind.

"*Fuck!* Zeus, where the fuck are you?"

Like a flower waning, the barriers of both enclosures dwindled, losing their potency. If the spell broke, Eros and Psyche would break out, their joint toxicity destroying all of Olympus. Despite the pure ambrosia fluttering through Athena's veins…she couldn't stop them.

For the first time in many, many years—similar to hours ago, with Cerberus—she feared for her immortal life, her soul.

She pushed into the door, twisted the knob as dread spread into her abdomen—

And froze.

The door wouldn't budge, locked from the outside. Someone had sealed her in with two deadly gods and their sobbing, useless daughter.

||26. GLORIOUS||
PSYCHE

"Your husband is right, Psyche."

Psyche covered her ears and rocked back and forth, similar to how Eros had only moments before. The concrete floor was cold and hard under her, and she missed the muddy grass she'd so often wandered on.

"I don't want to kill. I don't like murder," she mumbled, her voice low and breathy. "Because I'm a peaceful goddess."

"...all the same, all spoiled, righteous and crude, sex-loving, violence thriving bungholes!" Eros continued to spew out insults at their daughter, and his words only worsened Psyche's distress.

She squeezed her hands harder over her ears. "Stop! I refuse to hear him like this!" Warm tears trickled down her cheeks. "Please, whatever, whoever you are…the one controlling us…leave him be!" Pain pinched in her gut, and she screeched. "Take me, *take me!*"

Despite her cries, Eros' tone amplified, his curses becoming harsher, terrifying. Psyche tried to shut her eyes, to block out his rampage. But the poisonous being kept them open, forcing her to stare at her enraged husband as he shook his fists at Hedone.

And poor Hedone, backed against the opposite side of her cage, spasming with disgust, remained silent.

"See reality, Psyche. Poison or not...this was bound to happen."

She seethed, clenching her teeth through the agony, the roaring in her skull. "You're wrong, *you're wrong!*" The searing sensation continued, and she wondered if she should have been praying for death. Would that be her only relief?

"I needed the gods to rebel amongst themselves. To commence a civil war."

"Screw your civil war, you monster!" Psyche wanted to sound threatening, yet her words came out as a soft whisper. The pain was so intense it constricted her vocal chords. "Let...me speak...let me...denounce you!" But the harder she tried, the more strain she put on her throat, burning it.

"I needed conflict to start bloodshed among gods and *humans. To show my strength, make a point."*

Psyche threaded her fingers through her hair, pulling, twisting. "You're not making a point...you're destroying the world!" She cringed as tight knots formed in her belly.

"You and Eros were perfect pawns in my game... and now you'll both prove it."

Something else, something new swirled in Psyche's stomach. Like a storm brewing, waves swishing, clusters of crunchy leaves bristling in the wind. When she opened her mouth to yelp, to beg for help...no sounds came out.

"You've said enough, Psyche. You'll not interrupt anymore."

Again she sought to pry her lips apart, but only the faintest squeak—unheard under Eros' rambling—escaped.

"I have to start the process earlier than planned, since you let yourself be captured."

Her eyes blurred with so much liquid, she no longer noticed Athena who, when she'd last checked, was banging on the dungeon door, begging for support.

"Help won't come. That brat of a goddess won't interrupt, either."

Psyche's head involuntarily flipped over to where Athena yanked on the doorknob and kicked at the battered wood. *"Fuck, fuck, fuck,"* she said, between groans.

"...and I will kill *you* too, you disgraceful child." Eros' intonations turned raw and raspy. "You've accomplished nothing but run around and fill everyone with pleasure. And fuck with all the cupbearers and servants at Dionysus' orgies, too, last I checked. You're useless."

Tipping her head back, Psyche gaped at the molding ceiling, wishing it would crumble atop her. Squash her, eradicate her, get rid of that voice—

"Leave...him...alone," she managed, though each word scraped at her insides, boiled the linings of her throat. "He's a peaceful god...this temper...isn't him!"

Her captor chuckled.

"Peaceful? Do you not remember your past?"

In response, Psyche grimaced. "I do—"

"—How he kidnapped you, locked you up, commanded you to never look upon him?"

She yearned to claw at her scalp and rip the voice out. "Stop. Stop!"

"And when you, poor mortal, couldn't resist, he shunned you?"

"He...did not—"

"—Left you to be punished by his hysterical mother?"

The chuckle morphed into a witchy, gloomy cackle.

"Do you not recall that about your precious husband?"

Violent shivers racked her frame as flashes of the Aphrodite-induced madness she'd experienced consumed her thoughts. The trials, the confusion, the sorrow, the heartbreak—they resurfaced, vivid as if they'd happened yesterday.

"He changed! He is...not connected to his mother like that. She doesn't command his actions—"

The growling spiraled down to her abdomen and tugged at her innards, shredding through them, releasing more toxins, and pushing them further, deeper into her body.

"No, I command him now. I plan to bring back the wrathful, angry, selfish Eros."

The being twisted Psyche's neck to watch Eros as he smirked at Athena. He was like a demon; reddened cheeks, tangled, wild, matted blond curls, and eyes so dark and twisted they were scarier than how Psyche imagined the pits of Tartarus to be.

"He is already here."

Eros then swerved away, barring her from witnessing any more of the crazed flicker in his gaze.

Psyche breathed, and for a moment she lost her tension, shielded from her spouse's madness. Witnessing the whimpering Hedone, unable to respond to his horrid accusations, sparked the tiniest of fires in her stomach. *Her daughter.* The monster possessing Eros insulted her, demeaned her. Psyche wouldn't, *couldn't* have that.

Sudden flames of motherly rage ravaged the voice inside, fought it, and reminded Psyche she had to act. She had to protest, to ban this entity from controlling her. She'd shoved it down once, in the wilderness; so she had to do the same again here, in the Olympus dungeons. Though it admitted it had lowered its guard before, Psyche could only pray it would do so once more, to test her.

It likes testing me.

"Leave…us…be," she hissed, her voice barely audible but its vibrations still rattling her enclosure. "Leave us all be." Her fists tightened, nails slicing into the skin of her palms. "Who are you to attack us?" Her stuttering stopped, as if the being inside had been caught by surprise. A slither of energy returned to Psyche's extremities—energy that *she* controlled. "Who are you to decide how and when we should die?"

Her efforts, albeit tremendous, were short-lived. The creature giggled at her, its amusement fluttering up and down Psyche's spine, setting loose a horde of butterflies in her belly. Appeasing, soothing wings brushed within her, and she scrunched her eyebrows.

"Whoa…what is that? A change of heart?" She dared to smirk, thinking perhaps she'd succeeded, she'd drowned the creature with her sudden strength.

But when the voice giggled again, it was distorted, snarling, snake-like; and the butterflies exploded.

"Who am I, you ask?"

"Y-yes," Psyche's shoulders sank, the force of the explosion rendering her nauseous, "tell me."

"I'm powerful. Ancient. You should fear me, all of you. I will be glorious, and you'll regret it."

Wooziness settled in, wrapping around Psyche's limbs and loosening them. Exhausting them. Her knees buckled, and she toppled backward. Eros' speech fizzled away from her ears as her eyelids smashed together.

"No...*no*..."

She expected the internal monster to chortle, but it didn't; it hummed, its eerily melodious timbre embracing Psyche like a long-needed hug.

Though she slowly fell into a state of unconsciousness, she heard Eros scream, Hedone moan, Athena battling to open the door. Something hauled her far, far from them, plunging her into a coma.

"We are sealed in. Only Zeus can open that door...but something might have delayed him..."

As her body became weightless like cotton, Psyche craved to hurl herself at the metallic bars, to draw Athena's attention, to plead. But her legs were dead-weight, her arms glued to the ground, her core drawn to the earth. Slumber called, its tune a gentle lullaby, its tone icy but refreshing, calming.

"You'll sleep until I break Eros free. Then you'll resume your missions. We're not done."

Psyche's thoughts faded. Tranquil, obedient, she let the world around her disappear.

"All will go as plotted. I will be glorious."

Psyche's head dropped to the side as she entered a realm of dreams and fuzzy clouds; a place she might choose to never depart from.

||27. THE ROYAL SUMMONS||

ATHENA

How…*why* was the dungeon door locked?

Panicked, Athena turned away from the sealed exit, and her jaw dropped at the sight of Eros staring straight at her, his gaze dark and unwavering. He lifted his arms, his fingertips twinging with electricity as he directed them towards the cage. The bars rattled.

"No…" A slow moan slithered past Athena's chapped lips.

I can't take him on…the ambrosia is fizzling out of my system.

So drained from battling with the door and from the struggle of transporting Psyche and Hedone, her limbs quaked almost as much as the metal enclosure before her.

Eros' hands twitched as a bright, sizzling light swooshed out of thin air, and smacked into the bars.

"No!" Bracing for what she anticipated would be an explosion, Athena crouched, covering herself, begging her powers to shield her.

Instead, the prison door behind her blew open, sending her flying across the room.

Heart racing, she landed near Psyche's cage. She shook her head to regain her senses and peered over to see Zeus, Poseidon, and Ares, cramping in front of the threshold, their weapons pointed at

Eros.

Zeus raised his arm and his fingers glowed. "Now!"

Lightning streaked from his hands, filling the prison with blinding flashes. Poseidon's trident burst with a giant jet of sparkling water, and Ares' sword emitted a thick trail of red smoke. All three substances swirled and swirled around one another, combining as they collided against the cage, strengthening it, changing its hue from gold, to white, to black.

Ares and Poseidon lowered their weapons and stepped back, reeling from the strength of their attack. Zeus strode forward, resting his weapons—his hands—at his sides.

When Eros, unscathed but shaken up, opened his mouth to argue, the King of the gods blasted him with a snap of his fingers.

Another streak of lightning, less intense, knocked into his chest, and Eros soared to the other end of his cell, slamming into the wall.

Hedone and Athena gasped.

"It wasn't a fatal blow," said Zeus, wiping his hands on his gray tunic. "But it should keep him out of trouble for a while." The thunderous energy lingering about him dissipated as he glanced at his sibling. "I had no choice, you agree?"

Poseidon, regal in his favorite navy blue tunic, his glistening seashell and ruby crown nestled atop his charcoal and brown curls, nodded. "He's lethal. That poison is dangerous, brother. You must use more drastic measures."

Ares looked over Hedone before meandering over to Athena, offering her his hand, which she took reluctantly. "What a mess," he muttered, aiding Athena to her feet.

She dusted herself off and glared at him. "Your mess. He's your son! He and his wife…" When Ares' eyes narrowed, almost begging her to insult him so he had a reason to insult her in return, she grimaced. "I'm sorry. I'm tired, under pressure, and my list of suspects continues to grow. My personal disgust of you has no place here."

"Whoever's mess this is," Poseidon wandered over to Psyche's enclosure, "it's nasty."

Athena shoved past Ares and stormed up to her father. "Did you not get my message?"

"I did. But I was delayed. Had I known of *this,*" he exchanged a worried glance with Poseidon, "I would have tried harder. We must speak. Away from them."

Athena crossed her arms. "Delayed by what? Tell me, what would be more important than me returning to Olympus with Psyche? Father—"

He slapped an enormous palm over her mouth. "Hush. Not here."

Ares and Poseidon remained in the prison, keeping watch over the knocked out prisoners, as Zeus led the way upstairs, out of the dungeon. He walked fast, maintaining a slight distance between them.

Once out of the darkness, surrounded by the soothing paintings and cool breezes of the palace corridor, Zeus halted, his sandals squeaking on the marble floors.

He gaped at his daughter, at last. "Apollo has reached his wits' end. We must employ outside help. Someone with a thorough knowledge of potions, poisons…and witchcraft. Someone able to analyze what's in those two and extract whatever it is. Completely and permanently." He fidgeted, glancing about warily as if worried of being spied on.

"Outside—" Athena's brows furrowed when she understood who Zeus referred to. "Hecate? You'd trust her with such a delicate mission? She's at the top of my suspect list, and I have no doubt she's responsible for this—"

"—yes, I figured." Zeus' piercing scowl silenced her, shattering the complaints she'd been about to formulate. "But I *do* trust her, as should you. She assisted us in all our past battles and allowed us to succeed. Yes, she is a witch…but she isn't evil, and you know that."

"But I cannot deny the eerie feeling that she's more involved in all this than we imagine." Athena gulped, shriveling in her father's shadow. His anger made him taller, more impressive than usual. His undulating hair in vibrant hues of light ash with streaks of black, blue, yellow looked ready to wrap around her neck and choke her for daring to speak up.

"How would she be? She's been in the Underworld while all this happened. So unless she ordered Psyche around during one of her frenzies, I don't see how Hecate would have anything to do with Eros and Psyche and their rebellion against the gods."

"Yes, her frenzies." Athena lowered her voice, debating on whether to share her thoughts—but Zeus' insistent stormy eyes would slice into her if she didn't. "Has she had any as of late? Who's to say she's not liable for plotting with the main villain that poisoned the two rebels?" Zeus raised a hand to hush her, but in an action of bravery—or utter idiocy—she jammed it aside. "It's her potion that swims in them! She figured it out, since Persephone had been briefly infected, too! Father, it's her concoction that started all this! Does that not bother you?"

Zeus' hand dropped. "I…I did not—"

"—and that potion mysteriously disappeared, or was stolen, she claims. She'd stashed it in her private collection that only she has access to. A potion meant to be hidden, too dangerous to unleash on the world…so should you not punish her for that alone? For having such a weapon and keeping it as a secret?" Breathless, Athena sucked her lips in and exhaled. Reality caught up with her—she'd cut off the king. She'd yelled. At once, she sank to her knees. "Father…Heavens, forgive me. I am confused, exhausted, overwhelmed. It is no excuse for me to use such language and tones with you."

He frowned, but massaged her shoulders, urging her to stand again. "Dearest daughter, did it not occur to you that since Hecate knows this elixir, she'd know how to heal someone of it? Didn't she cure Persephone?"

"Well…yes, she did."

"Right." Zeus squeezed her, his touch furious and forgiving all at once. "It shocks me you didn't think to summon her here. She might be able to save our affected ones, and once she does, once their memories are restored…they will help you narrow down the list."

She shivered at his power as it coursed through her, flooding into her core, pulsating through her veins. "But I don't trust her. I can't." She wriggled, hoping to break from Zeus' hold, but he held on tight. "She loves Persephone but curing her might have been part of a ploy to convince us."

Zeus' nails clawed into her shoulder, tightening his grip; but to her surprise, within a few painful seconds, he released her. "Whether or not you approve, I have decided." He switched his gaze to something behind her; footsteps suddenly echoed in her ears. "Ah, Hermes!"

He leaned aside, and Hermes popped up beside Athena. She

swiveled to witness his approach; his eyes alert, his brown biceps shiny with sweat and flexed as if he'd just finished a work-out.

"Father, Athena, fancy meeting you here." He winked, and Athena gagged.

"Thank you for joining us, son." Zeus waved him closer.

"I thought you needed me in the dungeon?" The flirtatious god peeked between Zeus and Athena. "Why are you up here?"

"We handled that issue," Zeus cringed, "but I still have a task for you. Fetch Hecate from the Underworld. I require her help with healing Eros and Psyche."

Hermes cocked a brow, and the smallest of smiles graced his features before he shrugged it off. "Hecate? Me?"

Zeus laughed. "Are you not the herald of the gods?" Hermes rolled his eyes. "You have a connection to the Underworld, easy access." He clapped Hermes' upper back, smacking right into an oiled section of skin that sent droplets onto Athena's chin. "You were just there, so Hades may be wary of you returning so soon, but…go, quickly. Tell her it's an official summons from me, and if Hades asks, inform him I'll return her as soon as we're done. Her prolonged presence would attract questions I'm not willing to answer."

With a bow, and purposely avoiding Athena's inquisitive expression, Hermes scampered off.

"And you," Zeus seized Athena's jaw and dragged her close enough for their noses to touch, "need to remember that I'm the king, daughter." Any earlier pleasantness and apparent pardon of her attitude had faded. "I know what's best, and you'll stop questioning it." He dropped her, and her skin seared with pain. "Alert me when she arrives, then take her straight to Eros and Psyche." Without another word, he barreled down the hall, likely headed to the throne-room.

Biting her lip, she slanted against the wall. Hecate *could* cure them; but would she curse them instead, lying to the Olympians? What if her master plan was to pose as their savior, when in truth she only wanted to intoxicate all gods…and slay them?

"Eros and Psyche were a distraction…" Athena paced, clasping and unclasping her hands as a drum pounded in her head. "I must prepare. I don't trust her, and I'm not the only one who is suspicious of her manners. So I must enlist spies, allies, and others who will monitor her when I can't."

"Indeed." The sudden voice, so stony and stern as it slithered over from nearby, prompted Athena to kneel, to shield herself like she had earlier when Eros tried to escape.

A rustle of fabrics and clinking jewelry came from an adjacent corridor. As Athena looked up, gathering her bearings, a peacock-patterned tunic was swishing up to her.

"Hera?" Athena groaned as she straightened up. "What do you want?"

"To help you." The matriarch smirked as she adjusted her crown, stopping inches from Athena. "I have spies and allies who agree with your opinion of our dearest witch-goddess."

As a courtesy, Athena inclined her head, but she didn't wipe the disgust from her face as the queen's flowery scent invaded her nostrils. "You'd ally with me? The daughter you hate and who sickens you? To what do I owe this change of heart? Or should I say mind? Since you don't have a heart."

Hera snickered and flipped her satin tresses to the side. "I'm not allying myself. But I *align* myself with your views on Hecate. I think she's up to something, and I've thought it from the start, but didn't wish to share my opinions. Especially not with my husband who vouches for her at every turn." Her tone laced with its usual venom, but for once, it wasn't meant for Athena.

"So…" Athena looked at her feet, oddly struggling to find words, "what do you suggest?"

Hera got into Athena's space, her scent nauseating. She lowered her honeyed voice. "Investigate Hecate *our* way. We can't go against Zeus…but you've grown good at lying, and with your mind protected from us all…it could work. I have my tricks, too. I'm not asking for your trust, but your compliance. We are both against her." Despite her confidence, there was a subtle tremor in her words, and Athena spotted her looking left and right, not unlike how Zeus had moments before.

Tipping backward, Athena huffed. "Fine. But you're not scratched off my list yet." A sly grin smeared over her lips.

I'll play along, and perhaps our schemes will lead me to the truth.

Batting her lashes in satisfaction, Hera offered a hand—in a gesture of temporary peace. "So for old time's sake, like the humans say…we work together. It'll be like Troy, but this time we won't be fighting."

Athena accepted the handshake, and at the contact she clenched her stomach muscles, fighting the urge to recoil. "Deal."

Hera gave a quick nod and hastened off to the throne-room, leaving Athena to resume her pacing, wondering if somehow Hecate and Hera worked together.

‖28. NO ONE CAN KNOW‖
EROS

A weight settled on Eros' breastbone. The harder he tried to breathe, the heavier it became. He struggled to come to, but as he rubbed his eyes and the blurriness cleared, he realized…he wasn't alone. He had spectators.

The soreness of his limbs kept him stuck to his mattress. He had little mobility, but he needed to view his surroundings, to figure out who *they* were, what *they* wanted. Their scent wasn't sweet and tangy like Psyche's; nor was it the peppy and citrus aroma that Hedone gave off.

Hadn't his spouse and daughter been there earlier? He recalled talking to them, seeing them. Or was it a dream?

Gaping at the stone ceiling, he stopped trying to crane his neck towards his audience; he was frozen in place, unable to move. Would the rotting, flaky surface overhead crash onto him? It seemed to be getting closer, closer—

He tried to throw out his hands to shield himself, but nothing happened. His arms remained glued to his sides. In any case, no power would have shot from his fingertips, because he *had* no powers within his cage.

Cage…

"Fuck."

He'd attempted to destroy his cage. The voice inside had fueled him with rage, ordered him to hurl insults at everyone. Had that evil being left him, at last? Or was it still dormant, waiting for the right moment to resurface?

"I put you under a spell to immobilize you," said a feminine, breathy tone he didn't recognize. "More for my protection than for yours, I'll admit."

Not Psyche. Not Hedone. Not Mother or Athena. Who is *that?*

Delicate and light-footed steps came from close by; from inside the enclosure.

Eros yearned to crawl away, to hide under his dingy bed, to protect this individual from his fury. Or protect *himself* from its wrath; this individual was surely there for revenge on his behavior.

"You shouldn't be in here," he said, his throat aching, turning his voice to a raspy croak. "I'm lethal, out to kill the gods…"

Again, he willed his head to spin, to witness this creature's poor decision to enter his hell-hole of an enclosure, but he remained stiff as a board. Squinting, he dug into his tiny reserves of energy and slid his eyes as far to the side as possible.

Finally, he saw her—and somehow he became more rigid.

Her long robes of burgundy covered her feet as she strode up to him, not an ounce of hesitation in her approach. Her hair—jet black, streaked with crimson—tumbled over her shoulders and spiraled down her back. Voluminous, vivid, almost violent as it swayed with her every move. A dark ruby pendant dangled from her neck, gleaming in tune with her starry, purple eyes.

He'd rarely encountered her or spoken to her, but he'd never mistake this goddess for anyone else. Her obscure yet enticing aura was too familiar, too fascinating. Too frightening.

"H-Hecate?" His gut bubbled and a strange flash-back featuring her prompted him to wonder if he had seen her recently. "Is that...you?"

Whispers and gasps fogged his mind as she rushed to his side and leaned over him. "Quiet," she hissed, her gaze piercing into the abyss of his soul. All the beauty about her faded, fizzled into a haze of black smoke as she traced her sharp ebony nails near his temples. Was he imagining that? Or had she become some sort of demon, right before his eyes?

That demeanor brought on more memories. The exuberance, the lurking, creepy silhouette that she was, looming in the shadows...that was how he met her in the Underworld, next to Cerberus. When he met with Persephone. But *was* she there, or only an illusion? It was all so vague, so confusing. Hecate watched over Hades' wife, so her presence made sense, and yet Eros had no clue where she fit into the puzzle of his poisoning.

Hecate clapped a hand over his mouth. "Quiet your thoughts, too." Her snake-like pitch pushed through his skin and caused his organs to quake, his nerves to twitch.

He tensed as her fingertips tapped over his face, his torso, his abdomen, his legs. "But...how—"

"—Eros," she pressed a finger to his lips, "hush. I cannot heal you if you do not shut up and stay still."

Her voice was a soft, beautiful breath of Olympus air; but it shifted to a tenebrous timbre as she chanted in ancient Greek. The words were weighty, compressing, each letter tearing into Eros, devouring him. Every few sentences she swayed her hands back and forth over his body, and a tingling sensation coated his skin. Though she'd closed her eyes, Eros caught a glow seeping from beneath her sealed eyelids, morphing from an eerie scarlet to a vibrant violet, then the darkest of blacks.

A shimmering outline formed around Hecate as her chants continued, growing in volume. Muttering the spell under her breath, she extracted several vials from inside her robe. She sprinkled them over him—a combination of dazzling liquid, sparkling dust, and coarse powder. As each particle reached him, he flinched; but his limbs, still paralyzed, had no reaction.

She proceeded in a new language—a tongue Eros had never heard before, but he suspected it was one older than time itself.

Witch tongue.

His extremities numbed and slowly, his back lifted from the bed. His lower limbs, his arms, his head—all floated, suspended above his mattress. He'd seen such being used craft before, but never on him. Never had he been through the surreal experience of a healing ritual led by the world's oldest sorceress.

Hecate's incantation grew more obscure, and her timbre altered into hasty, demonic, terrifying tone. Eros squeezed his eyes shut, as if watching her would worsen the effect her words had on him.

Then came the agony. The pain of luring the toxins out of his body. Muscles ripped, veins tore, skin shredded to bits. Every inch of flesh was sliced, yanked from him, detaching from his bones. She slashed into him, drained him of blood and oxygen. Ambrosia and ichor poured from every wound, every orifice, dripping onto the floor with a deafening *splat*.

Eros couldn't cringe, couldn't scream, couldn't do a thing to protest, to stop her from killing him.

I deserve it...I deserve it.

He wished to pry his eyelids apart and glare at Hecate as she spilled his immortal blood, as she carved into him. But the pain twisting his entrails instead forced him to writhe about, to pray for it to end. To pray for death. Even his thoughts drizzled out of him, pulled by an invisible rope that separated his brain in two. His forehead was on fire and his temples thrummed, cracked by lightning, thunder booming within incessantly.

She wasn't curing him, she was destroying him. Were those her orders? To assassinate him as he'd assassinated the poor soulmates? Had Zeus lied? Had *all of them* lied?

He yearned to break free, to yelp at the top of his lungs that she was a miscreant, a devil. To call for his mother, for his father—

Hecate's chants sped up and grew louder, splitting into his skull and dividing his atoms like an earthquake dividing the soil. She triggered explosions in every cavity, like a thousand fireworks setting off all at once. Like a volcano spewing, spitting out its flames to burn him, scorch him.

That's it—I have to defend myself!

He mustered a semblance of courage to open his eyes, and braced for the carnage, for the destruction in her wake. For his limbs to be chopped off, his clothes torn and drenched in blood. Was he even alive? Or would his spirit zoom out of him and overlook the gruesome scene, then plunge into the depths of Tartarus? He pictured guts sprawling out and ichor everywhere; severed finger and toes, and protruding bones.

But he saw none of it. No remains, no lava, no flesh on the floor. When he sniffed the air, there was no stench of despair, no coppery flavor lingering on his tongue. He peered at his chest—not a scrape or a scar, not a single trace of Hecate's claws.

I wasn't hacked to pieces?

"That's what it feels like to have such a deadly poison snatched from the depths of one's soul," said Hecate, between her spells. "Now close your eyes again; this last part is tricky."

His momentary relief ended, as her words became vice-like, sharp. They seared into his rib-cage and brought him to tears. Fire skidded along his skin and melted through him. His lungs overflowed with air and water and his heart pounded, fast, fast, *faster,* on the brink of detonating. He fell into the pit of his suffering, lulled into the confines of Tartarus itself—

An unexpected but subtle hum in his ear ceased all pain and erased it, as if it had never happened. As if he'd hallucinated it all.

"You're healed," said Hecate, her lips brushing against the tips of his ears. *"But before you rise and recover your memories, I have a warning to give you. Nod if you understand—only you can hear me right now."*

He wasn't sure he understood anything anymore, but he nodded.

Her sleek, suave timbre came alive in his head. *"Do not divulge every memory that comes to you. No one can suspect me, and from what I analyzed in you earlier, you met me during your plotting."*

Visions of Eros' actions woke in him; his cruel ways, his carnivorous actions, the desperation to heed the voice commanding him. How he'd insulted his daughter, how he'd threatened to break loose and kill everyone.

Did you do this to me? Did you provoke us, poison my wife and me?

Hecate's *shush* was a whistling, breezy, soothing sound. *"I'm not the wrongdoer. But what you'd reveal about our acquaintance in the Underworld would point to me and distract from the real evil. I can't allow that. I want the truth uncovered, the culprit stopped. So do not mention me in any of your interrogations. Leave me out of this, or I swear by Zeus you'll fear for your safety more than in the past few months."* Her words imprinted onto his brain.

Do you know who it is? Who did this?

Like yanking a needle from his veins, she removed herself from their private trance. "The poison lodged itself deep in his heart and soul, but I extracted and exterminated it. Eros is cured."

He had no inkling who she addressed, but murmurs replied to her.

She sat at the edge of the bed, breaths ragged, exhaustion shrinking her to half the deity she usually was. "I need a few moments to gather my strength before attempting the same for Psyche."

Eros wiggled his fingers, lifted his arms, moved his feet. He rose into a seated position and groaned as he swiped at the sweat on his forehead and settled beside Hecate. As she glanced at him, a weak smile over her aubergine-hued lips, her eyes had reverted to purple— their normal shade, albeit laced with concern.

"Am I really cured?" He gulped. "Done with the murder and bloodshed? Am I the god of love again?"

Only then did he pick up on the shuffle of feet and sense the overwhelming presence in front of his cage. He sent a quick glance that way—and there they were. His parents, his daughter, his family.

He was still too fuzzy to recognize them all, but pleased they were there. Pleased they wanted him healed, and not dead for his crimes.

"You are, but," Hecate's gaze narrowed, "watch yourself. No one is safe, especially here, in Olympus." Small lines creased near her eyelids as she pivoted from him and lowered her voice. "Prepare your spouse, because she will battle through the process more than you did. I believe her poisoning reached a deeper level."

He hesitated to move, to attempt to stand. Something about Hecate's shriveling frame didn't reassure him. Yes, she was tired; but there was angst in her mannerisms, a twitch to her motions that he didn't find reassuring.

"Do it," she said, glowering at him. "And stop thinking."

His cell was open, and Hedone waited at the doorway, beaming. "Father!" She embraced him, and he fell into her, at ease, calm, no erratic ideas screaming about in his mind.

As he spewed out apologies that she deflected—*you were poisoned, Dad*—she guided him to Psyche, who was unconscious in her cell.

She lay unconscious, peaceful, but probably immensely troubled on the inside. Her blonde tresses tumbled over her rosy cheeks, and despite her distress, she was alluring as ever, delicious in her slumber.

But her dreams are flooded with death, as were mine.

Hedone squeezed Eros' shoulders. "It's okay. She…is okay. She will be."

It would all be over soon. Psyche would heal as he did. A tear slipped down his cheek as he understood he was free, truly free, at last. No more horror, no more blood, no more urges to make his charges eat one another.

The real Eros was home.

||29. SUSPICIOUS WITCH||
ATHENA

Watching Hecate's ritual was, Athena had to admit, quite the show. But the details—the request to shield the cage from all thoughts and disallow Hecate's and Eros' from seeping out—still bothered her.

Did the witch-goddess think they'd all be deterred by Eros' demeanor during the spell? No one had been spared from his cruelty after his capture, and it would shock no one to hear him spew out more crude comments in the process. So why the secrecy? Did Hecate have something to hide?

Hecate's gown swished over the dusty concrete as she followed Eros into Psyche's enclosure. Her eyes were glittery, loaded with insight and secrets.

I don't trust her.

Hedone was at her heels, filled with joy and hope for her parents' speedy recoveries. Uncaring of the methods, unaware of the eerie ways Hecate worked her magic, all she wanted was for everyone to survive and for the gruesome deaths to stop.

The brief whispering after Eros awoke had also disturbed Athena. What did the witch say to him? What words did she mutter to finalize her incantation? Whatever they had been, they'd sparked a curious gloom in Eros' gaze. He'd stiffened, questioned her, then relaxed; but the act hadn't convinced Athena. Something else was going on.

Hecate shooed Hedone out of the cell, and the latter scampered over between Aphrodite and the surprisingly solemn Ares. Zeus and Poseidon, farther off, conversed in hushed tones, and Hera readjusted her posture against the wall. Her peacock-patterned tunic scrunched at her feet as she sighed and wiped her knuckles on her bosom. This was no place for a queen like her; Athena doubted she'd ever visited the dungeon before now.

Apollo dawdled behind Athena, shifting his weight, impatient to view the spell a second time—to witness what he was powerless to do.

None of the gods present for this healing event harbored the concerns that Athena did. When slipping into their minds, while they were distracted with witnessing Hecate's wonders, she realized all of them—except for Hera, whose thoughts were melodious hums—believed in the witch-goddess and her magic.

How do they have such blind faith in her?

The swift spell-work escaped Hecate's mouth. Psyche's once immobile body began to shake, twist, contort every which way in manners Athena found unnerving. She wriggled like a snake, shimmied about like a cat's furious tail.

Eros sat atop her body to stabilize her before she hurt herself. He watched Hecate with quivering lips and hunched shoulders, desperate for the incantation to take, for the toxin to pour from his wife.

He'd endured his fair share of pain during the ritual, from how he writhed and seethed and hissed. Now, as Psyche whimpered, he had to suffer her pain, be with her as she went through the same sordid ordeal. It would succeed, Athena knew; Hecate had extracted the poison—*her* poison—from him, so why not from Psyche?

Yet the feeblest of voices in Athena's head watered the doubt she already felt blooming within. What if Hecate left *something* in Eros' bloodstream? A tiny trace of the virus that would ignite and prompt him to start his rebellion again at an opportune moment of Hecate's choosing?

Psyche's wails drew Athena from her overthinking, and she returned to the scene. Psyche's eyelashes fluttered as she grasped Eros' arm, moaning, screeching, gasping for air.

"It's okay, love," said Eros, his tone crackling. "Hush now…let Hecate pull the venom from you." This was a softer, more docile Eros; the *real* Eros. Not the carnivorous monster hurling cruelties at everyone he encountered.

Thank Olympus for his return.

Forehead pressed to the metal bars, Hedone couldn't keep still. Athena focused on her but was still unable to fully decipher her thoughts. Everyone—Hecate, especially—had dismissed her role in her mother's madness. Without an interrogation, basing themselves on Hecate's quick analysis, it was decided she wasn't poisoned, wasn't a risk.

But Athena, of course, didn't agree.

She followed Psyche for weeks, but is unscathed? How?

Since when was Hecate's word law in Olympus? She was no queen, and didn't rule over anyone. So why had Zeus guzzled up all her claims as if they were the purest of ambrosias?

The witch's voice crescendoed, taking on a more threatening depth than it had with Eros. Her spell discharged from her mouth like overflowing rivers in a storm. The words tumbled over Psyche, drenching her. Her body rose, her arms limp at her sides—and Eros straddled her still, unaffected as they flew several inches above ground.

Hecate's palms shot towards the ceiling as she threw out string after string of incomprehensible and violent sentences.

"She must be more resistant," whispered Apollo, peering over Athena's shoulder. "Eros was contained for days, so the poison had a chance to settle…easier for Hecate to coach out. But Psyche is still wild."

Athena nodded, pretending to care about Apollo's thirst for knowledge and magic. In truth, she wished for her own alternatives to extract more facts out of Hecate. For ways to get her alone, get her to speak.

I'm on to her, and she must be made aware.

Psyche let out a few more ear-splitting groans, but with one final grunt and a sharp intake of air, she and Eris splattered to the ground, crashing against the concrete.

Her eyes rolled open, at once drawn to Eros. "My love?" Her timbre was frail yet sprinkled with honey and sugar. Back to normal. "Am I…are we…what happened?"

Eros cupped her chin and smothered her cheeks with kisses. He glowed with glee, as he always did before chaos had erupted inside him. "It's all right," he said, plastering his lips atop hers and engaging in a smoldering kiss.

At that, even Athena couldn't hide her smirk. He was definitely back to himself if he engaged in explicit sensual smooches in front of the entire family.

Hecate crouched to catch her breath, but her gaze fluttered to

Zeus. "It was more difficult than anticipated, but she is also cured." As she straightened up, she flinched, though a flicker of relief slashed over her face. "Eros and Psyche are rid of that nasty virus."

Zeus and Poseidon applauded, imitated by Aphrodite, Ares, and Apollo. Hera flashed a quick—and painfully fake—smile before exiting the dungeon without a word.

Though reluctant to lose sight of Hecate for even a second, Athena spun to watch Hera depart, carefully listening to whatever might have passed through her mind. But she heard nothing.

If only I could be in two places at once.

Zeus issued one last clap. "Let us go to the throne-room. I'll have a small feast put together later. But," he wrinkled his brows, "we can't let our guard down. We'll thank our dear Hecate for her involvement, but we won't make a raging party out of it." As he twirled, his stormy gaze caught Athena's and relaxed. He approached her, everything about his demeanor comforting and calm. "My sweet," he whispered, a few strands of his graying beard brushing against her brow as he kissed her forehead. "All is well. You may release your tension. Everyone is home."

But we haven't uncovered the culprit.

She feigned a grin as he took off, Poseidon close after him. He acknowledged her too—a rare occasion—and jutted his chin at the door. "You deserve rest and praise, Athena. You found her."

Teeth gritting behind her increasingly uncomfortable smile, Athena inclined her head in respect. "Thank you, Uncle. I will join shortly."

Aphrodite slithered up to her, beaming so brightly, it was like the sun spilled from her pores. She took hold of Athena's hands, her warmth causing Athena's stomach to gurgle. "I'll never forget this. I am in your debt for saving my family."

Ares said nothing, but Athena sensed his gratefulness. Hedone, squeezed between them, mumbled a few Greek prayers to show her own gratitude.

Eros and Psyche lingered close to the cage exit, hugging, touching, kissing. Athena gagged, and despite his distraction, Eros spotted her disgust. With a chuckle, he linked arms with his wife, and they wandered over, both still wobbly on their feet.

"Athena." Any amusement once sprawled over his features dissipated. "I must—"

"—no." Athena stepped backwards, out of their overwhelming circle of love. "You may thank me later once you're at full strength. Once we've located and terminated the threat. Go, everyone wants to welcome you home." She switched to Psyche. "You as well, dearest. I imagine Hestia will concoct something delicious for us all."

They trudged out, annoyingly adorable despite their drawn-out, exhausted steps.

From the corner of her eye, Athena noticed Hecate sitting on the bed in Psyche's enclosure, still reeling from the powers she'd used to save the beloved couple.

Athena grinned; and didn't fake it this time.

The Fates are with me. This is my moment.

Swift as a gust of wind, Athena lunged forward and snapped the cell bars shut, waving a hand to seal them—and confining Hecate inside.

Hecate jerked her chin up. "Huh?" She peeped at Athena, and at the metal separating them. "What's this? What are you doing?"

"Don't play with me, witch." Athena crossed her arms, elongating her spine to appear threatening, intimidating. "These enchantments won't hold you long. I need you to answer my questions…then, I'll consider releasing you."

Hecate stood up, her legs obviously wobbling beneath her thick skirts. "You're interrogating me? Am I still a suspect? I thought we established in my crypt that I'm a victim." She took a few strides closer, and a savage storm came to life in her eyes as the corners of her lips tugged downward.

"*I* never established anything." Athena wouldn't budge, even as the goddess' energy struck through the bars and swirled about like toxic clouds about to suffocate her.

I will not show weakness. She's a witch, but I am wisdom embodied.

"I don't believe a word you said. As lead investigator on this case, I demand a proper explanation…or I'll expose your treachery to Zeus and Hades."

"Treachery? You still think I'm lying?" Genuine shock painted into Hecate's expression. "That I made it all up? Stole my own potion, poisoned Persephone, located an ally up here to poison Eros and Psyche, and waited for evil to unfurl?" Bitterness weaved into her tone; a brittle bark Athena disliked.

"It's too obvious." Athena's arms pressed harder into her torso. "Everything points to you. You made that poison, you stashed it away, you told no one about it. You likely had illegal frenzies while Eros and Psyche roamed about inflicting their damage on the world; you fed them victims. Would you not be suspicious in my shoes?"

Hecate paced back and forth, every step cautious and calculated. "Yes. But I beg you to look past that." Her fingertips twirled, wiggling to and fro as if preparing a spell. "My track record is squeaky clean, and you cannot deny that. I've been a neutral force for centuries. Reformed from my old ways. I have no business wanting the gods dead…and if I did, I'd not go about it in such drawn out ways, would I? No. I'm not poisoning gods, Athena. I'd lose my home, my purpose, my life. And the frenzies?" She scoffed. "They're out of my control, but I never harmed anyone. Never sent any of my acolytes to Eros and Psyche. Nor was I near those two when they lost their minds."

Athena tried her damndest not to snort. "Excuses. Do you have witnesses to prove this?"

As her eyes sparked with red and violet flares, Hecate zoomed up to the bars, her black nails almost melting, digging into the metal. "Melinoë. Hades. Thanatos. They can attest my frenzies of late have been in South America and Africa. I've not come near the United States or Europe."

"Then why are you so closely tied into this?" Athena stomped a foot, angry at her emotions that shot out like bullets. She'd wanted to be level-headed, stern, serious; but the urge to smack the evil out of the witch-goddess kept hammering in her skull. "Why is your name written all over it? Tell me!" A foreign electricity pumped through her and fizzled at her fingertips. "Or will you stand there and continue to scream about your innocence? Ha! I bet you'll tell me you were framed."

When Hecate quirked a brow, her mouth gaping open, her limbs stiffening, Athena immobilized. That body language wasn't pretend. The angst undulating up Hecate's arms in obvious tremors wasn't fake. *Was* she tricked into this position? *Was* she innocent?

Athena inhaled, rethinking her words, rehashing her feelings.

Framed…I did not anticipate that option.

"Athena," began Hecate, her complexion paling, turning her

face to a light, sickening charcoal shade.

She didn't have time to finish, as the dungeon door blasted open, and Zeus thundered in.

Electric rage simmered in his wake as he barreled up to the cage and unlocked it. "Hecate, pardon my daughter's rudeness." He waved the gate open and offered his hand to help the witch-goddess out.

"Sire," Hecate's chin dipped, "all is well." A sudden frailty washed over her, transforming her into a cowering girl, a woman in terror. She cringed and marched out of the enclosure, avoiding looking at Zeus or Athena.

"I should hope so." Zeus twisted to scowl at Athena as he led Hecate out. "Eros and Psyche await *you*. They have revelations, and I wish for us everyone to listen before we enjoy any festivities." He was direct, his voice pinched, soft.

Athena shivered; such softness, coming from Zeus, meant danger. Trouble. It meant that soon *she* might find herself behind bars for disobedience.

Once Hecate had passed the threshold, Zeus beckoned Athena closer. The lightning dancing in his gaze was fierce, forceful, and deadly. "I'll deal with you later."

It took all of Athena's might to fumble her way upstairs.

‖ 30. LET'S HEAR THE TRUTH ‖

EROS

Stepping into the throne-room threw Eros back in time. Back to the days when he'd been summoned for this or that adventure by Zeus, or the reprimands for spreading too much love. Or when he'd plead his case to keep Psyche in Olympus, to marry her, to spite his mother.

The gleaming seats and marble pillars covered in flowery vines had always marveled him, and still did, though hours ago he'd wished to destroy them. As he wreaked havoc across the United States, shredding soulmates to pieces, he'd craved to see the thrones shattered and the ceiling caving in.

But this ceiling would hold, and those thrones were occupied, preventing them from being targeted. The occupants—the Greek gods of Olympus that he'd wanted dead mere hours ago—glanced at him as if surprised to discover him alive, somewhat well, recovered. Weeks ago he'd been a mess, a panicked paranoid on a quest to locate his wife, and they'd all ignored him.

Not today. Today, though they remained silent, they watched. Waited. They were receptive. Their postures were regal and reverent, but their eyes were inquisitive, penetrating, painful to behold.

Settled in his *interrogation chair,* placed at the bottom of the dais, before the semicircle of thrones, Eros basked in the glowing orbs of light sprinkled between pillars.

To relax his nerves, he hummed a peppy tune, determined to appease his woes—but when the king's recognizable footsteps rang behind him, he quieted. Stiff and sore, he perked up and bit his lip.

Zeus marched by his right side, with a wary-looking Hecate beside him. Athena sulked past his other side, worried but scorned, her fingertips twitching with electricity. The energy between them was furious, flickering with fear.

Something had happened between the three of them in the dungeons, and Eros hated to realize it likely had to do with him.

A few feet to his left, Psyche wriggled about in her own interrogation seat, her eyes tired and her skin sickeningly pallid. But her heart was healthy, he heard it; she was safe, her soul pure once more.

Despite all we've done and the verdicts to come...we survived.

With a grunt, Zeus lowered into his throne, atop the podium, and directly across from Eros. Hecate, her auburn skirts brushing against the tiles, stood by him, squeezed between his seat and Hera's. Her gaze darted about the area, suspicious. Nervous.

The goddess of wisdom dropped into her seat and peered into her lap, her shoulders drooping. An unlikely sight—Athena wasn't one to cower, ever.

"We start with you, Eros," said Zeus, his booming tone tearing Eros from his thoughts. "Tell us all that you recall, from the beginning. Especially whatever might help us understand who or *what* did this, and for what purpose."

Eros gulped. "I vaguely recall the day before I noticed Psyche's disappearance. I sensed *something* following me. Like a light effect, an orb…but I couldn't identify it, so I dismissed it as a sort of presence. Nothing harmful, nothing uncommon for a home such as ours."

Psyche mumbled in agreement. Hera whispered to herself, and Athena's brows itched to hike up. Everyone else kept their focus on Eros.

"But I soon realized…this *thing*, it had a heart." A few gasps interrupted him, and Zeus shushed them, waving at Eros to pursue. "A heart blackened by violence and anger. No evil, but rage. Whatever it was expressed a lot of frustration. But again, I let it slide. I expected it was Father's usual mood-swings," he winced, side-eyeing Ares, who groaned, "or an unhappy human's emotions gliding up to us. Which has happened before. So I carried on with my business, and the next day…Psyche was gone. The madness I'd perceived in that being, in its heart, was in me. Identical fits of indignation grew inside me."

On instinct, he shriveled. So used to the soul-crushing agony he'd endured for weeks, he expected his heart to thump out of control, his limbs to numb, a frenzy to unfurl in his brain and command his senses.

But his heartbeat remained steady, and he didn't black out, didn't become weak and carnivorous.

I'm finally free of the rage that once consumed me.

"And only the next morning you felt this, yes?" Zeus' voice startled him, reminding him the interrogation was far from over. "What tossed you over the edge? The same *thing* that followed you the night before, that had possessed you?"

Eros dug through his remembrances, seeking the details. "That thing…everything *it* felt woke in me. It spoke to me, it told me Psyche had left. Upon checking, I understood it had given me the truth. No one had noticed her absence…which riled the fury within more. I searched the palace and everyone else acted normal, had no worry or care that Psyche hadn't begun her usual tasks. So…it irked me, spiked my blood. And this voice…" his hands balled into fists, "it commanded me to leave, to find her, and to do that, I'd have to kill."

The gasps grew louder, and even Zeus, whose expression had remained neutral until then, propped his mouth open. "And…do you remember where you went next?" He scratched his chin, shoving aside his bushy beard.

Eros anticipated his internal monster would growl now, urge him to attack; but only a solemn silence reigned in his mind. Only regret filled his core. Only flashes of a meeting in the Underworld, one he'd promised to conceal. He had to be wary; Zeus could read minds, and if he caught a hint of the earlier conversation in the prison with his healer, who knew what would happen.

"I traveled to the Underworld. Snuck through a passage under a lake…I followed Hermes to it." Hermes' jaw sank, and Athena turned to him, shoulders tensing. "I guided myself with the rivers and came upon Cerberus and…well, that's where I met Persephone, who warned me I'd need blood. *Blood from the beast*, she said. It would be of great use to me." He imagined if Hades were there, he'd be glaring at him. "She was off, not herself, but…so was I. I never questioned her demeanor." Acid bubbled up in his throat. "She helped me obtain the substance. After that, it's all a bit blurry."

Zeus shot to his feet and traipsed towards Eros. "Hecate cured Persephone. But Persephone didn't remember speaking with you.

Her affliction was less intense, but it hindered her memories much more."

Eros stole a quick glance at Hecate, who kept her gaze focused on her sandals. Her heart sped up, but Eros didn't sense it as blackened and evil, like the being that had taken over him. Hers was white, pulsating, drowned in angst and confusion. Until then, he hadn't been strong enough to sniff her out, to gauge her intentions.

She isn't the culprit. She can't be.

Zeus inched closer, eyes widened. "Ah?"

Realizing his mistake, Eros grimaced. "Shit."

"Shit indeed," said the king, not a trace of amusement in his darkening features. "Would you care to share these thoughts? Who is *she*, and how is it that she isn't the culprit?"

Psyche hiccuped, Hecate chewed on her lip, and Hera leaned forward, intrigued.

Eros didn't realize Zeus was still able to read his thoughts. He swallowed. "*She…*" He winced as daggers lined his throat. "As in Persephone. *Persephone* isn't the culprit. I was only reminding myself of that. You are correct, she didn't have the level of infliction as my wife and me. That internal voice…it didn't fuel her as it did us. Didn't force her to attack humans and make them eat each other's hearts. But she might have had another role." He inhaled and exhaled. "A distraction, perhaps?"

Zeus squinted, pursed his lips, then slid backwards. "Perhaps. Or *you* were the distraction from Psyche. She transformed individuals into flesh-eating creatures. Why…*why* weren't you searching for her, as you claimed you needed to? Why did you instead concentrate on pushing soulmates to destruction?" He joined his hands behind his back, glimpsing Eros with one brow quirked.

Was I *the distraction?*

Zeus nodded. "Share with the class, Eros."

"The voice…it instructed me to target humans, soulmates, and doing that would lead me to Psyche. Killing them would draw us together, draw the gods out, and…" He clapped a hand over his mouth, but Zeus urged him to continue. "It did. The voice was right. *You* are right. My killings were the interference."

Psyche whimpered and he veered to her, viewing her chin sinking and her chest heaving. "He…" she moaned, and Zeus flipped his attention to her. A cup-bearer rushed up and fanned her face, and another seized her hands, squeezing, mumbling soft words to soothe her.

With a shudder, more memories flicked to life in Eros' brain, reminding him that the being had controlled his actions, his emotions, *for weeks*. "I didn't comprehend it then, but I had no clue the voice was its own separate entity. I accepted it as my conscience, and believed its words were mine. And I wanted you, all of you…dead."

Hera, Artemis, and Demeter sneered. Their heartbeats raced, raging in their chests. The others ingested his comments in silence, remaining relaxed, aware he no longer wished for their deaths. He was no longer a menace to them.

After a heavy sigh, Zeus meandered to his throne. "It wanted to blind you with Psyche's disappearance. Give you a purpose, a reason to go insane. It made you unaware you were poisoned." The usual storminess evaporated from his eyes, and a subtle sternness sprinkled into his features as he gaped at Psyche. "So it all comes down to you, my dear. The creature manipulated you most. It used Eros and Persephone to fool us, but you were part of its true plan."

Everyone switched their focus to Psyche, who sucked in a deep breath and closed her eyes.

She shooed the cup-bearers away and struggled to sit up straight. "Me."

"My love," said Eros, desperate to reach her, hold her, reassure her. "It'll be okay. You weren't yourself, and we all know it. They'll forgive you as they did me. *I* forgive you." Though his words came out soft and pleasant, a twinge of fear pinched his belly.

Would she be all right? Would she recover from the long-term damage of what she'd done?

Zeus is correct—this affected her most.

Zeus sent one leg over the other and gripped the armrests of his throne. "Yes. You will be forgiven. So tell me, Psyche; what do you remember?"

||31. PSYCHE'S REVELATIONS||

PSYCHE

Psyche readied for the backlash. For the cringing, the cruel glares, the anger.

But the growling ache that once unfurled in her belly, the bitter voice that once screamed and took control…never came. Her thoughts were her own. She was alone to confront a mob of confused and unhappy gods.

Zeus leaned back in his seat, a sympathetic smile swiping over his lips. "We're not unhappy with you. You were poisoned, and we only wish to understand why. To eliminate suspects." He flinched, his gaze flashing at Hecate, then Athena, then returning to Psyche. "Athena's list has grown since her investigation began, and I don't like it."

Psyche cleared her throat. "Most of the day before my…disappearance…I was sick. In a humanly way, as if my once mortal soul was perturbed. Weighed down, depressed, loaded with a sorrow I didn't understand. An awkward block of negativity inside me. I shared my woes with my daughter," she exchanged a glance with Hedone, who stood off to the side, "but she told me to rest, and I'd get better." Struggling to focus on Zeus' concerned features, she dipped her chin. "Well…I didn't."

She sensed Eros to her right, but he was too far. The gods claimed that the two love-birds needed physical distance in order to get accurate recounts of their experiences. Though Psyche agreed, she needed Eros now, as she recounted her horror. Relief had flooded her being when she became lucid again, finding herself in his warm arms, no longer drowning in toxins. Without his touch, she couldn't relax.

Can we be safe? What is coming for us?

"I barely ate that night. The food tasted sour. I assumed my illness caused that, so I mentioned nothing of it to Eros or Hedone. We went straight to bed." Her jaw weighed a thousand pounds as she fought to stop it from drooping. "He fell asleep peacefully as ever, but I was restless. Which is unusual." Eros grumbled in agreement. "I kept hearing things. Things that intrigued me, that summoned me. Beckoning me away from the blankets. I refused to get up, at first, because I was hallucinating, but…" The gods were so absorbed in her story, so focused, chills undulated up her spine. "Someone whispered in my ear. Loudly. It unsettled me, and when Eros didn't react to the noise, I suspected I had imagined it. But it advised me it was real. And it *felt* real. It gave me instructions."

Zeus fidgeted. "To make humans eat raw animal meat?"

"No," Psyche grimaced, "not like that. It advised me to go to earth, to fix humans. To mingle amongst them and treat them, help them. It told me only I had the ability to do so, because no other god would have the patience, would take the time. It compelled me, tugged at my heartstrings…so I obeyed. And next…" Silence enveloped her in its sweet embrace, and she wished they would all read her mind, so she wouldn't have to say the truth out loud, wouldn't have to formulate it. "Athena found me in that field. Dirty, bloody, and insane."

"And you…" Hera pressed forward as if about to lunge on her. "You recall nothing between those moments?"

"No." Psyche shivered as blinding flashes that made no sense flickered to and fro before her. Guts and flesh and deerskin and green smoke. "And after that…I blacked out again, only to awaken on the concrete floors of the dungeons. That's it." She coughed as she glimpsed Zeus. "Your Majesty."

Every ounce of her courage drizzled out as she tore away from her audience. She looked into her lap, at her hands that ached as if she'd punched walls for days. Weeks. Her mouth overflowed with the acidic, abnormal taste of venom, and droplets of sweat gathered on her forehead. Tears gushed down her cheeks, and the liquid that fell onto her skin was red, violet, blue. Blood, poison, pain.

Apollo had helped her change her bloody tunic, he'd healed her external bruises, mended her sore, scabbed feet. But her insides still ripped at the seams and agony poured out, leaving her hopeless and breathless.

Why is this so hard? Why do I only have flashbacks?

A shadow loomed over her, and she jerked her head up to find Zeus. He placed his hands on the arm-rests and glanced at her not with anger, but with concern.

"Can you share these flashbacks with us? Try to describe them?" He kneeled, his eyes like a bright blue sky. Tender, fatherly. "Deliver them to us so that we might analyze them?"

She peered around Zeus' massive frame and caught Hera wincing, Athena holding her breath and steepling her fingers, Hermes shaking his head, Apollo whispering to himself. Poseidon had risen and was pacing before his throne, wiping his dampened forehead.

"You," Psyche bit her lip, "you wouldn't understand them, you wouldn't get it, and I can't—"

Zeus seized her chin and forced her to look at him. "We need to hear it, child. No matter how messy, we will figure it out. You're safe here, never forget that."

Once I confess, they will kick me out of the palace.

"I never…never should have listened to that voice," she said, her arms racking with tremors.

Zeus held her chin tighter, the pads of his thumbs somehow soothing to her. "You had no alternative. So speak, before I choose to dig into your mind—and trust me, that wouldn't be pleasant." He released her, but stayed close, urging her to come clean.

She tucked a strand of her golden curls behind her ears. "The voice and I…we argued. A lot. It punished me whenever I disagreed with its goals. It drove me to believe I was helping mortals by forcing them to…to eat…" She convulsed, moaned in displeasure, sensed something swirling up her throat—

Eros arrived before her, shoving Zeus out of the way. "Love," he said, docile and calming as he set his hands on her knees and kissed her exposed calves. "It's okay. It's okay. Talk, let it out, it will free you." His amber eyes soaked with tears.

No one yanked Eros off her, so she contracted all her muscles and prayed the shivers away. "It kept telling me this was for the best. That I would save humanity. I knew it was lying, but the insanity consumed me. Hurt me. I had no other option. Those flashbacks…they revealed that I was driving humans to be as mad as I was. I poisoned them." Her lower limbs stiffened as she tugged them to her chest and wrapped her arms around her knees, rocking back and forth. "I can't live with it, I can't." So broken, so frail, she rocked and rocked as her eyes clogged. She zoned out into a world where no one would judge, no one would hold grudges against her mistakes.

Someone else approached, but Psyche didn't realize who it was until she spoke. "You needn't let the guilt eat you up, Psyche." Artemis' strong and feminine tone was careful, but reassuring. "I sent my best huntresses down to control the populace. Apollo sent healers, and Hecate will, too. We'll fix this." She placed a kiss on Psyche's forehead, then returned to her seat.

Too much saliva bubbled in Psyche's mouth, and she couldn't reply.

Zeus weaved his fingers through his graying mane. "How many distractions does this cruel being need?"

Poseidon sauntered over, clenching his trident, as if bracing to hurl its magic at the next person who entered the room. "So she was a distraction too, you think?" He shrugged. "Three disturbances?"

"If not more." The King of the sky blew out his cheeks as he pivoted to his brother. "But no, not her…the individuals she infused with toxins? *They* were the distraction."

A few deities broke out in hushed comments, but Psyche trained her gaze on the two brothers.

"To conceal true motives?" The ruler of the seas spared a quick glance at her.

"And to then fake heal them…and gain trust from all mortals. They wanted to stop a plague, make themselves look godly." Zeus shifted his weight, his tunic swaying near his knees. "Maybe. There are endless possibilities. Whatever the case…someone is attempting to lead us astray while they set their actual plan in motion. Someone hopes to fool the gods of Olympus."

Dionysus almost spilled his wine; Ares growled; Aphrodite let out a high-pitched shriek.

Zeus wrenched around to face them all and slammed a foot to the floor. "Setting gods out to destroy humans, hoping to divide us...yet making it easy for us to capture and tame those causing chaos? Yes, the healing process was hard, but what if that was an ambush of its own? Time wasted on curing them while something happened *somewhere else?*" His back muscles tensed, throbbing. "Choosing two gods with an established link—a loving husband and wife—and separating them, dropping clues to confuse us, leading us nowhere?"

Eros snuck to Psyche's side, his fingers curling around hers. "Distractions within distractions?"

Poseidon shuddered so deeply the ground quaked beneath him. His dark hair shot up, as if electrified, like a cat's fur when threatened. "Someone is setting a trap, preparing something bigger?"

"Someone wants us dead," corrected Zeus, jutting his chin at Eros. "He said so himself."

Psyche recoiled.

Who would want to kill Olympian gods?

"Sabotage." Poseidon snorted and crossed his arms, clutching his trident in the crook of his elbow. "I see it, brother. A god among us thinks he or she is smarter, wants to overthrow us. Hades would agree. We're too familiar with such wars, aren't we?"

The word *war* drew Ares from his post. "Father?" He planted before Zeus, a fist pumping to his chest.

Athena—the other deity connected to battle—soon followed. She kneeled before her father and inclined her head. "Should we brace for war, Father?" Fear laced into her tone, coiled around her like a snake.

Ares crouched beside her, his helmet trembling in his grip. "Whatever you command, we'll do."

So odd to see them agreeing, for once.

Psyche knew it was her doing. She'd caused them all to panic, and they had no inkling why, no notion who sought to create such discord.

"We recognize the signs as you do," said Athena, sending a brief side-glance at her half-brother. "The signs of a diversion, of a declaration of battle, of the pain to come."

"Heart-eating creatures, a horde of zombies..." Ares frowned, straightened up, and offered his arm to Athena; another shocking sight. "Not to mention easy access to Cerberus...it all smells like a fight. A big one."

"Clear warnings. Unlikely and unusual, but impossible to ignore," added Athena.

"As gods of this planet, we are to protect these humans. And to do so..." Ares turned to Athena, "we must protect ourselves."

"You are both correct." Zeus' nostrils flared. "It's all too coincidental. Phenomena like these only announce something much worse to come."

"But who is provoking them?" Hera's svelte figure swished over, her lengthy train trailing behind her like a peacock's tail. "Who would dare cause such atrocious acts of diversion—*human death*—to steal our attention and trick us?" A few others voiced agreement, though none dared declare it like Hera. "You said our first list of suspects was too long, but we cannot change that if we don't know where to start." She weaseled between Zeus and Poseidon, hands on her hips, and her demeanor filled with spite as she narrowed her gaze on Psyche. "What more do you know? A single, slight detail might topple the balance in our favor."

Eros snarled at her tone, but Psyche snatched his hand and prevented him from attacking the queen. "No, she's right."

He fought her grip. "Perhaps, but you don't have to respond to her taunts—"

Psyche dug her nails into his skin and, legs wobbly, she heaved up from her seat. Zeus and Poseidon veered to her, Hera blinked, and Athena and Ares stilled.

"There *is* a minor detail that might help." Closing her eyes, Psyche prayed for peace, for forgiveness. That by saying this information out loud, she'd be absolved of all her crimes. "I don't know who spoke to me, nor how they melted my thoughts and forged their way into my skull, but I *can* tell you the voice was feminine. It was a woman."

|| 32. ACHING TRUTHS ||
ATHENA

A woman?

The gods had long since fled the throne-room, but Athena, stuck to her chair, her mind swimming with pictures and portraits of female goddesses, hadn't moved. She pinched the bridge of her nose for the fiftieth time and let out yet another exasperated sigh.

It was intelligence that would benefit her investigation, but it highlighted several names on her list in big, scary, ways. There were so many female deities in Olympus or with easy access to it, and many others who were guests. And many with friends who swung by for visits, with powers beyond her knowledge. Not to forget the serving staff and the lesser goddesses who came and went.

So who out of them all could possess someone's mind at a distance?

She tucked her head between her palms and moaned. Whoever this culprit was, *she* played with human lives by manipulating a married couple and causing discord among the gods. Did this woman want to spare humans from her chaos? Or were they only pawns in her plans? She'd torn their hearts out and poisoned them without scruple, and without even making them ingest anything. And she'd known the Olympians would prioritize the mortals and abandon the palace to help—

She sat up straight. "That was Psyche's role! To create a zombie army to draw us from the palace."

Squeezing the arm-rests, she squinted at the empty seats before her, where Psyche and Eros had perched earlier. Where they'd plead, and Athena had begged to understand their muffled thoughts, yearned to decipher the flashes that crashed through their minds.

The Titans? The Giants? Or minor gods? All had attempted to replace Zeus in centuries past. This new situation was too similar for her to not have picked up on the pattern.

A cold sensation trickled down her neck. "First, Aphrodite was dispatched to earth and never meant to return," she inhaled and exhaled, "and then me. Sent after Psyche. Was I also never supposed to make it home?"

This creature had guessed Zeus would send a mother after her erratic son. And a wise goddess after a wandering woman spreading a virus among mortals. This individual also knew Athena would sneak into the Underworld to talk to Hades—

She shot to her feet, but her nails clawed into the marble arm-rests. "No. No, I told him!"

Only someone with unimaginable power and foresight would be able to learn such things. Only someone with unlimited resources and a deep knowledge of all the gods would scheme all this.

A vision seeped into her brain; a womanly figure with violet and scarlet eyes, crimson streaks in her ebony hair, her auburn skirts swishing, a smirk of secrecy across her dark-painted lips—

"It *was* Hecate. She must have orchestrated it and was aware I'd show up downstairs."

Rage burned in her belly, so hot and powerful that it scorched the linings of her stomach. Hecate had expected her, hadn't she? She'd prepared to be interrogated, invented the missing potion to waste time, to keep Athena in the Underworld while she furthered her agenda. But she wasn't alone; she'd have an accomplice. Another female ally in Olympus had helped her poison Eros and Psyche.

Zeus' swears made no sense and wouldn't dissuade Athena. How did he not read through the Underworld sorceress' fake exterior? She'd been practicing her pretty manners and niceties for centuries; why was Athena the only one who noticed it? It broke her heart to witness the toxicity radiating from every inch of the witch-goddesses' skin, permeating the pure Olympus air with foul ploys and cruel intentions.

But why would she want to take Zeus' crown and dismantle Olympus? Why would she reenact former rebellions and turn all the gods against each other?

"And she has succeeded," Athena whispered to herself, punching a hand into her other palm. "Father and I are in disagreement over her. Hera took my side, and her children will team up with us, as will her sisters. Meaning Hecate has already created a civil war."

Overcome with doubt, Athena spun on herself and scanned the area. She didn't trust anyone, not even the men—any could be weaving a web of chaos for Hecate at that very moment.

Who works for whom? Who is on the good *side?*

So absorbed in her internal accusations, she screeched when someone approached from her right, slinking up with such stealth it caught her by surprise.

She twisted towards the being, recognizing them almost at once, though they hunched, keeping to the shadows. She knew that sly stance.

"Hermes? What are you doing?"

He smirked and cocked his head as he wandered closer to her. "All this has put you quite on edge, hasn't it? But fear not; I don't have the right body parts to be a suspect." He stopped before her and trailed his fingertips along the outline of his manhood, eyebrows wiggling as he slid his tongue across his teeth.

Athena gagged. "What do you want? I don't have time for your games."

"Well," he resumed his strides towards her, his chest puffing out, "I was about to take Hecate home, but she asked—no, demanded—to chat with you first. I had hoped for some…uh…quality alone time with her, but I suppose it must wait." He pivoted and jutted his chin towards the exit. "She's outside, by the gates."

Athena didn't delay for him to tell her twice—she whipped by her sex-hungry brother and raced out of the throne-room.

Was it an ambush? Had Hecate realized none of her ruses had taken?

She wouldn't let the witch-goddess escape so quickly, but a twinge of fear prompted her to turn around as she passed the threshold. Hermes was powerful, had knowledge, and…

Oh crap.

She shuffled off, worried that he was the accomplice working from Olympus. She'd thought it before, and dismissed it, but could he have a network of serving girls and nymphs aiding him to further Hecate's cause?

She wouldn't confront Hecate without protection. So as she approached the massive entry doors, she skidded sideways to a concealed door leading to a downward staircase. At the bottom was a place she heavily disliked—Hephaestus' workshop.

It was a last resort. She abhorred the blacksmith deity based on their past, but he had what she needed.

She didn't knock, and stole inside the dingy space, her gaze meeting his as she slammed the heavy door shut behind her. "I need your help."

All manners of rusty and polished weapons decorated the walls, and a massive furnace rested at the end of the room.

Hephaestus dropped the hammer he'd been holding and wiped his hands on his apron. "Of course." Though his hellish eyes brightened, he appeared otherwise undisturbed by her presence. He might have been anticipating it. "What is it?"

He owes me, and he hasn't forgotten.

"I need…" she peered about the area, a copper and steel scent slipping into her nostrils, "pure ambrosia. And a weapon strong enough to kill a witch."

"Ah." His eyebrows quirked up, but he didn't question her as he reached for a box below his workstation and extracted a vial. "Here's the ambrosia, but the weapon will take a little longer. Especially for *that* witch, since she's also a goddess."

Athena's heart sank. Hephaestus usually concocted armor and swords out of thin air, so she hadn't expected this.

His lips bunched as he scratched at his temple, near the scar Athena remembered giving him in their youth. "However…I do have something that might incapacitate her." He handed her the vial and limped off to a closet near the furnace.

Athena didn't hesitate and drained the ambrosia into her mouth. Immediately, godly power swelled in her veins and enriched her blood, infused her bones, and fortified her muscles.

Try me now, Hecate.

Hephaestus returned with a hammer resembling the one he'd been using, but shinier, glowing. He tossed it at her, and she caught it so fast a *whoosh* of wind knocked over a few papers nearby.

"That should do it." He shrugged a few matted raven curls from his glistening forehead. "It was powerful enough to knock out Dionysus and extricate him from one of his frenzies, so it might destabilize her for a spell. Do you need backup?"

Athena was already halfway out the door, clutching the hammer as a fizzing sensation swirled up her arms. "No, but if you hear me scream…fetch Zeus and Ares."

Moments later, when Athena burst through the palace doors, she tightened her grip on her weapon when she noticed Hecate pacing a few feet away.

At the sight of Athena, she froze. "I…"

The goddess of wisdom stormed over, and the witch threw her hands up in surrender, sighting the iridescent hammer. The vibrant crimson in her eyes faded, replaced by a neutral, nearly bland purple.

Ambrosia bubbled inside Athena. "Don't start with me, witch. I've had enough of your tales, and enough of my father covering up for you. I want the truth." The tip of her sandals traipsed over the hem of Hecate's gown, gluing her in place should she try to rush off. "Or I'll bash your head in and throw you in the dungeon."

Athena cringed; she sounded too much like Ares.

Hecate swallowed and dipped her chin. Actual fear poured from her aura, and for a moment, Athena wondered why. Her hair was tangled, her skin pallid, her shoulders drawn inward.

"You're right, okay?" Hecate looked up, and her lower lip

trembled. "There is a distraction, but by accusing me you're playing into it. *I* am a distraction, too! My poison, Eros, Psyche, even my darling Persephone—we're all involved without wanting to be. The humans sacrificed…are also part of this. If you give in to your hunches, if you don't see reason, she'll win!"

Athena's hands became clammy as she grasped the hammer, bracing to lift it. "What are you saying? Are you trying to delay me, throw me off the scent? Take the blame off yourself? What are you playing at, Hecate? Why are you so damn suspicious?"

The witch-goddess sank to her knees, palms clasped in prayer. "Please…speak with Eros. Privately. He…he saw my heart, he encountered me in the Underworld, and I…" She let out a tiny whimper and shook her head. "I was manipulated, Athena. But not poisoned. Nor did I poison anyone. I know more than I should, but I swore an oath of secrecy on the Styx." Multicolored tears splashed on the stones beneath her.

Athena lowered the hammer. "What sort of nonsense is this? A trap?"

Grabbing at Athena's mid-length dress, Hecate sobbed. "Please look at the facts. The diversion was meant to pull the strongest of you out of Olympus, to leave Zeus vulnerable…as he is now. Listen to me, and you may return to him, to keep him safe. His throne is at stake. Someone works against him…several people, in fact, but I can only reveal one, due to my oath."

Every fiber of her core screamed at her to not lower her guard, but Athena had to hear Hecate's story. "I'm listening."

The witch didn't miss a beat and gaped up at Athena, scarlet swirls animating in her eyes, coming to life. "Think. Who hasn't left Olympus recently? Who hasn't been sent out on a mission and has full access to the palace? Besides Zeus, who fits that profile?"

A chill slithered down Athena's spine. "The spy in Olympus…the monster among us."

"Yes," Hecate let go of her dress, "now go on, list those you're distrustful of, and you'll find the pattern."

"Dionysus and Apollo…cleared, as the first is a drunk, and the second helped with all the healing." Athena tapped a finger to her chin. "Ares was here too, but Eros is his son, so he wouldn't. That concern he had…it was real, I sensed it." She shrugged. "Despise him as I might, Poseidon is in the clear, as he hastened home to his kingdom. Hades left the Underworld at Zeus' behest but was otherwise in his realm. Hermes was with me."

Hecate said nothing, leaning back and crossing her arms, waiting.

"And the women…I rule Aphrodite out—she is one of the strong ones you referred to, assigned to stop Eros. Demeter wouldn't dare harm Persephone. Artemis wouldn't do anything her brother would shame her for, and she'd never permit animals to be devoured like so. Hestia is sworn to peace and quit the Olympian council."

"So do you get it, yet?" Wobbly, Hecate heaved to her feet. "Do you understand?"

Athena narrowed her gaze. "With all those deities ruled out, it leaves—" she stumbled backwards, her balance tested, "—oh. *Oh.*"

Hecate nodded. "You realize who may be a bigger part in this than she claimed. I wouldn't say she's the mastermind, but she has a say, no? Zeus is too blind to figure it out, but you and I…we can."

A sickening throbbing resonated in Athena's skull. "So…you're accusing her? But how…how can I trust you? You're full of deceit and have had this knowledge for a while without admitting it. You lied to me."

"I did, and I promise you I had no alternative. And yes," Hecate perked up, her fiery attitude reviving, "I accuse her, outright and without a doubt. You can count on me, because Zeus does. He is the only one you should trust." She sucked in a heavy breath of Olympus oxygen. "*Ask Eros.* I made him promise to keep our interaction a secret, but he can attest I've always been pure-hearted. Trust me. It's her you should be wary of."

The doors opened behind them, and light footsteps paraded up to them. Athena swiveled to find Hermes, a falsely innocent smile swiping across his lips.

"Are you two finished? I see there's been no bloodshed, so you've chosen not to massacre each other." He gawked at Athena. "Can I take her to the Underworld now, Highness?"

She exchanged a last glance with Hecate, trying her hardest to see beyond the veil of cruelty she'd always envisioned around her. "Go. Something's afoot here, and all Olympians must be home. Hurry. Tell Hades to be on his guard."

Hecate and Hermes both acquiesced, and as they walked away, Athena heard him ask *"what was that about?"* before they jumped into the clouds.

Athena set her sights on the gleaming golden doors, her lungs tight, her soul in agony.

Hera. It's all Hera, isn't it?

‖ 33. SMELLS LIKE A PARTY ‖
EROS

Watching the Olympian nymphs dance and sing in tune to Apollo's lyre usually put Eros in a lovely mood. He'd admire his daughter as she joined in, spreading pleasurable energy all around. He'd beam at the Muses who accompanied Apollo's instrument, dazzling everyone with their heavenly voices. And he'd squeeze his beautiful wife's hand while imagining himself stripping off her clothes and having his way with her.

Today, he saw nothing but drowned colors, like a ruined watercolor painting. A gray cloud hovered over him. Dread weighed like a thousand tons in his gut, and he smelled danger despite the delicious scents sneaking into the courtyard from the kitchens.

How could everyone be so festive with the impending doom looming over their heads?

As he dwelled on his negativity, the music faded. The laughter and cheer died, and everything happened in slow motion. He cringed as he pictured himself zooming up to Apollo, plunging his fingers into his rib-cage, extracting his lively heart, and tossing it to the ground. Then he envisioned a nymph crawling up to eat it, licking its juices from the stone.

With a shudder, he tuned back in to reality. To where Hedone whirled and whirled, waving at him and Psyche; but he didn't wave back. He couldn't, too frozen by his vision to move.

Why were these visions plaguing him again? Wasn't he cured? No one noticed his agony, all too preoccupied by the celebrations to care. What did they celebrate? The threat was still out there, and Athena's list of suspects only became larger. Instead of investigating, the ever-lavish Olympians threw a giant party.

Athena didn't attend it, Eros noticed. She hadn't made an appearance since they'd all departed the throne-room, but no one seemed disturbed by her absence.

He and Psyche sat atop flowery garden chairs mounted on a flat-topped rock, elevating them above everyone else, showing them as guests of honor. Aphrodite and Ares flirted in a dark corner, Demeter waved her hands enchantingly, producing fruit and flowers with her touch. Artemis kept watch over her nymphs, bobbing her head to the melody, and Zeus stood in the doorway, smiling at his family.

Eros spotted something off about his smile. It didn't quite reach his ears; it didn't glow and bask his people in sunlight. A storm raged on in his gaze, but it was so cloudy, so hard to discern, no one paid it any mind.

Except for Eros.

Why did he want this party? What does he hope to gain from it?

Psyche brushed her hand against Eros' arm. "My love?" He twisted to find her soft blue eyes welling with worry. "What's wrong? Are you not enjoying yourself?" Her gentle fingertips grazed his cheeks, spiraling shivers down his spine.

Her touch always relaxed him, yet today it only exacerbated his tension. "I can't do this." He shifted his position, uncrossed his legs, huffed. "I can't sit here, venerated, because I'm no longer a bloody killing machine. It's like everyone forgot, like they don't care what's going on."

The tunes muffled his speech to all but Psyche, who removed her fingers from his skin. "It's a temporary break, that is all. We all need it. It means they forgive us, they realize we were not responsible for our actions. But they will never forget. *We* will never forget."

Hedone gaped over at them, grinning as she danced, relieved to have her parents back to normal. Though her demeanor should have pleased Eros, he visualized himself shooting an arrow at her. He viewed it smashing into her chest, staining her tunic with crimson as the Muses crammed their hands into her torso and tore out her heart. Blood splashed everywhere, splattering the courtyard's polished cobblestone. Apollo's lyre notes distorted, deep and dreary.

Eros' temples pounded as he shoved the horrid flashes down, trying to return to the moment. Past, potential future, present—all the images interlaced, forming a pattern of blood and death, flesh and carcasses. He was nauseous, and glad he was sitting down.

He fanned himself, praying to drown his dizziness. "Do you not get flashes of rage, of violence, still?" He nudged Psyche. "Do you not still feel the angst? Are you not still suffering?"

She shuddered as she peeked at her hands. "I…I *do,* but I cannot let them overtake me. We must be strong, my love. All of us. Strong for what's to come. We've defeated the toxins within, and Hecate saved us! This creature can no longer manipulate our thoughts and force us to hurt others. And that is cause to celebrate." She tried to smile though her lips trembled, and her shoulders hunched.

Eros closed his eyes, remembering Hecate and her fear. Her pure and innocent heart filled with an atrocious level of fright and terror. But why?

Why wouldn't she tell me more? Why would she leave me so clueless?

He gaped about the garden, realizing other gods had departed. Hera had fled who knew where, Hestia had run to the kitchens, and Hephaestus had returned to his workshop, not one for festivities. Hecate and Hermes had excused themselves, too, to take off for the Underworld.

"You're still not reassured, husband." Psyche stiffened as she veered away from him. "Shall we withdraw to our room, lay down for a while? Relax in our own way?"

Eros chewed on his tongue; usually such an offer would be more than tempting, and he wouldn't hesitate to sweep his spouse off her feet and tug her clothes off before they even arrived at their bedroom door. But today, haunted by his murderous tendencies, dragged down by torment, reminded of the bloodshed, the cruelty— he was blocked. He was part of a ploy to divert the gods while someone attacked his home.

But Psyche was right about the need to withdraw from the party. The positivity that surrounded him worsened his mood. Even with the poison extracted, he wasn't the same Eros as before. Still the god of love, but not sweet as he once was.

I don't think I'll ever be the same again.

He turned to his wife. "Yes, good idea."

They rose, and as their sandaled feet reached the ground, someone clapped. Following the sound, Eros' gaze landed on Zeus, who had meandered farther into the courtyard, a stubborn sternness written all over his expression.

"Our lovebirds need some privacy." He winked at Eros and Psyche but maintained a firm tone as he spoke. "Tidy up and retire to your rooms. I'll summon you all again soon, as I have several special guests joining us to help in this sordid affair."

Psyche took Eros' arm, and he sensed her tension.

Guests?

As they passed by Zeus, he leaned in to Eros, his voice lowered to a whisper. "I won't summon you two immediately. You deserve rest. Alert a cup-bearer if you need more seclusion, and I'll grant it."

Eros inclined his head in thanks, but something didn't sit right with him.

Once out of earshot, Psyche made it clear she agreed as she released his arm and groaned. "Guests? *Guests?*" All the calm once peppering her aura dissipated, replaced by confusion. Eros felt her heart turning scarlet, thumping and growing and loading with anger. "In a time like this, he'd invite more people to Olympus? Who would he possibly trust?"

Squinting through the corridor, wary of shadows and mists and voices, he snatched Psyche's waist and pulled her close as he led them to their quarters. "I don't know, but I don't like it either. Not one bit."

||34. OUTSIDE HELP||
ATHENA

As she walked, her heels clicking while her gaze fixed on Olympian portraits hanging from the ivory walls, Athena shook out her hands. Waves of shudders continued to spiral around her limbs, seeking to incapacitate her—but she wouldn't let them.

Each god in the murals stared back, knowing her questions. They watched her, they twitched, and she could have sworn they pointed at the painting of her now number one suspect.

Hera.

She peered at said painting; the image of a majestic, proud lady in an emerald tunic-dress draping down her womanly shape. A bejeweled crown nestled atop her head, and her eyes glowed with knowledge. Or spite or deceit, Athena couldn't tell. Peacocks posed beside her, tails fanned out, glaring at Athena as if protecting their queen.

Athena grunted as she spun away, unable to bear the weight of the artwork. Was Hera the one damaging Olympus this whole time? She had pushed Athena out of the palace. She likely urged Zeus to send Aphrodite off, too.

Athena resumed her march to the throne-room; her steps uneven, her conscience screaming at her. Hera was renowned for driving gods and heroes mad; but it was usually in retaliation for Zeus being unfaithful…and he hadn't cheated on her in centuries.

As she passed landscapes of forests and beaches, populated with lesser deities and mythical creatures, Athena took a sharp turn, and the throne-room doors came into view.

She slowed her pace, unwilling to accept that Hera would seek to discipline her husband again. It had been too long. Zeus had learned his lesson—right?

What other motive would she have to distract her family and go after her spouse's crown?

One peep into the massive room revealed no one had returned from the festivities; Athena would have the area to herself for a while. She snuck in and plopped onto her throne, wriggling about atop its uncomfortable marble and stone surface.

"Why would the queen need to dethrone her own husband?" She scratched her chin and drummed her fingertips on the armchair. "She never trifles with human lives, and cares for her worshipers…unless her desires have changed?" Her rhythmic drumming ceased. "Has she decided humans are no longer important to her? That they must be…sacrificed for whatever her sordid goal is?"

Thundering footsteps in the distance urged her to jump up from her seat. Had the culprit—Hera, or whoever she worked with—heard her formulations and elected to confront her?

Athena's tension released, and she blew out a breath of reprieve when she noticed Zeus slipping into the space, his expression determined as ever.

"There you are," he said, rushing up to her. "I confined everyone to their rooms, for now. Guests are arriving shortly, and I need to bring them up to speed before we attack them with questions."

She quirked a brow. "You're inviting more gods?" She wanted to snort, to question his actions; but she knew she'd tested his patience enough as of late. "Is that wise, Father?"

Zeus brushed a few graying locks from his face. "Not if it were anyone else...but these gods are ones we can trust. They're family...folk I have never doubted." His gaze darkened as he scanned his favorite daughter's features. Did he hope to eliminate the cloak concealing her thoughts? Was he tired of trying to understand her?

Crap. And here he is to take me off the case. He'll give it to one of his guests...

"You're sure?" She gnawed on her lip, yelling at her internal self to shut up before she said something she regretted.

"You've gone above my orders, daughter. If we're talking of trust...I have wondered often about *you*, lately." He didn't grimace, but Athena had no trouble seeing beneath his facade. He was pissed.

"Father, I—"

"—I have also wondered if you trust *me*." He crossed his arms, and his veins glowed blue and purple—a sure sign of irritation that he was trying to suppress.

She gulped. "Of course I do, I would never—"

"—no need to spend hours debating it." He huffed as he squeezed her shoulders. "I have one last mission for you, and it is a delicate, time-sensitive issue."

Her mouth plopped open, shocked that he still wanted her to do anything in relation to the case. After her errors in judgment, her talking back...why would he keep her as his investigator?

She nodded, and he moved away from her. "Yes, Father.

Whatever you ask."

Zeus unleashed a breath so heavy it might have provoked an avalanche. "The new arrivals will be of tremendous aid in our situation, but…they won't be enough. We need more help, and that's where you come in. I need you to fetch someone else for me." He pivoted and joined his hands behind his back as he paced to the middle of the room.

"Fetch someone?" Athena's shoulders sagged, but her legs stiffened as she shifted in her chair. "Ah…yes, Hermes is gone, and he is your usual messenger. I understand."

She struggled to hide her frown. It wasn't a reward, or a second chance; it was a job, and she wasn't even his first choice to do it. The momentary relief that had flooded her lungs soared out and disappeared.

He is still angry with me and seeks to punish me.

Zeus swiveled to her and winced. "Do not take it that way—"

"—no, it is fine." She stretched and got to her feet. "So, the Underworld, I presume? I told Hermes to warn Hades, so…who? The judges?" Realization hit her so fast she nearly tumbled back into her seat. "The judges. Naturally. They can help! They see deep within souls and judge crimes, view inner selves like no one else…I should have thought of that!" She perked up, a wave of anticipation coursing through her. She admired the judges and looked forward to bringing them an official summons from the King of the skies. "I'll fly to them at once. Do you want all three? I can reach them now, thanks to Hermes—"

Zeus whipped his arm up and shot a blast of air to knock her into her chair, to stop her tirade. "Enough." He shook his head as he meandered over and again pressed his hands to her shoulders. "Stop anticipating and start listening. I applaud your quick thinking, and you are right…but the judges are to stay downstairs at all times. They cannot follow you up here. If I need them, I will go to them myself."

"That's fair, I suppose." She shriveled under her father's touch. "But then who? Persephone? Mnemosyne? The Erinyes? Few are those in that realm who might help us, unless you plan on somehow transporting Cerberus in the hopes he'd intimidate the culprit into talking…"

Zeus kneeled before her, setting his hands on her knees. He smiled, and it was so unexpected Athena leaned backwards. "I never said the Underworld, daughter of mine. You assumed it." He pinched her cheek then sat on the throne beside hers where he sighed, then slanted towards her. "You're to go to earth, as I first requested. But this time…to retrieve Lukus Arvantis, the human who aided Aphrodite when she searched for Eros."

Her jaw dropped. "A human?" Her insides turned to butter, her skin burned, her temples thrummed in agony. Too many emotions cruised through her at once, and she felt her limbs melting into her throne. "You want me to desert my family up here to recover a mortal?" Fury, fear, guilt, confusion—all jumbled into one giant bubble in her belly, and she became nauseous. "I don't understand."

"I lack the time for details." Zeus' voice strained. "I need his expertise. His experience as an investigator will come in handy. And he's not fully human, Athena. He has a connection to the gods that he's unaware of."

Her extremities numbed, and she almost bit her tongue. "What?" She wanted to stand, but the energy from her ambrosia infusion earlier had faded, leaving her weak and astonished at Zeus' revelation. A fog of anxiety coated her movements, dulled her heartbeats. "Lukus, the mortal? He…is he…" she smacked a hand over her mouth, "are you saying he is…a direct descendant?" Her voice was muffled as her nails dug into the skin around her lips. "I thought they were all gone!"

A twinkle of knowledge sparked in Zeus' eyes. "I'm sorry, but as I said…no time. I cannot explain or confirm anything." His forehead glistened, and Athena prayed to read through it, to discover his thoughts. "Aphrodite is aware of this connection, though not its specifics…and my sources made it clear he's destined to join us. To help solve our mystery."

Athena scrunched her brows.

Sources—does he mean the Fates? Or someone else?

She shrank, her head spinning with theories and questions. "What in Tartarus are you hiding from us, Father?"

He waved at her dismissively as he rose from his throne. "It's not your concern, not yet. You're not my only council," he said, extending his arm, waiting for her to grab it. She did, but not without a flinch. "It's no coincidence Lukus is so skilled in finding criminals. He will be of great assistance to us. So you will locate him, return the memories Aphrodite plucked from him, and bring him here. I'll take care of the rest."

"But I…" she fumbled, nearly tripping as she took a few steps away from her throne. "I can't leave."

Isn't that what Hera wants?

She let her chin sink as acid brewed in her throat. She had to tell him, warn him, inform him of what Hecate said. He trusted her…so would he believe her?

When she looked up and cleared her throat, oncoming footfalls halted her. They were light and breezy, accompanied by a sickeningly sugary stench she abhorred; a stance and a familiar rustle of skirts she hated to recognize.

Crap—before I had a chance to denounce her. Did she know?

Hera sauntered in, a sly smirk tattooed on her face. She had the appearance of someone who'd been lurking, waiting for the opportune occasion to pop in and ensure Athena didn't have an opportunity to voice her suspicions.

Athena's fists tightened as a slow-burning anger awoke in her. She couldn't accuse Hera without proof, and less so in her presence. Why did she interfere at such an ideal moment? Had she listened to the conversation with Hecate?

Hera ambled over to Zeus. "Dearest—"

"—you're supposed to remain in your quarters, wife," said Zeus, whirling to her, his brows furrowed.

Eager to escape the argument to come, Athena bowed at them and scurried off, out of their space. "I'll return as fast as possible, majesties."

"Oh, but *she* can leave?" Hera sneered. "I dislike your favoritism, husband."

Zeus sidled in front of her and peeked at Athena. "Thank you. I will reward your aid in time." He then whooshed around, and though Athena couldn't see him, she pictured his stormy glare.

Hera's boastful posture faltered as she cringed, but Athena didn't linger to allow their gazes to connect.

You haven't won yet, dearest step-mother.

She'd get her proof, eventually; the intelligence to interrogate the Queen of the gods in front of all. Enough pertinent information to shame her and hold her responsible for her despicable actions. But before that, and before shimmying down to earth, she had one pit-stop to make. One person to consult about her new mission.

The goddess of beauty—the woman who knew Lukus Arvantis better than anyone.

||35. GUESTS OF HONOR||
EROS

The smooth silk sheets cooled Eros' burning skin. Weeks of not sleeping and days of torture on the concrete floors of the dungeon made him appreciate his bed more than he ever had. The cushion under his head relaxed his neck, and the feel of the plush mattress under him allowed him to unwind.

He crossed one foot over the other. Could he enjoy the luxury? Did he deserve it?

He glanced at his beautiful bride beside him, basking in her soft luminosity.

Do either of us deserve it?

This perfect creature of the heavens, nestled against him, her gentle breaths soothing, had been as evil as he was, only days ago. He'd been blood; she'd been poison—what a pair they made.

"It's all too odd," said Psyche, breaking their silent trance.

He slipped his fingers through her golden mane and twirled a few strands. "I agree. I fear you and I are destined to detect plots and ulterior motives in everything. We will never be our old selves again."

She pressed her nose into his bare chest. "Ah, so the facade I sought to hold up isn't as strong as I thought?" She let out a weak giggle, but Eros caught a trace of anxiety, a strain in the usually arousing sound. "Even with the toxin gone, I…that voice, I—"

"—yes, I still hear it too." He heaved himself into a seated position and tugged her up with him. "Though mine is different. But you…you had it much worse, didn't you?" He flinched at her grimace, his heart pinching to see her in pain. "You did, and I'm so sorry, I've been so selfish."

She scoffed. "*You?* Selfish? You took off in search of me!" She nuzzled into his torso again. "And in doing so you…you had to witness your charges eating their own hearts! We both had it rough, albeit in different ways. So our best option now…" Trailing her fingertips along his nipples then down to his belly, she pouted as she connected her beautiful blue gaze with his. "We must put it behind us and move forward, my love."

Her nails dug through the light tunic covering the top of his abdomen, sending pleasurable shivers up his legs, his spine, his neck. In other times he would have seized her, ripped her dress off, planted her skin with firm and feverish kisses—but he couldn't. A glacial sensation fluttered in his lungs instead, and he took her fingers and pressed them to his lips.

"No, we cannot. We must use our memories to help. Even if it scars us more. It's our duty."

Psyche's brows furrowed as she snatched her hand from him. "We owe them nothing. We barely remember anything, anyway, so how would we assist them?" She sat up straight and frowned as she crossed her arms. "We'd best stay out of the way and let the big players handle it now. Athena…she'll figure it all out."

Her sorrowful gaze broke his heart to pieces. He had never denied her affection before. But his head wasn't in the game, his libido drowned beneath his guilt, his fear, his confusion.

He stared at the pictures plastered on his crimson-colored walls—lovers, soulmates, fictional characters, charges. Figures he'd helped, couples he'd united with his arrows, others he'd yet to entice to fall in love.

People he'd killed.

He yanked at his blond curls and groaned. "I can't, Psyche, I just…can't." It wasn't anger bubbling in him; it was a deep sense of self-reproach, immense and troubling and impossible to move past. "You would recognize that voice if you heard it again, right? You said yours was not yourself. The one in me sounded like my conscience, but you…"

Psyche recoiled. "I…no, Eros, please—"

"—you have precious information. You are aware of the vocabulary she used, her intonations, her plans…might you at least be able to narrow Athena's list a little?"

Dragging herself to the edge of the bed, Psyche turned away from him. She let her bare feet dangle from the mattress as she sighed. "I do not want to share it. It's too painful to recall. Sure, I could extract the recollections from where I stashed them, but she wounded me. Mentally, physically…could I go through that again?"

Eros pulled on the blankets, which drew Psyche back to him. He wrapped his arms around her and squeezed. "She's not controlling you anymore. And this time, you're not alone. You have me, and you're safe." He spun her and kissed her forehead. She cringed, pretending to be disgusted, yet he caught her smirking. "So how about we talk, you and me? Debate? Throw out a few names to determine if they match voices we've encountered before?"

"Debate?" She squinted at him.

"If we detect a pattern, or anything relevant…then we report it to Zeus."

Closing her eyes, she inhaled, exhaled, loosened up. "Well…"

Come on, love. Unveil your bruised soul and help find the culprit.

When she pried her eyelids apart, Psyche nodded. "Fine. But you know more goddesses than I do, so you should be the one to toss out names."

He cracked his knuckles. "Great. So who among the females may be responsible for driving us mad because she holds a grudge against gods and wouldn't hesitate to use humans in her plots? Who would have no trouble sacrificing innocents, possibly the planet itself, to make a point?"

Psyche stood up. "For starters, who is one of the biggest troublemakers here, your mother aside?"

They exchanged a glance of knowing.

"Hera," they said in unison.

Eros got to his feet and set his fists on his hips. "Zeus already dismissed Hecate, and I concur, as I saw inside her heart and it was pure. But there are other witches who might gain access to Olympus, right? Circe, perhaps? Any of her disciples? I've never listened to her speak."

"Then we must count any lesser goddess on earth. Any who might have recently visited Olympus and that Zeus might have offended." Psyche tapped a finger to her chin. "He may have slowed down his sinful actions, but he *has* tried to ravish and rape many a pretty deity."

"Right." Eros paced by the bed. "And let's not forget sea monsters or earth-ridden beasts who might have struck a deal with a goddess. Or a nymph." He rubbed the back of his neck as discomfort spiraled through his nerves. "They're notoriously fickle."

"And cup-bearers!" Psyche snapped. "I'm sure some are mad at Zeus. Most are his daughters, but who knows how he treats them behind closed doors."

Exhausted as more and more images seeped into his brain, Eros collapsed onto the mattress. The crisp sheets no longer calmed him. "This was a terrible idea. Now we have too many options."

Psyche huffed as she sat next to him. "Agreed."

"Poor Gaia would be ashamed of all her children and grandchildren bickering like this." He kicked at the air and grunted. "Plotting to overthrow one another by using humans and cruel tricks? It would outrage her. She made our planet, rendered it fruitful and magnificent, and now it's in danger because of one stupid, egotistical act. One stupid situation probably caused by Zeus and his oversized ego."

Psyche opened her mouth to reply, but a knock on the door prompted her to freeze.

"Did someone overhear us?" she whispered, her arms tensing.

Eros shrugged as he rose from the bed and shushed her. He gaped at the door. "Yes? Who is it?"

Has Zeus decided to interrupt us after all?

The door opened, but instead of a cup-bearer or a herald summoning them to the king, two other individuals stood in the threshold. Two glowing, mature, stiff but majestic women, their beauty blinding, their expressions inquisitive.

Eros recognized both at once and his knees buckled.

Oh, my Zeus, to what do we owe this visit?

The first, her hair such a vibrant shade of scarlet it hurt to look at, so bouffant it filled up the doorway, took a stride closer. Her light-emerald tunic-dress seemed to plunge into the floor, and her muddy eyes shone as they fixed on Eros. "Well, hello to you, too!"

He regained his bearings and threw himself at her feet. "Gaia, oh…what an honor to meet you again." He kneeled before her, his spine tingling with chills.

The one and only Mother Earth making house calls—that was a rare privilege.

Psyche squeaked as she ran into the other woman's arms; a gorgeous brunette almost identical in appearance to Hera, but her aura warmer, more welcoming. Her lengthy orange sleeves wrapped around Eros' spouse as she smiled.

Rhea, mother of Olympians. Always a delight.

Gaia helped Eros up, her grin bright as the sun. "Now, now, no need for formalities."

Psyche extracted herself from the second goddess's embrace. She bent her knees, bracing to thrust herself before Gaia, but Eros grabbed her and held her close.

"Psyche, is it?" Gaia's gaze glazed over the golden-haired goddess of the soul, and her cheeks reddened. "We've never met, but I am glad to see you for myself, finally."

Eros beamed at his wife, enthused to present her to the mother of all gods, all things, all creatures. The primordial deity of the earth; the revered Queen of everything. "Dearest, I introduce: Gaia. Though in truth, she *needs* no introduction."

"Gaia, at our doorstep?" Psyche tried her hardest to hold in her squeals, but she was ready to burst with excitement. "What an absolute pleasure." Her smile somehow widened further as she twisted to Rhea. "And you, how lovely to see you after so long!"

Rhea's wild, jungle-scented perfume permeated the bedroom as she slid further inside. Eros hugged her, then returned to his wife's side.

"Indeed, it has been a while," said Rhea, setting a hand to her heart. "I've been traveling, ensuring all our precious creatures are happy and healthy. Harder work than one might believe—"

Gaia's savage locks flipped against Rhea's face, interrupting her. "Yes, *yes,* we'll catch up later with your adventures, daughter, but Zeus asked us to come and here we are." The edges of her skirts were like vines, tangling around hers and Rhea's limbs, hypnotizing and dazzling all at once. "I insisted we speak with you first, since this devilish fiend affected you most, from what I understood."

Rhea stepped out of her mother's spotlight without a word.

Eros gulped; the two powerful deities wanted to communicate with *him?*

Psyche's shoulders squared as she fought to keep her balance. "Wait…you are Zeus' surprise guests?"

Rhea's eyes darkened as they narrowed. "Is that an issue?" All the force of a lioness radiated in her energy, in her voice, but her claws were retracted—she'd never attack a family member without cause.

Eros clapped, dismissing the unwelcomed tension. "On the contrary!" A long-needed positivity infused him as Rhea smirked and Gaia inclined her head. "It's genius. It disappoints me that no one thought of this sooner." He whirled to Psyche, who was staring at Gaia's undulating gown, stuck in a daze. "These are the wisest, strongest deities in our history…and both watched their husbands overthrown because of evil. They witnessed Zeus taking the throne and they'd fight tooth and nail to keep him there."

Gaia's once iridescent features dimmed. "Yes…and Rhea and I have an inkling on who and what you're dealing with." She swallowed, and all her immensity diminished, as if fading, turning off, losing strength. She—the worldly creator—was afraid. "It's most likely one of my own children—a titan."

‖ 36. TRAITOROUS ALLIES ‖
PSYCHE

A titan?

A toxic, tart flavor fizzled in Psyche's mouth; one that reminded her of the poison that once bubbled inside.

Unable to listen or even try to focus, she zoned out as Eros detailed his experience to Gaia and Rhea. Lingering near the bed, she hugged herself, wondering how a titan would be responsible for such chaos. The malevolent ones had been locked up for centuries, and those left had proved themselves as benevolent—Rhea included.

So what had changed?

Psyche had participated little in the wars of the gods, but she'd read of the battles with titans. And aside from Rhea, she didn't know these beings well. A few of the women visited Olympus from time to time, and some even lived there, but they rarely showed themselves.

One thing stood out, and Psyche embraced herself tighter as the idea swelled in her mind—most of the free titans…were female. Meaning if Gaia and Rhea's theory was true, any of them might have had a part in the recent insanity.

"Tethys?" Gaia's voice grew louder as she listed off titanesses. "Themis, Eos. Phoebe…hm, not so much. And Leto, when Hera's too busy."

Though unsure what Gaia referred to, Psyche recognized those names. They were temporary or permanent Olympus residents, or popular visitors.

When she tried to associate the names with faces, she struggled. Her temples ached and pain shot to her sinuses.

I'd never recognize these ancient goddesses by their voice alone. Can they disguise themselves?

Coming to reality, she peered at Eros, stuck in a heated argument with Rhea, who sneered at him, her gaze fiery.

"But would you really dismiss that possibility?" Eros' fists clenched at his sides. "It's not like she couldn't transform back into a titaness if she wanted to."

Rhea's chestnut hair curled and coiled, morphing into a bushy lion's mane, rattling like snakes ready to attack. "Do not raise your tone with me, young man—"

Gaia stepped between them before either could retort. "Titanesses and goddesses have changed their appearances to escape Zeus before, daughter." Her soothing energy was like fresh dirt, like a blooming flower, a comfortable patch of grass. "Asteria became an island, Aura turned into a stream, Eos shifted into a grasshopper— the list is long. So we cannot dismiss what our dear god of love is suggesting."

Psyche didn't know much of the vast powers titanesses held, but she doubted any of them would return to their original forms on their own; they'd have help. But except for Hecate—who was actually a younger generation of titaness—she had no knowledge of who would cast such spells.

And Hecate is not a suspect, though Athena seemed wary.

Psyche admired Eros' bravery and his willingness to weed

through his horrible memories to identify the wrong-doer. But as she tuned in to him and his family arguing, she realized it was impossible. The options piled up the longer they spoke, and the number of women scorned by Zeus was too enormous to narrow down. One woman in particular paced back and forth in Psyche's mind—Hera, Queen of the gods, and number one scorned among all those Zeus had hurt. A suspect to any outsider, and a questionable figure to those who lived in the palace.

But why would she want to dethrone her own husband?

Rhea emitted a snorting, snarling cackle that drew Psyche away from her thoughts. "But to presume any of that is possible—"

Gaia cut her off in ancient Greek. An insult, a warning—Psyche had no clue. But Eros appeared to understand it, as he gasped and leaned backwards.

Rhea rounded on her mother, shouting back in the same hissing tongue.

Rhea—*she* had reasons to rebel, now that Psyche thought about it. She was so similar to her daughter, with an identical rage flowing through her, but she concealed it better beneath her mask of maturity and poise. Here, she unleashed it, and with each gesture—waving her arms, glaring, spitting—she resembled Hera in ways that made Psyche's knees buckle.

Despite the attitude, the tension, Psyche struggled to believe Hera—or Rhea, for that matter—was responsible for all this…at least, not alone. Every theory came down to that—to the fact that whoever the culprit was, they didn't act on their own.

Veering from the scene of Gaia and Rhea screaming at each other, Psyche wandered to the oversized dresser and focused on the heart-shaped ornaments decorating its top.

Perhaps if they first found the ally, that would lead them to the main evil-doer. Because it became clearer by the minute that this ally had to be one of the titanesses dwelling in Olympus.

A sudden and heavy silence filled the area. An odd chill broke through and covered Psyche's skin in tiny goosebumps. In the mirror, she saw Gaia approaching her from behind, her eyes sparking into a mossy green.

Oh dear... she heard me, and I offended her.

"No," said the primordial goddess, her timbre obscure but not laced with hatred. "You are the only one who is thinking clearly. Unlike them," she jabbed a thumb towards Eros and Rhea, both frozen in their spots, "and their arguments and theories about shape-shifting titanesses or my idiot sons escaping Tartarus. It's not feasible, and besides—we seek a woman."

Psyche hadn't overheard *that* conversation, so deep in her own reflections of Hera and titanesses. "You've been listening to my thoughts?" She twisted to the powerful deity of the earth, her throat constricting as she bit her lip.

A glimmer in Gaia's eyes revealed not fury, but sympathy. "I multitask better than anyone, dearest. And did I not accuse all my daughters myself? I agree with you. Something is afoot in our family."

She lifted her arms a few inches from her sides, and the hem of her tunic molded into the floor, crawling to the bed-frame, blooming like savage jungle vines as its fabric wrapped around everything in sight. It grazed over the walls and paraded up to the ceiling; and soon, the entire room was cloaked in emerald satin. Soundproof, concealed.

She wants privacy?

Gaia nodded. "No one can hear these formulations yet."

Flashes of orange and yellow flickered in Rhea's otherwise demure brown eyes. "What is it? Eros and I can't have several conversations at once, like you, so explain yourself."

With a scoff, Eros sidled up to Psyche. "Please, share with us."

A few more tendrils of Gaia's gown weaved up, dressing like pillars around the four of them. Like antennas to pick up on interference, surveying the vicinity in case anyone tried to pry into their discussion. "There's definitely a traitor amidst us. Among titans and gods. A treacherous alliance, and a powerful one."

Eros' eyebrows lurched upward. "Two deities working together?"

"And," Psyche shivered as the silky dress fabric undulated near her, "you don't disagree that Hera might be involved, as I was thinking? You would accuse your own granddaughter?"

Rhea shrugged. "Well…we can't discount her, no. She has every reason to wish harm upon Zeus, no matter his exemplary behavior in recent years. Daughter or not, I know her. She's wrathful." She glanced at Gaia and grimaced. "But we cannot be certain, because others have similar motives. Goddesses who aren't always stationed here, who pass through, or lurk in the shadows. Servants, Muses, Seasons, and the like."

Gaia's mouth widened as she was about to reply, but her gown vibrated, creasing and folding as if punched into or tugged on. "Postpone this." She yanked her sleeve and at once, the texture of her garb rolled back into place, draping her figure as normal. "We have company."

A knock came from the door, which opened at once to reveal Zeus. He scrunched his nose at the sight of the small assembly that had gathered without him.

"Ah, cloaking the walls, are we?" His shoulders tensed as he set one foot over the threshold. "Would you care to join us in the throne-room, instead? If you're done with this side-bar, that is."

Despite their elder status and superior presence, Gaia and Rhea bowed to him with smiles, their earlier woes and fury evaporated.

"Of course, my beloved grandson," said the former, shimmying out, leaving a forest and earth breeze in her spot.

Rhea followed, brushing her fingertips on Zeus' cheek as she passed him.

When Zeus flipped to the exit, Eros snatched Psyche and pressed their foreheads together. "Keep quiet, okay? Let them do the speculating for now. You did your part by communicating your concerns. Allow Gaia to present them to the court…they'll be better received coming from her."

Though she acquiesced and glided out, hand in hand with the man she loved, Psyche cringed. Her stomach wouldn't settle, her lungs wouldn't take in the appropriate amount of oxygen to keep her breathing, and her heart wouldn't stop fluttering.

A titaness-goddess duo? Two fearless ladies in charge, desperate to steal a crown and inflict suffering in their wake? Two creatures craving worldwide chaos?

As she trailed along the corridor, she swore she sensed a gentle gust swishing up her arms, and a soft whisper caressing her ears, though she didn't grasp what it said. She shoved both off; never again would she allow anyone to control her.

We'll find you, culprits. No one messes with the Olympian gods.

||37. TIME FOR A CHANGE||
ATHENA

"Aphrodite." Athena's knuckles rapped against the goddess of beauty's door. "I wish to speak with you. It's urgent."

She'd prepared for the worst; grumbles echoing under the door-frame, or a naked Ares to answer in Aphrodite's stead, or no reaction at all. But to her shock, none of that happened.

The door opened, and Aphrodite appeared, clad in a peach satin robe. "Come in," she said, her voice low, cautious.

Upon passing the threshold, Athena froze. Last time she'd seen the deity's bedroom, it was sprinkled with ornate sculptures, intricate ocean-themed paintings, priceless heirlooms, dramatic drapings over the windows, and covered in gold and silver. But this chamber was white, its walls bare, the bed-sheets a pale, soothing lavender.

A subtle sea scent wafted up her nostrils as Aphrodite chuckled. "Stunning, right?" She drew her strawberry blond curls over one shoulder. "After what occurred on earth…I disposed of most of my materialistic possessions. I changed." She hastened to her bed and sat, her robe sideways slipping to expose a breast.

Athena shuddered and peered askance.

No, you haven't changed at all.

"Sorry, I often forget that you are a prude." Aphrodite adjusted her garment and waved at Athena to join her. "You said it was urgent?" She lounged, turning to the side and propping herself up on one elbow. The edges of her gown again dropped, revealing her milky smooth skin.

Athena cleared her throat as she lowered to the mattress. "Speaking of your time on earth…I need to find out more about that. Specifically about your human, Lukus."

Aphrodite straightened up and pulled her robe to her chest. "Lukus?" Clutching the soft material with one hand, she used her other to twirl her hair. "What…what about him? And why?"

Unsure how to interpret Aphrodite's change in attitude— excited, confused, aroused, maybe all three—Athena clasped her hands in her lap and focused on them. "Zeus wishes to summon him here, and I'm to fetch him. I'll likely work alongside him, since our king wants his help to investigate our situation."

Aphrodite clapped a palm over her lips. "He what?"

"Tell me about him. I must leave now, that's why this is urgent," said Athena, wiggling her fingers, her heels tapping to the floor in an unsteady rhythm.

Aphrodite jumped up and marched to her dresser. "Zeus summoned Lukus? That's dramatic. And unexpected." She fiddled with the fabric draped over her and pressed her face up to the mirror, batting her lashes. "*Lukus.*"

"He claims Lukus is a gifted inspector, and he will shed light on what we cannot." Athena caught Aphrodite pouting her lips at her reflection. "Being an outsider to the case…he might have answers we need."

Aphrodite jolted around with a huff, her cheeks inflamed, her breasts popping out again. "He *is* gifted, but he isn't an outsider.

You…" she squinted and cocked her head, "you *know* about him, about his true nature, don't you? Zeus told you."

Flinching, Athena crossed one leg over the other. "Not the details…but yes. I'm still unclear on Lukus' purpose and destiny. Which I'll discover in due time, I imagine, but for now…I'm in a bit of a hurry, Aphrodite. What can you tell me about him?"

Aphrodite's brows lifted. "*I* don't know his destiny either." She swirled back to her mirror, dabbing her fingertips over her mouth as if evening out her lipstick. "But he's not fully human. It's not fair of our king to throw you into this blindly—"

"—to set me up for failure?" Athena glared at the floor as Aphrodite's robe slithered to her waist, baring her entire chest as she put herself on display. "Yes, I thought so too, but again…no time to worry over it."

When Aphrodite whirled back to her, a sheer turquoise gown covered her body. Athena couldn't help but unleash a quick sigh of relief as the goddess leaned against the wardrobe, clothed at last.

"Well, he's a skeptic. A big one. He had to be transformed into one of Eros' heart-eating zombies before he grasped that something supernatural was at play. Even after temporarily returning his memories, to speak with him about what had happened…he was tough to convince." She let out a weighty breath and tucked her locks behind her ears. "He won't come easily."

Athena rolled her eyes. "Delightful. A reluctant and powerless human is who Zeus believes to be our savior." She scratched the back of her head. "How is it possible? If he is a descendant I'd understand giving him access to Olympus, but he's not fully immortal, is he? He's some mortal man with a fate that's intertwined in ours."

Aphrodite shrugged. "It puzzles me, too." Her eyes widened.

"Oh, and he was persuaded I was his soulmate. I'm uncertain if my memory spell changed that, so be on the alert. He became quite infatuated, poor thing, especially when I left. He may still be obsessed with me."

Sneering, Athena waved her hand. "That's nothing new." Aphrodite grimaced at her, then swerved to her mirror. "But that news might actually be useful should he get too difficult to deal with. I could use you to sway him."

Pinching her cheeks, Aphrodite emitted a moan. "Perhaps…but he's smarter than you think. Witty, observant, thoughtful." As she twirled, her mane shimmered and landed on her bare shoulders. "Now that I think about it…he does have abilities that would aid us. His intuition. Despite his wariness, that part of him is flawless. Beware, though—he might outwit even you."

Perfect. This was what I needed.

Athena rose from the mattress. "I appreciate your help. I'll be sure to mention your contribution to this investigation once we uncover the culprit." She proceeded to the door, but Aphrodite caught her arm and yanked her to the dresser. "What the—"

"—I only want us all to be safe," said the goddess of beauty, her expression softening. "Including Lukus. If you pull that off, that's all that matters. I need no reward or special mentions."

Athena smiled.

I may have been wrong—she is *changing.*

She rushed to her chambers, eager to change into a fresh tunic and brace for another trip to earth. Another encounter with a confusing mortal awaited her—though this mortal might be a piece of the Olympian future.

She switched to a travel-friendly dress that stopped at her ankles and showed off her upper arms. The baby blue hue worked well with her complexion, and as she hurried to her mirror, she fixed her hair.

I must appear wise, welcoming, godly. Lukus must believe I'm a goddess, but not be afraid of me.

As she was about to hasten out, she noticed a golden envelope on her dresser—one that hadn't been there earlier. Interest sparking, she picked it up, balanced it in her hands, testing its weight.

"What's this?" She flipped it around and gasped at the thunder seal atop it. "Zeus? When did he deliver this?"

She tore the thing open and plucked out a thin sheet of paper, with a few words scribbled in Zeus' thick but proper handwriting. As she read, she held her breath, her heart hammering a million miles a minute in her rib-cage.

"Lukus," she said, lowering the message and glimpsing her stupefied self in the mirror. "He *is* a long-lost descendant? It is confirmed. But…of who?"

Why Zeus chose to inform her when he'd initially said he couldn't, she didn't know; but this was precious intelligence she hoped to use to her advantage.

She stashed the letter in her bustier and dashed out.

Distracted, she didn't hear the breathless giggle that emanated from a corner next to her wardrobe. She didn't visualize the near-transparent cloud of purple and green that shot up the ceiling, leaving a faded cerulean mark on its way.

||38. HUMAN||

???

Red. Vivid images. Vibrant flashes. Splashes of colors, glimpses of eyes, hands, skin—and *red*.

Nightmares.

He bit into something—a chunk of meat, he thought—and tore through it like an animal, gnawing at the flesh like a hungry, rabid beast. His heartbeat echoed in his ears and muffled sobs resonated nearby. He smelled a metallic, delicious scent that called him, begged him.

No…*she* begged him. The one sobbing; *she* beseeched him to stop.

Lukus jolted up, the dreams buzzing off like bees as his notebook dropped to the ground. The bottle of vodka he'd been hugging spilled onto the hardwood floors.

"Shit." He swiped his damp hair out of his face and groaned.

"Such foul language," said a fierce, feminine voice—one that shouldn't have been in his living room, where he'd been laying.

He jumped to his feet, ignoring the thrumming in his temples. "What the fuck?"

He spun to the source of the noise occurring from the other side of the couch. Instinctively, he reached near his belt—but of course, he didn't have his gun on him. He'd been sleeping, it was nighttime, he was safe.

No...not safe.

Though his eyesight was blurry, and he was groggy from his nightmare, he viewed a woman drifting from behind the sofa. She'd propped herself a few feet away from him, her energy overpowering and strong, and the outline of her body...glowing.

He scrubbed his eyes, which only worsened his blurred vision. "Who the fuck are you, and how did you get into my apartment?"

At a loss for a means to defend himself, he snatched the half-empty vodka bottle and aimed it at her. He never hit women, but this one needed to explain herself before he changed his mind.

His sight adjusted. The woman was as tall as him, her hair dark brown, long and wavy, flowing in the wind; but where was this wind coming from? His windows were closed. He couldn't see her eyes, but they illuminated the area, scintillating in an unreal, inhuman way. Were they yellow?

What the fuck is happening?

She wore a blue wrap-around style dress that stopped at her ankles, not unlike a Greek toga. A breastplate over the top portion of her body smooshed her breasts, and her arms were muscular, veiny.

As his vision continued to normalize, Lukus realized she was beautiful. Whoever she was, she radiated confidence and power, an aura of trust and clarity that rolled off her tanned skin.

His knees buckled and he couldn't move, mesmerized by the glitter, the luminescence dripping from her in heaps. He shielded his eyes, hoping his jaw hadn't sunk too low.

Am I drooling?

"Swell," she said, her tone smooth but so cold and impatient it broke his trance. "Are you awake now? Alert?"

"Who are you?" He tightened his grip on the liquor bottle.

She chuckled; a melodious, enticing sound that sent chills down his spine, fluttering up and down his arms.

She breaks into my condo and laughs when I ask who she is? What the fuck?

Her giggle was oddly familiar, reminiscent of someone else's. The more he stared at her attire, her demeanor, her exuberance, the more something pinched at the nerves in his brain. That outfit, its style, the glow of her silhouette...had he seen something, some*one* like that before?

Still thrusting the bottle before him, he crouched and picked up his notebook. As he straightened up, he squeezed the vodka jug between his legs and flipped through the pages until he came to the first one.

"Strawberry blonde hair...no, yours is brown...but...ah, yes, there it is. *Pearly porcelain skin. Wore a long golden dress, cute sandals on her feet.*" He peered at the intruder and cocked his head. "Your skin is darker, and your dress is blue, though it's the same style. You do have the right shoes."

Had he met her before? How? When? She wasn't the woman he'd described in his notes, and yet she gave him serious deja vu.

"I don't have time for this, human." The energy she showered on him fizzled and darkened. "You're to come with me. You're a descendant of the gods, and we need your assistance."

"Whoa, *whoa.*" Lukus' lower limbs quaked, and the bottle slipped from between them. "I'm a what?" The notebook escaped his grasp as his eyebrows elevated.

Human? Does she call people that for fun, or...?

She took a step closer. "Heavens, she told me you'd be difficult, but she didn't mention you'd be daft."

Lukus scrambled backwards so fast he bumped into a wall. "Hey now, can we talk this over like adults before you kidnap me, you psycho?" He arched his spine, unwilling to divulge the panic surging in his veins. He was an FBI agent, for crying out loud—why would he fear her? She was tall, she looked strong, but she wouldn't intimidate him.

A few blinks later, he lunged to his vodka bottle and lifted again it as he bent his knees, bracing for her attack.

She was faster, and swerved up to him with a *whoosh*. She tapped the bottle with her fingertips and sent it smashing to the floor. "You think I'm that easy to trick? That alcohol container won't protect you from what's to come. You have a lot to learn, Lukus."

Lukus puffed his chest out and glared at her. "How the fuck do you know my name? Who are—"

"—I'm not an enemy, so calm down." She strode aside, slinking past the cluttered coffee table. "I'm here to take you with me, as you're destined to help save us. Fated to solve a mystery that might spare the world from chaos."

Despite the fright slithering all over his limbs in waves of shivers, Lukus was overcome with an urge to guffaw. "Chaos?" Unable to hold back, he puffed out a few laughs and slapped his thighs. "You're funny, you know that?" A few tears strolled down his cheeks. "Jeez, you almost fooled me!" He pictured his boss watching some sort of live-feed in his office, cursing because his prank didn't work. "Where did they find you, huh? Did I pass the old man's test? Is he trying to figure out if I'm fit to come back to work?"

The woman narrowed her gaze and mumbled something under

her breath as she marched forward, stopping once her nose pressed into his. "Enough."

His laughter ceased at once, but before he could shove her off, she seized his arm and threw him onto the couch. He landed with a *thud*, melting into the cushions.

"What the—"

She pinned him down and placed her fingers on his temples, massaging them, as if weaving knowledge into his brain. The gesture, invasive as it was, felt familiar.

He couldn't fight her off, and soon an eerie warmth emanated from her touch as his eyes closed.

His earlier nightmares flickered to life inside his mind. Pools of blood, bits of flesh, crime scene tape. Ashes, dust, camera flashes, and curious onlookers gawking at the spectacle.

This wasn't a nightmare—this was real. He'd been there, in that spot, in his FBI jacket, jotting down notes, barking orders. And in the notebook, he saw what he'd written. *Cannibalistic murders.*

Seconds later, he was in a hotel lobby, watching as an elegant strawberry blonde approached him, a trench coat covering her emerald dress.

"*I am Agnes,*" she said, her voice like silk.

Her image fogged as the background faded into a gloomy, abandoned warehouse.

So not nightmares...but memories? Is this chick the one from my notes?

The woman in question was lying on the ground in front of him, pallid and panicked, eyes shifting from blue to green to purple. Her arm had been chomped into; blood gushed from the wound and pieces of muscle and veins slid out.

To his left he located a man clad in leather, with golden hair falling in short locks over his iridescent amber eyes. He held a bow in one hand and pointed at Lukus with the other.

"Eat," he said, motioning at the squirming woman on the floor.

Eat? Eat her?

Lukus observed the woman's arm and patted his face. His lips were wet, and a coppery flavor swirled on his tongue. A morsel of skin hung loose—

"Agnes!"

His eyes wrenched open; but he was back in his apartment. Sweat clung to his shirt and glued him to the sofa.

The overpowered brunette still held him down, and he thrust her off. "Where is Agnes? What happened? Where'd she go?" He got up, but nausea bubbled in his gut as more recollections poured in, drowning him.

"Agnes?" The lady crossed her arms as her brows furrowed.

"Shit." He rubbed the back of his neck. "That…that wasn't her real name. She visited me in the hospital." He hissed as another memory pinged in his brain. "Aphrodite. *Aphrodite,* that's who that was. Where is she?"

The blue-garbed woman allowed a weak smile to grow across her lips. "She's in Olympus." Her eyes shifted to gray as she set her hands on her hips.

"Olympus." He browsed through the Greek myths that lolled in the depths of his mind. "She's home. Okay, so…" He frowned. "Wait, who are you, then? Why did she erase my memory?"

The woman inclined her head as she pressed a hand to her heart. "Sorry for the brutality…I'm Athena."

Athena…goddess of wisdom?

He shuddered; this goddess was one his mother had always revered, had praised. "What do you need me for?" He shifted his weight, his feet numb and his calves tight. "First this goddess of beauty swooshes into my life, introduces me to her fucked-up son, then leaves. And now *you?*" He racked his fingers through his perspiration-coated hair. "I'd rather not be involved, thanks. Last time I got roped into your godly bullshit, I was turned into a fucking zombie! Hell, I *ate* her! Why would you guys want me up there?"

Athena cleared her throat. "Yes, you were a heart-eating monster, for a spell. But we stopped him; Eros, I mean. Bigger issues have risen, Lukus. According to my father, you are essential in helping us." She extended her arm. "Will you please join me? I don't wish to use force."

"No." Lukus shimmied away. "No, I'm done. I'll end up turned to mush. It took weeks for me to recover from having chowed down on Aphrodite's flesh."

Athena pinched the bridge of her nose. "She's up there. Waiting. So if you want to be with her again..." she leaned close, "come. She's still as beautiful as before. If not more. And Olympus is magnificent."

"But I'm..." he jabbed a thumb into his chest and sneered, "I'm human. How could I go to...Olympus? And her?" He scoffed. "I barely saw her godly form without losing it. I'd die."

"Lukus." Electricity flickered off Athena's skin, its effects dazzling Lukus as she touched his wrist. "You're not mortal. Not one hundred percent. You have a destiny among the gods."

Lukus' mouth turned sour, his saliva dried, his teeth stuck together. "But..."

She took no note of his distress as she laced her fingers with his and tugged. "I'm sorry to be so blunt, but we have no time. We must leave for Olympus now."

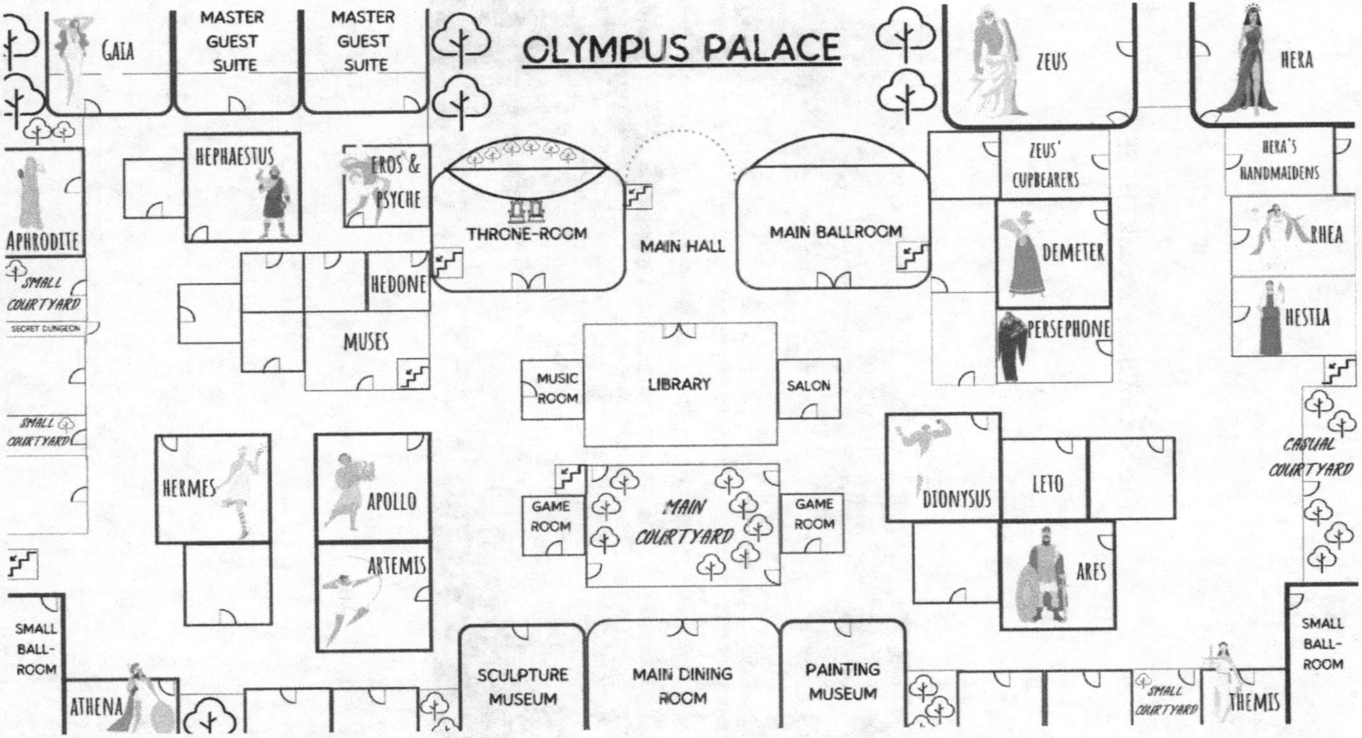

OLYMPUS PALACE
HERA
HERA'S HANDMAIDENS
RHEA
HESTIA
CASUAL COURTYARD
SMALL BALL-ROOM
THEMIS
SMALL COURTYARD
ZEUS
ZEUS' CUPBEARERS
DEMETER
PERSEPHONE
LETO
ARES
DIONYSUS
MAIN BALLROOM
SALON
GAME ROOM
LIBRARY
MAIN COURTYARD
PAINTING MUSEUM
MAIN HALL
MUSIC ROOM
GAME ROOM
MAIN DINING ROOM
THRONE-ROOM
SCULPTURE MUSEUM
MASTER GUEST SUITE
MASTER GUEST SUITE
EROS & PSYCHE
HEDONE
MUSES
APOLLO
ARTEMIS
HEPHAESTUS
HERMES
GAIA
APHRODITE
SMALL COURTYARD
SECRET DUNGEON
SMALL COURTYARD
SMALL BALL-ROOM
ATHENA

To be continued in book THREE

RAVENOUS RHEA

ANGRY GREEK GODS SERIES BOOK 3

AUTHOR'S NOTE
&
ACKNOWLEDGMENTS

"POISONOUS PSYCHE" is the continuation of a project dear to my heart. When I wrote the prequel, CARNIVOROUS CUPID, I had no idea where I was going or what I was doing—I just wanted to write about Greek Mythology. At the time of composing this acknowledgment section, the series is slowly getting traction and reviews, and I'm so excited to share this second novel with you!

Publishing this wouldn't have been possible without the help of five fantastic beta-readers and editors: **Vee, Danielle, Kat, Natali, and Selena**. You were all so incredibly supportive and positive about Psyche's journey, and I appreciate the time and effort you all put into this story!

To my family, thank you for your support, for spreading the word about my novels, and for displaying them so proudly in your homes. I love you all.

To Matt—for being the most incredible boyfriend and tolerating my rants and listening to me ramble on about my novels. You're an amazing human with the kindest soul, and I love you deeply.

To all my online friends and authors who bought and read and reviewed Carnivorous Cupid, encouraging me to pursue my self-publishing journey, *thank you!* Your help and kindness have been essential in the creation of this mythological world.

And finally, to those starting out in this field, or still struggling to make it—don't give up!

ABOUT THE AUTHOR

Stephanie Rose is an author based in Nevada, but her heart lives in Paris, France, where she resided for almost twelve years. When she's not writing, she spends her time going on adventures with her boyfriend, catching up on TV-shows, or snuggling her tuxedo cat, Crowley.

"POISONOUS PSYCHE" is the second in a four-book series, inspired by her obsession with Greek mythology. For updates on upcoming works and exclusive content about the Angry Greek Gods world, visit her website: www.stephanierose.online